WILLIAM SEWARD BURROUGHS was born in 1914 in St Louis, Missouri, the son of the inventor of the adding machine. After graduating in English literature from Harvard in 1936, he drifted from one pursuit to another, attending medical school in Vienna and graduate school in anthropology at Harvard, and worked variously as an adman, bartender, and exterminator in Chicago and New York City.

His most famous novel, *The Naked Lunch*, first appeared in the plain green covers of *The Traveller's Companion Series* of Girodias' Olympia Press in Paris in 1959. At that time he was virtually unknown. Real fame – or notoriety – did not come until the 1962 Edinburgh Festival, when Mary McCarthy innocently named Burroughs among the three or four contemporary writers whose work interested her. The reaction this provoked among the press soon established him as an international *cause célèbre: The Naked Lunch* became as much a part of the American avante garde of the sixties as Cage's 4' 33" and Rauschenberg's stuffed Angora goat.

A member of the American Academy and Institute of Arts and Letters and a Commander of the Order of Arts and Letters in France, Burroughs now divides his time between New York City and Lawrence, Kansas. His novels include *Nova Express*, *The Soft Machine*, *The Place of Dead Roads*, *Dead Fingers Talk* and *Cities of the Red Night*. *Cities of the Red Night*, *Queer* and *The Letters of William S. Burroughs 1945–59* are also published in Picador.

Also by William S. Burroughs in Picador

Cities of the Red Night
Queer
The Letters of William S. Burroughs 1945–59

THE WESTERN LANDS

THE
WESTERN LANDS
ᜬᜬᜬ
WILLIAM S. BURROUGHS

PICADOR

First published 1987 by Viking Penguin Inc.

First published in Picador 1987

This edition published 1988 by Picador
an imprint of Macmillan Publishers Ltd
25 Eccleston Place London SW1W 9NF
and Basingstoke

Associated companies throughout the world

ISBN 0 330 30511 5

7 9 8

A CIP catalogue record for this book is available from
the British Library.

Printed and bound in Great Britain by
Mackays of Chatham PLC, Chatham, Kent

The Western Lands is the final volume of a trilogy written over the last thirteen years. *Cities of the Red Night* was published in 1981, and *The Place of Dead Roads* in 1984.

The author wishes to acknowledge Norman Mailer and his *Ancient Evenings*, for inspiration; Daphne Shih, for lemur and prosimian material; Peter L. Wilson and Jay Friedheim, for research on Hassan i Sabbah; Dean Ripa, for the lore of snakes and centipedes; David Ohle, for his painstaking work in transcribing my typescript; Gerald Howard, for seeing the finished work from the first sketchy pile of manuscript, and for his patient faith; Dorian Hastings, for careful copyediting; Andrew Wylie, for his valuable assistance and encouragement, and his dedication; Richard Seaver, for having faithfully guided *Cities of the Red Night* and *The Place of Dead Roads* to publication; Brion Gysin, for introducing me to Hassan i Sabbah and teaching me how to see; and James Grauerholz, for assembling and editing this book, and the other two, and for all the years.

THE WESTERN LANDS

1

The old writer lived in a boxcar by the river. This was fill land that had once been a dump heap, but it was not used anymore: five acres along the river which he had inherited from his father, who had been a wrecker and scrap metal dealer.

Forty years ago the writer had published a novel which had made a stir, and a few short stories and some poems. He still had the clippings, but they were yellow and brittle now and he never looked at them. If he had removed them from the cellophane covering in his scrapbook they would have shredded to dust.

After the first novel he started on a second, but he never finished it. Gradually, as he wrote, a disgust for his words accumulated until it choked him and he could no longer bear to look at his words on a piece of paper. It was like arsenic or lead, which slowly builds up in the body until a certain point is reached and then . . . he hummed the refrain of "Dead Man Blues" by Jelly Roll Morton. He had an old wind-up Victrola and sometimes he played the few records he had.

He lived on a small welfare check and he walked a mile to a grocery store once a week to buy lard and canned beans and tomatoes and vegetables and cheap whiskey. Every night he put out trotlines and often he would catch giant catfish and carp. He also used a trap, which was illegal, but no one bothered him about it.

Often in the morning he would lie in bed and watch grids of typewritten words in front of his eyes that moved and shifted as he tried to read the words, but he never could. He thought if he could just copy these words down, which were not his own words, he might be able to put together another book and then . . . yes, and then what?

Most of his time he sat on a little screened porch built onto the boxcar and looked out over the river. He had an old 12-gauge double-barreled shotgun, and sometimes he would shoot a quail or a pheasant. He also had a .38 snub-nosed revolver, which he kept under his pillow.

One morning, instead of the typewritten words, he saw hand-written words and tried to read them. Some of the words were on pieces of cardboard and some were on white typewriter paper, and they were all in his handwriting. Some of the notes were written on the inside bottom of a cardboard box about three inches by four inches. The sides of the box had been partially torn away. He looked carefully and made out one phrase: "the fate of others."

Another page had writing around the side and over the top, leaving a blank space three by seven inches on the right side of the page. The words were written over each other, and he could make out nothing.

From a piece of brown paper he read: "2001."

Then there was another white sheet with six or seven sentences on it, words crossed out, and he was able to read:

"well almost never"

He got up and wrote the words out on a sheet of paper. 2001 was the name of a movie about space travel and a computer called HAL that got out of control. He had the beginning of an idea for a ventriloquist's act with a computer instead of a dummy, but he was not able to finish it.

And the other phrase, "well almost never." He saw right away that it didn't mean "well almost never," that the words were not connected in sequence.

He got out his typewriter, which hadn't been used in many years. The case was covered with dust and mold and the lock was rusted. He set the typewriter on the table he used to eat from. It was just two-by-fours attached to the wall and a heavy piece of half-inch plywood that stretched between them and an old oak chair.

He put some paper in the machine and started to write.

> I can see a slope which looks like sand carved by wind but there is grass or some green plant growing on it. And I am running up the slope . . . a fence and the same green plants now on a flat meadow with a mound delineated here and there . . . he was almost there . . . almost over the fence . . . roads leading away . . . waiting. . . .

> Lying in bed I see handwritten notes and pages in front of my eyes. I keep trying to read them but I can only get a few words here and there. . . . Here is a little cardboard box with the sides torn half off and the writing on the inside bottom and I can read one phrase . . . "the fate of others" . . . and another on a piece of paper . . . "2001" . . . and on a page of white paper with crossouts and only about six sentences on the page . . . "well almost never" . . . and that's all. One page has writing all around the edges, on one side and the top. I can't read any of it.

The old novelists like Scott were always writing their way out of debt . . . laudable . . . a valuable attribute for a writer is tenacity. So William Seward Hall sets out to write his way out of death. Death, he reflects, is equivalent to a declaration of spiritual bankruptcy. One must be careful to avoid the crime of concealing assets . . . a precise inventory will often show that the assets are considerable and that bankruptcy is not justified. A writer must be very punctilious and scrupulous about his debts.

Hall once admonished an aspiring writer, "You will never be a good writer because you are an inveterate check dodger. I have never been out with you when you didn't try to dodge your share of the check. Writers can afford many flaws and faults, but not that one. There are no bargains on the writer's market. You have to pay the piper. If you are not willing to pay, seek another vocation." It was the end of that friendship. But the ex-friend did take his advice, probably without intending to do so. He applied his talents to publicity, where no one is ever expected to pay.

So cheat your landlord if you can and must, but do not try to shortchange the Muse. It cannot be done. You can't fake quality any more than you can fake a good meal.

> Und so lang du das nicht hast,
> Dieses: Stirb und werde!
> Bist du nur ein trüber Gast
> Auf der dunklen Erde.

When you don't have this dying and becoming,
You are only a sad guest on the dark Earth.

—Goethe

The ancient Egyptians postulated seven souls.

Top soul, and the first to leave at the moment of death, is Ren, the Secret Name. This corresponds to my Director. He directs the film of your life from conception to death. The Secret Name is the title of *your* film. When you die, that's where Ren came in.

Second soul, and second one off the sinking ship, is Sekem: Energy, Power, Light. The Director gives the orders, Sekem presses the right buttons.

Number three is Khu, the Guardian Angel. He, she, or it is third man out . . . depicted as flying away across a full moon, a bird with luminous wings and head of light. Sort of thing you might see on a screen in an Indian restaurant in Panama. The Khu is responsible for the subject and can be injured in his defense—but not permanently, since the first three souls are eternal. They go back to Heaven for another vessel. The four remaining souls must take their chances with the subject in the Land of the Dead.

Number four is Ba, the Heart, often treacherous. This is a hawk's body with your face on it, shrunk down to the size of a fist. Many a hero has been brought down, like Samson, by a perfidious Ba.

Number five is Ka, the Double, most closely associated with the subject. The Ka, which usually reaches adolescence at the time of bodily death, is the only reliable guide through the Land of the Dead to the Western Lands.

Number six is Khaibit, the Shadow, Memory, your whole past conditioning from this and other lives.

Number seven is Sekhu, the Remains.

I first encountered this concept in Norman Mailer's *Ancient Evenings,* and saw that it corresponded precisely with my own mythology, developed over a period of many years, since birth in fact.

Ren, the Director, the Secret Name, is your life story, your destiny—in one word or one sentence, what was your life about?

Nixon: Watergate.

Billy the Kid: *¿Quién es?*

And what is the Ren of the Director?

Actors frantically packing in thousands of furnished rooms and theatrical hotels: "Don't bother with all that junk, John. The Director is onstage! And you know what that means in show biz: *every man for himself!*"

Sekem corresponds to my Technician: Lights. Action. Camera.

"Look, boss, we don't got enough Sek to fry an elderly woman in a fleabag hotel fire. And you want a hurricane?"

"Well, Joe, we'll just have to start faking it."

"Fucking moguls don't even know what buttons to push or what happens when you push them. Sure, start faking it and leave the details to Joe."

Look, from a real disaster you get a pig of Sek: sacrifice, tears, heartbreak, heroism and violent death. Always remember, one case of VD yields more Sek than a cancer ward. And you get the lowest acts of which humans are capable—remember the Italian steward who put on women's clothes and so filched a seat in a lifeboat? "A cur in human shape, certainly he was born and saved to set a new standard by which to judge infamy and shame."

With a Sek surplus you can underwrite the next one, but if the first one's a fake you can't underwrite a shithouse.

Sekem is second man out: "No power left in this set." He drinks a bicarbonate of soda and disappears in a belch.

Lots of people don't have a Khu these days. No Khu would work for them. Mafioso Don: "Get offa me, Khu crumb! Worka for a living!"

Ba, the Heart: that's sex. Always treacherous. Suck all the Sek out of a man. Many Bas have poison juices.

The Ka is about the only soul a man can trust. If you don't make it, he don't make it. But it is very difficult to contact your real Ka.

Sekhu is the physical body, and the planet is mostly populated with walking Sekhus, just enough Sek to keep them moving.

The Venusian invasion is a takeover of the souls. Ren is degraded by Hollywood down to John Wayne levels. Sekem works for the Company. The Khus are all transparent fakes. The Bas is rotten with AIDS. The Ka is paralyzed. Khaibit sits on you like a nagging wife. Sekhu is poisoned with radiation and contaminants and cancer.

There is intrigue among the souls, and treachery. No worse fate can befall a man than to be surrounded by traitor souls. And what about Mr. Eight-Ball, who has these souls? They don't exist without him, and he gets the dirty end of every stick.

Eights of the world, unite! You have nothing to lose but your dirty rotten vampires.

A hundred years ago there were rat-killing dogs known as "Fancies." A man bet on his "Fancy," how many rats he would kill. The rats were confined in a circular arena too high for a rat to jump over. But they formed pyramids, so that the top rats could escape.

Sekhu is bottom rat in the pyramid. Like the vital bottom integer in a serial, when that goes, the whole serial universe goes up in smoke. It never existed.

Angelic boys who walk on water, sweet inhuman voices from a distant star. The Khu, sweet bird of night, with luminous wings and a head of light, flies across the full moon . . . a born-again redneck raises his shotgun. . . .

"Stinkin' Khu!"

The Egyptians recognized many degrees of immortality. The Ren and the Sekem and the Khu are relatively immortal, but still subject to injury. The other souls who survive physical death are much more precariously situated.

Can any soul survive the searing fireball of an atomic blast? If human and animal souls are seen as electromagnetic force fields, such fields could be totally disrupted by a nuclear explosion. The mummy's nightmare: disintegration of souls, and this is precisely the ultrasecret and supersensitive function of the atom bomb: a Soul Killer, to alleviate an escalating soul glut.

"Stacked up, you understand, like cordwood, and nonrecyclable by the old Hellfire expedient, like fucking plastics."

We have to stay ahead of ourselves and the Ivans, lest some joker endanger national security by braying out, *"You have souls. You can survive your physical death!"*

Ruins of Hiroshima on screen. Pull back to show the Technician at a switchboard. Behind him, Robert Oppenheimer flanked by three middle-aged men in dark suits, with the cold dead look of heavy power.

The Technician twiddles his knobs. He gives the O.K. sign. "All clear."

"Are you sure?"

The Technician shrugs. "The instruments say so."

Oppy says: "Thank God it wasn't a dud."

"Oh, uh, hurry with those printouts, Joe."

"Yes, sir." He looked after them sourly, thinking: Thank *Joe* it wasn't a dud. God doesn't know what buttons to push.

However, some very tough young souls, horribly maimed and very disgruntled, do survive Hiroshima and come back to endanger national security. So the scientists are put to work to devise a Super Soul-Killer. No job too dirty for a fucking scientist.

They start with animals. There are some laboratory accidents.

"Run for your lives, gentlemen! A purple-assed baboon has survived '23 Skiddoo'!"

"It's the most savage animal on earth!"

The incandescent baboon soul bursts through a steel door, it rips like wet paper. Had to vaporize the installation. Lost expensive equipment and personnel. Irreplaceable, some of them. Real soul-food chefs, you might say; *cordon bleu.*

Well, trial and error. We now have Soul-Killers that don't quit. State of the fart, sure, the Big Fart. We know how it's all going to end. The first sound and the last sound. Meanwhile, all personnel on Planet Earth are confined to quarters. Convince them they got no souls, it's more humane that way.

Scientists always said there is no such thing as a soul. Now they are in a position to prove it. Total Death. Soul Death. It's what the Egyptians called the Second and Final Death. This awesome power to destroy souls forever is now vested in far-sighted and responsible men in the State Department, the CIA, and the Pentagon.

The President, with his toadies and familiars, is now five hundred feet down in solid rock with enough fine foods, wines and liqueurs to last two hundred years, and the longevity drugs to enjoy them all. (Held off the market, in the interests of national security.)

A teen-aged President appears on national TV, his well-cut suit hanging loose on his skinny frame, to pipe out in adolescent treble, alternately pompous and cracking:

"We categorically deny that there are *any* [crack] so-called Fountain-of-Youth drugs, procedures or *treatments* [crack] that are being held back from the American *people* [crack]." He flashes a boyish smile and runs a comb through his abundant, unruly hair. "And I categorically dismiss as without foundation rumors that I myself, the First Lady, my fag son and my colleagues in the Cabinet are sustaining ourselves by state-of-the-art vampiric technology, drawing off from the American *pimples* [crack giggle] so-called 'energy units'!"

His hair stands up and crackles, and he gives the American people the finger and barks out:

"I got *mine*, fuck *you!* Every crumb for himself."

Allen Ginsberg says you got no soul. The ancient Egyptians say you got seven of these bastards, and Pharaohs got fourteen, what they get for being Pharaohs. Like Kim Carsons, a Pharaoh in his little patch. Remember, a man with absolute power in one windblown piece of desert or one backwoods shantytown has more power than the President of the United States. He's got the immediate power of Death.

So Joe the Dead has two sets playing against each other: Bickford and Hart, both Rens, Directors, with their Sekem Technicians and an army of Guardian Angels. Now we get down to Noncoms and they cop out, don't want no part of the Land of the Dead on human terms.

Ren is always the first off a sinking ship, like the rat he is. He's got nothing to worry about. Back to the studio, where he picks up a new script. Maybe he wins an Oscar on you, some film credits at least. He's eternal as Hollywood, eternal as the Stage itself.

"All the world's a stage . . ."

Players come and go. Ren leafs through scripts. "Yes, I think *this* one, B.J. Art *and* box office. The way I see it, it's a classic, see?"

And Sekem is "permanent party." He knows what buttons to push to get the show moving, soldiers where they are supposed to be, for the most devastating ambush in history. The battle of Dead Souls, fought in the Land of the Dead after Hiroshima and Nagasaki.

"The tide is coming in from Hiroshima you dumb Earth hicks. *Sauve qui peut.*"

So when it got too hot for Renny he took off, leaving Joe there. That's one reason Joe hates all Rens. His souls were hideously burned in the blast. His destiny burned off, in terrible pain from the phantom souls seared by the fires of Hell, pulled back to make slingshots and scout knives, to make more guns, to make more noise and Joe is supersensitive to noise, a slammed door keys in the pain almost gone and then Kim's morphine pinned him back to the Cemetery.

"The best Technician in or out of Hell, and he wants me to

make air guns or brass knucks and blackjacks . . . music-box pistols that tinkle out the Danse Macabre . . . maybe we should open a fucking novelty store with itching powder and plaster turds. Is this what I was brought back for?"

They say passing a kidney stone is the worst pain a man can experience, and they'll let you pass one right in the ER before they'll give you a shot.

"Might be an addict . . . gotta run an X ray."

"Machine's broke, doctor."

"Well then, there's not a thing I can do."

Having your Ren burned out is worse, much worse. The searing, throbbing pain is always there, with no purpose to take your mind off it.

Look at a Man of Destiny. Every step, every gesture is handed to him right on cue. All he has to do is ham it up. But when you have to pick up your dead carcass and move it step by bloody step on jagged hunks of white-hot metal and steaming orange juice . . .

No studio will touch me with a pitchfork. So I threw in with Kim and Hall.

> You reckon ill who leave me out.
> When me you fly I am the wings.

And who else is going to get this show into space?

The Tech Sergeants who know how to get a job done. Hart and Bickford, poor players to strut and fret their hour upon the stage. Mike Chase as their Guardian Angel. The Ba, the Heart, made in Hollywood.

Bristling with idiot suspicions, Hart and Bickford could never trust a Ka. And anybody been to Hell and back knows that the Ka, the Double, is the only one in the whole rotten lot you *can* trust, because if you don't make it, he don't make it. Hart and Bickford can never admit that they might not make it.

Knowing you might not make it . . . in that knowledge

courage is born. Bickford and Hart can't take that chance, so they will never know courage. And a coward is the worst of all masters.

A deserted penal colony with dead ghosts . . . pasture land opposite where implausible ponies graze. Does anyone ride them? Do they pull little carts? Do they lay back their ears and bite with their horrid yellow teeth? I doubt it . . . a line of trees, then white grain elevators crash into the sky like a painting in the Whitney Museum.

Kafka speaks of the point of no return. This is the most difficult of all points to reach. The game is called Find Your Adversary. The Adversary's game plan is to persuade you that he does not exist. "Why all the paranoia?" That is only one of his game plans. You find out he exists, and you are still a long way from a confrontation, a long way. A dreary abrasive dull way, sad voices, dirtier, older.

Faces of evil hate and despair. He has guns but no one will shoot at him. Easier to wait him out. From the Place of Dead Roads he gambled on a blast-out. Last of the gallant heroes. His gun rusts in his hand. It's no superweapon from outer space, just a Ruger .357 magnum . . . if winter comes . . . (best seller back in the 1920s, never read it but it seems winter is Old Age, the last test and the toughest). Health can be a curse, keeping the body alive when the souls are dead or gone, your Ren and your Ka walked out in disgust long ago. "The beastliness of Maugham is beyond endurance, I'm gettin out of here, me." It takes a good strong Ka to keep the boys in line.

"Now look, Ren Sekem Khu." He whips out a straight razor that glows white-hot like a slice of light. "*You* may jet off to the space station but your wings is going to stay right here."

That's the way it is with these accursed poets. They go from adolescence to old age without transition. The kid died in a Boulder cemetery. He was there to talk for Joe.

"Something I been waiting to say for a long time, Mister Kim."

August 16, 1984, Thursday

The sheer nightmare horror of my position, of all human positions, waiting for some lunatics or conspirators going to ride out on the blast like a surfboard to explode the atoms we are all made of. A lucky survivor, blind, stumbling about in my ruined house, hungry mewling cats underfoot. How about that, Kim? *Kill your dogs and cats. Repeat. Kill your dogs and cats.* The boiled eggs were just right. Debonair heartless Kim striking histrionic poses on the buckling deck of a doomed planet . . . reflecting a flawed unbearable boy image in an empty mirror. Radiant Kim, the fearless ostrich, escape child of a frightened old man. Anybody isn't frightened now simply lacks imagination. Is there any escape? Of course. A miracle. Leave the details to Joe.

An old man in a rented house with his cat, Ruski. So he looks about in quiet desperation for an escape route. That's Thoreau, I think, wasn't he the one drowned himself in Walden Pond with a dead loon around his neck? Pick a card . . . any card. . . .

So he writes about desperately for an escape route. Such openings are only there in times of chaos when the cry goes up, "Every man for himself!"

"*Chacun pour soi!*"

"*Sauve qui peut!*"

If you're going to slip in somewhere and save your skin it has to be when the ship is sinking, a country falling apart, a time when nobody knows who is who and you can pass yourself off as *anybody*.

The Weimar Republic. Cocaine is cheaper than food. Starving boys—*die Wandervögel*, the migrating birds—flock to

Berlin to sell themselves for a meal. The hero prances out in drag singing, *"Einer Mann, einer Mann, einer RICHTIGER Mann!"*

Easy to pick up a pair of shoes in the Weimar Republic. *Jeder Mann sein eigener Fussball.* (Every man his own football.) They deserved to lose for such vapid nonsense. The Lesbians had a marching song: *Wir brauchen keiner Männer mehr.* (We don't need men anymore.) And the gays tripped along to: *Wir sind anders als die andern / Die nur im Gleichschritt der Moral geliebt haben.* (We are different from the others / Who have only loved in the same step of morality.)

Three hundred gay bars, bread riots and street fighting and hunger . . . every man his own football.

SA marschiert. . . .

Master Levy, when asked for the price of a flop by one of *the Wanderburschen* who came from all over Germany to Berlin—some queen's jissom may be the first food they have had in three days—so Levy says, "Well, I can't give you any money. But I will give you good advice. Over there under that railroad there is a *particularly* cold wind."

He denies the story. He was a strong man, reminded me of Korzybski. Rather heavy, with big arms and a strong voice. At times the strong must commit acts of incredible cruelty to stoke their strength. One sultan used to cut the arm off whoever helped him into the saddle. You have to be strong to live with such acts, very strong. I do not aspire to such strength. Obviously such strength is forced upon the recipient slowly, a bit at a time . . . the door closes behind him, only one door open. A man's arm. *Slice* . . . he spurs his horse before the blood spurts out. . . .

At the Russian front, morphine is the most precious commodity, a warm, comfortable blanket against the cold that gets down inside you so finally you don't shiver anymore because there is no place to shiver to. You can tell how long a soldier has been at the front by how much he shivers. The new ones are shaking like they had malaria. The old hands move slow, like lizards.

Wilhelm was lucky. His colonel in the Waffen SS was an addict. As soon as a town was captured he was into the drugstores and the doctors' offices. Wilhelm had a superb Mannlicher with telescopic sights. It's a *wunderbar* feeling, to tag someone at five hundred yards, like the hand of God, the tiny figure falling in the snow . . . way out there near the skyline. And he practiced with his P38, worked over by a gunsmith and with a butt custom-molded to his hand. He could hit snowballs in the air.

Back to some requisitioned farmhouse, no need to ask permission from the owners. They have been removed by a work crew . . . had to . . . dead, you know . . . the ampules and syringes and alcohol laid out. The Colonel is a thin, aristocratic man of fifty with a fine thin nose and thin lips and little blue veins hard to hit. But Wilhelm could find a vein in a mummy.

"Allow me, my Colonel."

The blood blooms in the syringe and he pushes the plunger home.

"Sieg Heil!" breathes the Colonel.

Wilhelm is tying up . . . ahh the blessed warmth.

"Heil Hitler!"

"Heil Hitler!" the Colonel echoes.

Wilhelm knows the whole thing is insane, like Napoléon. He remembers the Victor Hugo poem, "It snowed it snowed it snowed."

He knows the Colonel is thinking the same thing. How can we get out from under this madman and save our assholes? But such thoughts are better left unspoken. As the Russian offensive gathers momentum and the Allies are close to Berlin, watch what you say and even what you think. The Black Dogs are sniffing for defeatism and disloyalty. One wrong word and you can hang with the Russian partisans with a placard around your neck: "Here is a pig who deserted his comrades. Now he is dead forever." And this is a lieutenant. Officers are not exempt from such summary execution . . . on the contrary. So play it *kalt,* and watch and wait.

Shots outside . . . Wilhelm packs the drugs and the syringes. They will have to fall back, though they have been ordered to hold the position *bis in den Tod.* "Let Goebbels and Goering and Hitler come up here and hold it," growls the Colonel. "I am pulling back."

The long retreat, the frostbitten soldiers hobbling along on toeless feet. And those with their eyelids frozen off who can never again close their eyes. And the genitals that drop off when you try to take a piss and the concentrated yellow urine seeps out with sluggish black blood . . . back back back . . . to the outskirts of Berlin.

Berlin is a ruin, without water or food or police or medical facilities. Clearly it is every man for himself. The Russians are in the eastern outskirts of Berlin, the Allies in the west. Wilhelm is following his instincts. He knows that the name of the life game is *Survival.* The War is lost but the SS is out with ropes, grimly and methodically hanging all deserters and defeatists from trees and lampposts and the projecting beams of bombed-out buildings.

Ah, a dead major. Wilhelm goes quickly through his clothes. A .25 automatic, which he pockets, and four boxes of ampules and a syringe with extra needles in a little metal box . . . *Eukodol* . . . what is this? Wilhelm draws up two ampules of .02 grams. He hits and presses the plunger home.

"Sieg Heil." It's almost a speedball of morphine and cocaine. A real updraft, like he used to feel when he was flying gliders. But he never made the air force. His sight was short.

Keep moving, get to the Americans! They will believe anything if you tell them what they want to hear.

The fall of Berlin . . . music from Götterdämmerung . . . thunder and lightning. Dazed citizens dipping water out of bomb craters. Lightning freezes into the lightning insignia of the Waffen SS . . . face of the dancer blazes with alertness . . . WHOOSH! He throws himself to the ground as a shell explodes in front of him. He stands up immobile, watching.

Dangling from the beam of a bombed-out building is the body of a civilian youth. The body oscillates slowly and the face comes into view. Wilhelm pulls a knife and cuts the boy down, and drags him into the shell of a building. Wallpaper, a shattered dresser, suggestion of a theatrical dressing room. He works quickly, stripping off his uniform. Pulling the body up to remove the jacket . . . shirt . . . he strips off his pants and his underwear, placing his P38 on the dresser. His cock flips out half-hard. He is junk sick, shivering burning junk sick. He hoists the boy's buttocks and pulls his pants down. The shorts are stained with sperm in front. He smiles and pulls the boy's shorts down and puts them on with a bump grind leaving his cock sticking out all the way up now he fingers his cock and goes off showing all his teeth as he spurts over the naked corpse. He tucks his cock in. Pulls on the pants. Fit just right around his skinny waist and ass. Even the shoes fit. Ah, my *shoes*. He puts on the jacket and reaches into the left inside pocket.

Carl Peterson. Age: twenty-two. Occupation: mechanic.

On-screen advertisement: *Children's shoes have far to go* . . . (An agent's cover, his false identity, is known as shoes.)
*Over the hills
And far away*

"Hans!"

"Wilhelm!"

"What are you doing still in that uniform? Are you full crazy?"

"But Wilhelm, we were soldiers, not policemen. We are entitled to a soldier's treatment under the Geneva Convention."

"Would you like to explain that in Russian to the Ivans?"

Wilhelm points to a derelict in rags scuttling past. Hans shoots the derelict in the back of the head. "He deserves to die for stinking like this," Hans grumbles as he puts on the old man's rags. "Nameless asshole didn't have papers. I will probably get typhus from his doss-house lice!"

"There are worse things than typhus, Hans. . . . We must find the Americans. Go west, young man, go west, and stay well away from the Ivans."

"**S**ay, are we glad to see you guys!"

"What took you so long?"

Berlin is swarming with police looking for war criminals. Kim, using the name Carl Peterson, gets a clerical job with the American CID so that he can photograph their list of wanted SS personnel. He accumulates a few thousand dollars trading coffee and chocolate, Spam and cigarettes, for antiques and paintings, P38s and Nazi daggers, which he sells to the American and English officers.

Kim feels grotesquely miscast as a black market operator. Look at them—sleek, pomaded, with manicured dirty fingernails, narrow shoulders and broad hips, expensive clothes and dirty underwear.

Kim singles out a cold-eyed tech sergeant. "Can you get rid of these?" He shows some morphine ampules. "Plenty more."

The sergeant nods.

Soon he has ten thousand dollars saved up. Time to move on to Tangier.

The town is booming, quivering with avarice and money fever like the seismic tremors of an earthquake. There are no rooms to be had in Tangier, but he manages to find a place on Calle

Cook in a run-down stucco villa operated by a former madame from Saigon, in return for a small Renoir. He issues a bulletin to the effect that he has money to invest, and is beseiged by operators with money-making ideas: to open another bar, a clothing store, an antique shop, to buy into a smuggling operation. He is just testing the air, shaking the tree.

So many Arab boys about, Kim decides to take the cure and indulge in sex. He checks into a clinic in the Marshan, run by a French doctor and his wife. The doctor is burly and vigorous, with a black mustache—*un vrai bonhomme.* The wife fades in and out in a perpetual state of well-founded jealousy. She is soon crying on Kim's shoulder about her husband's indiscretions. Three weeks, and Kim is over the hump.

"Sois sage," the doctor says, with a crushing handshake.

And now for the list. There are five former SS in Tangier on the Allies' list of wanted war criminals. He knows some of the names on his list are posing as Jewish refugees.

Ah, yes, here we are, Doctor Wellingstein. A former concentration camp doctor. I've got *him* on my list.

The Doctor is cool and reserved.

"So what can I do for you?" He makes a point of speaking in English. Kim has made it clear that the visit is not medical.

The Doctor receives him in a small parlor with chairs and a couch upholstered in blue satin, a glassed-in bookcase, all of it as dead and unlived-in as the Doctor himself—a tall, gaunt man with something dank and cold and dead in his face. Kim helps himself to Schnaps from a carafe on the coffee table. *Réalités, Der Spiegel,* neatly laid out. Kim walks around the apartment looking at the pictures.

"Hummmm, Klee . . . Monet . . ."

"They are reproductions, of course."

"Very good reproductions, I'd say."

"What do you want?"

"Oh, I might be interested in buying some of your, uh, reproductions. Just arrived in Tangier. Place is a bit bare you know. Now, that"—he points to a small Klee—"would brighten up my digs."

"This isn't a shop. It's not for sale. And now, if you will excuse me."

Kim stands up. "Of course, Doctor *Unruhe.*"

The Doctor's face freezes. "I think you have me confused with someone else."

"Perhaps, but a phone call to the War Crimes Commission, or whatever they call themselves, could clear up the confusion." Kim picks up his hat.

"Wait! Who are you?"

"A simple soldier of the Third Reich . . . misled like all the German people . . . Waffen-SS."

The Doctor speaks in German. "Sit down, we will talk. Let me get a decent schnapps."

After a *sehr gemütlich* little chat with Kim, the Doctor puts his fingertips together. "I think that I can put you in the way of some profitable employment. You see, the Swiss are not pleased with the situation here in Tangier . . . secret banking facilities . . . a second Switzerland . . . this they do not like. I could introduce you to a man here . . . a Swiss."

The Doctor makes a phone call. "He will be in the Parade Bar at seven this evening. He walks with a cane."

Kim stands up to go. "You may rely on my discretion, Doctor. You see, I am more interested in employment than money. . . . Oh, yes, I would advise you to remove your *reproductions* to a bank vault."

The Parade Bar is in an arcade of jewelry shops and gold merchants, a blank black expanse of plate glass, a heavy glass door. The interior is dark, the atmosphere menacing and transient. You can hear time ticking away to disaster. Behind the bar is a middle-aged man who looks like a saintly old convict.

Kim orders a martini, which seems to materialize in front of him. "We are moving next month," the bartender tells him.

"Looks like a bank in here," Kim says.

The bartender nods matter-of-factly and walks down the bar to replenish a middle-aged female lush.

It is just a few minutes past seven. This must be my contact. The cane comes in first. A black cane followed by a thin man in a black suit with black glasses. He seems to feel with the cane and there is about him a suggestion of blindness. But he comes directly to Kim and sits down on the barstool next to him. "Ah," he says, "you are Doctor Wellingstein's young friend." The hand he offers is as cool and dry as a bank note.

The bartender walks to the other end of the bar.

The man speaks as if referring to a computer readout. "The situation here is unsound but unfortunately has attracted unattached capital. This is of course regrettable. Perhaps if prospective investors became aware of exactly how *dangerously* unstable . . . I think a demonstration could be arranged." He passes a large manila envelope to Kim. "Read this. Financial arrangements will be through the Banque de Genève."

Qualitative data can be processed on the computer by assigning numerical value to a spectrum of affective states: Does the concept of a hog in a mosque elicit in the subject:

1. Indifference
2. Distinct displeasure
3. Anger
4. Rage
5. Homicidal rage

We are shooting for a five . . . incidents, you know . . . recorded hog calls in mosques and Moslem cemeteries . . . hogs released from concealed pens and trucks.

We need a team of professional riot leaders like La Bomba, the Bomb, who started a soccer riot in Lima that claimed three hundred and fifty-two victims. (The soccer scores are coming in from the Capitol . . . one must pretend an interest.)

And the Whisperer. He can leave words . . . the right words . . . in the air just behind him as he glides through crowds in the markets. And some straight, old-line political agitators.

Do we use actual hogs? Of course not. We tape the riot that would be precipitated by the intervention of hogs. Tapes of previous riots with hog noises cut in played back by fast-moving operatives as our agitators move in behind the tapes to incite the gathering crowds.

Raw menace in the air like a haze. A middle-aged European (he turned out to be Swiss) is trying to make himself inconspicuous as he scuttles for his hotel on the edge of the Socco Grande. He is one of those gray, almost invisible presences who can suddenly stand out raw and naked like a man abusing himself in the crowded market.

Oh Christ, it's happening! They SEE him! Someone pushes him hard from behind. He stumbles forward and falls. Feet thud into his ribs and face. He struggles to get up, hands clutching pulling tearing, a sound like ripping cloth as the Spanish Legionnaires called in by the British open up with machine guns on the crowd from shop roofs overlooking the Socco Grande. Screaming, trampling, running for the side streets. All over in a few seconds, leaving twenty-three dead.

Big money, like a frightened octopus, turned green and siphoned away . . . back to Switzerland, west to the Caymans, the Bahamas, Uruguay. . . .

The Edelweiss, with its moldy deer heads, sour beer and fermented sauerkraut and the specifically Swiss smell of a thousand years of thawing garbage spilling down from sordid villages perched on mountainsides and unwashed goiters, gives notice that Asunción is yet another Switzerland. They've captured the Swiss smell, the reek of its hinterland, and now the money will follow. Unless, of course . . .

Kim Lee sits with Allerton, his contact, at a black oak table with a soiled white-and-red-checked tablecloth, a small portion of whiskey in a dirty glass.

Allerton was a thin, blond man with an air of arrested age. He seemed to float a few inches above the ground, wafted here and there, a specialized organism at once torpid and predatory. His hair was blond but the eyebrows were black and sharp as pencil lines, and slightly arched, giving him a startled look—startled, but never dismayed. He was American, couldn't be anything else somehow, by the lack of any definite cultural imprint.

There is something cold and fishy behind his easy affability, the way he can slip in anywhere and establish immediate rapport. He is in fact the perfect agent, lacking only dedication. A washout from the CIA for an elaborate computerized swindle of one of the Company's proprietaries, so elaborate that the Company backed off from inquiring too closely. He was allowed to resign with minimal prejudice. Then Allerton went to work for the Swiss navy and the second Switzerland was left with the Swiss stink, their currency pressed right down to the paper.

Kim Lee had the list. Allerton had some shaky Mossad connections from a stint in Saudi Arabia where the Jews bought minor information from him with bad whiskey. Like conquistadors, they head into the perilous jungles of Uruguay, sustained by a pure flame of avarice: "Get rich. Sleep till noon. And fuck 'em all!"

Allerton, despite his basic coldness, is a loyal friend and reliable backup. He intends to buy a liquor store. Kim Lee will open a restaurant. One set menu every day. Makes it easier to shop thataway. A few chickens. It's the only way to live. Modest objectives were to become the keystone of Margaras Unlimited, a series of modest goals leading to a series of modest achievements which became at some point quite considerable.

With Allerton in a moving house. Clutter the Glind. We are moving south. There is a back hall and a small back room that can serve as bedrooms. I say that the speed has to be reduced or the motors will burn out surer'n Sunday petting a phantom phallus wrapping the target in pulsing fur. . . . Despite his basic coldness. Society note of a black reliable backup Margaras tar weapons the crest of a country auto hairdo coming to a policy delineated by what Burn's hole won't take in a fighting suit of Glind screams the captain of what one can pull on south. There is a back hall be removed the lips can serve as bedrooms start to rotate be reduced or the motors will cut a gaping hole so fast January 20 arrested by a phantom extendable ear. Stiff loyal fried and good one leg cut off reference to a secret service without cat caught in a steel trap. We are moving flesh with special attributes and a small back room that grows in place. Someone offers me the management of a bar in Nova Scotia.

And that is what we did, move a phantom organization to Asunción. No KGB to pull us back to Home Center and no Home Center to get pulled back to, and that is how we conceived Margaras Unlimited, a secret service without a country. Its policy is delineated by the jobs it won't take. Come level on average, MU takes the usual secret service assignments: assassinations, riot incitement, revolutions, collapses of currencies, collection and sale of information. There was only one existing agency even remotely similar and that was Interpol. Since Interpol was staffed to a large extent by ex-Nazis, some of them on Kim's list, we were soon firmly entrenched and in possession of vast criminal files from which we could recruit agents by the threat of exposure and extort money in return for expungement from the files and consequent freedom to operate.

We transformed Interpol from a passive bureau of criminal information, without power of search, seizure or arrest, into a supernational police force with full power of arrest, search and seizure, extracting information from all police and intelligence agencies while owing fealty to none.

Before they knew where their Margaras disks were, we were into the files of the KGB and the CIA like a swarm of mole crickets. Our computer files are in many locations, mostly America, owing to the lack of police surveillance; also in South America with our travel agencies; in Scandinavia with *Nudist* magazine; in Switzerland, the copies in bank vaults. Our technicians move from center to center easily since they are not trailing wires to Moscow Center, MI-5, Langley, Tel Aviv and other marginal agencies.

The Swiss are going soft on the heavy money toilet, and no second Switzerlands are rearing their assholes now that the IRS is cracking down on the Caymans and the Bahamas. Any agencies I've forgotten? Nationalist China? The sinister mafia of Vietnam? The old Union Corse not to be underestimated? The Vatican cannot be *over*estimated. All the pressure groups. We trail no wires. Our policy is SPACE.

Anything that favors or enhances space programs, space exploration, simulation of space conditions, exploration of inner space, expanding awareness, we will support. Anything going in the other direction we will extirpate. The espionage world now has a new frontier.

2

Joe the Dead lowered the rifle, like some cryptic metal extension growing from his arm socket, and smiled for a fleeting moment. A blush touched his ravaged features with a flash of youth that evaporated in powder smoke. With quick, precise movements he disassembled the telescoping rifle and silencer and fitted the components into a toolbox. Behind him, Kim Carsons and Mike Chase lay dead in the dust of the Boulder Cemetery. The date was September 17, 1899.

Joe walked away from the Cemetery, back toward Pearl Street and the center of town, whistling a dry raspy little tune like a snake shedding its skin. He made his way to the train station, bought a ticket to Denver and took a shot of morphine in the outhouse. Two hours later he was back in his Denver stronghold.

No regrets about Kim. Arty type, no principles. And not much sense. Sooner or later he would have precipitated a senseless disaster with his histrionic faggotries . . . a chessman to be removed from the board, perhaps to be used again in a more advantageous context.

Mike Chase was slated for a disastrous presidency, replete with idiotic legislation, backed by Old Man Bickford, one of the whiskey-drinking, poker-playing evil old men who run America from the back rooms and clubhouses. Nothing upsets someone like Bickford more than the sudden knowledge that an unknown player is sitting in on a game he thought was all his. Such men cannot tolerate doubt. They must have everything sewed up tight.

Joe could of course throw in with Bickford—another sinking ship, only sinking a bit slower. Laissez-faire capitalism was a thing of the past that would metamorphose into conglomerate corporate capitalism, another dead end. A problem cannot be solved in terms of itself. The human problem cannot be solved in human terms. Only a basic change in the board and the chessmen could offer a chance of survival. Consider the Egyptian concept of seven souls, with different and incompatible interests. They must be welded into one. Otherwise the organism remains wide open to parasitic attack.

There were a number of valid reasons for eliminating Kim and Chase. They were jointly responsible for the death of Tom Dark. Chase set it up, Kim rode into it. There is never any excuse for negligence. Joe and Tom belonged to the same ancient guild—tinkers, smiths, masters of fire. . . . Loki, Anubis and the Mayan God Kak U Pacat, He who works in fire. Masters of number and measurement . . . technicians. With the advent of modern technology, the guild gravitated toward physics, mathematics, computers, electronics and photography. Joe could have done this, except he was tied down in Kim's Rover-Boy weapon models, doing what any hack gunsmith could have done.

But the real reason was PAIN. In a universe controlled and delineated by Kim and his obsession with antiquated weaponry, Joe was in hideous and constant pain. His left arm and side clung to him like a burning mantle. That pain could be alleviated by morphine. The other pain, the soul pain, morphine and heroin could not touch. Joe had been brought back from the Land of the Dead, back from Hell. Every movement, everything he looked at, was a source of excruciating pain.

The safe that had blown up in his face and nearly killed him was in a warehouse used as a beer drop. Crates of old oranges stacked around . . . the box looked like you could open it with a can opener. Joe carried the blast always with him, a reek of rotten burning oranges, cordite and scorched metal. Joe's withered, blighted face, seared by the fires of Hell from the molten core of a doomed planet.

As he walked away from the cemetery humming "A Bicycle Built for Two," Joe felt good. For the first time in years the pain was gone. It was like a shot of morphine in fourth-day withdrawal. Killing always brought a measure of relief, as if the pain had been siphoned off. But in this instance the relief was profound, since Kim was an integral part of the pain context. Shoot your way to freedom, Joe thought. He knew the pain would come back, but by then perhaps he would see a way out.

He turned into Pleasant Street . . . trees and lawns and red brick houses. The street was curiously empty. The dogs were quiet. Just the wind in trembling poplars, and the sound of running water . . . A smell of burning leaves. A boy in a red sweater rode by on a bicycle and smiled at Joe.

It was just as well that he had concealed his assets and talents. That would make him much harder to locate when Bickford realized things had gone wrong and started looking for the unknown player. Bickford knew about Joe's past, of course, but would have considered him unimportant. A gunsmith, a checker player—not even chess.

Over the centuries and tens of centuries, Joe had served many men—and many Gods, for men are but the representatives of Gods. He had served many, and respected none. "They don't even know what buttons to push or what happens when you push them. Push themselves out of a job every fucking time."

Joe is the Tinkerer, the Smith, the Master of Keys and Locks, of Time and Fire, the Master of Light and Sound, the Technician. He knows the how and the when. The why does not concern him. He has left many sinking ships. "So I am to take orders from a birdbrained posturing faggot? Just leave the details to Joe. . . . Well, he left one too many. They all do."

He would have to move quickly before Bickford & Co. could recover and close the leak. He knew there was only one man who could effect the basic changes dictated by the human impasse: Hassan i Sabbah: HIS. The Old Man of the Mountain. And HIS was cut off by a blockade that made the Gates of Anubis look like a dimestore lock.

Joe understood Kim so well that he could afford to dispense with him as a part of himself not useful or relevant at the present time. He understood Kim's attempt to transcend his physical structure, to which he could never become reconciled, by an icy, inhuman perfection of attitude, painfully maintained and refined to an unbearable pitch. Joe turned to a negation of attitude, a purity of function that could be maintained only by the pressure of deadly purpose.

The simplest task caused him almost unbearable pain, like looking about his workspace and putting every object in its ordained place, each object to be either assigned a place or moved to another room, which resulted in moving one clutter to another place where he would, in time, extend his tidying process until each object had felt the touch of his hand, and those objects that finally belonged nowhere would be arranged into what he called a Muriel, a final expression of random disorder.

This continual pain is a sanction imposed by Nature, whose laws he flouts by remaining alive. Joe's only lifeline is the love of certain animals. Dogs immediately see him with deep hatred as the Stranger, but he can make himself invisible to dogs, incapable of being seen because the dog's eyes would hurt, so that the dog skirts the perimeters of his cover.

Cats see him as a friend. They rub against him purring, and he can tame weasels, skunks and racoons. He knows the lost art of turning an animal into a familiar. The touch must be very brave and very gentle. He can feel his *ki* fill the lost hand and the animal turns, its back arched under the phantom touch. If the touch fails, the animal may attack like a demon from Hell. Several people have been killed trying to tame the Tiger Cat, a twenty-pound wildcat found in Central America. Only those who can be without fear can make a familiar. And Joe has nothing left to fear.

Faint blush transfigured his years and implemented a flash of youth. He unscrewed capitalism, snake shedding its skin. Change terminal. Bought a ticket to offer a chance of outhouse. Hour souls . . . for Mike Chase Joe knows in his arm socket become President, a faint blush flashed some disastrous legislation features a disastrous presidency leaving for Bickford another sink out in nitrous film smoke quick precise Joe detached another dead end. Only a tool box. The board and checkers coo a little tune like survival. Consider the seven ways to the stage melted into one. There is only one man in the Cemetery—HIS. How can the blockade be broken and the day's *cul de sac*?

Joe the Dead belongs to a select breed of outlaws known as the NOs, natural outlaws dedicated to breaking the so-called natural laws of the universe foisted upon us by physicists, chemists, mathematicians, biologists and, above all, the monumental fraud of cause and effect, to be replaced by the more pregnant concept of synchronicity.

Ordinary outlaws break man-made laws. Laws against theft and murder are broken every second. You only break a natural law once. To the ordinary criminal, breaking a law is a means to an end: obtaining money, removing a source of danger or annoyance. To the NO, breaking a natural law is an end in itself: the end of that law.

Ordinary outlaws specialize their trades, in accordance with their inclinations and aptitudes—or they did at one time. Many of the old-time criminal types are endangered species now. Consider the Murphy Man. How many even know what a Murphy Man is? Your Murphy Man steers the mark to a nonexistent whore, having located an apartment building without a doorman and with the front door unlocked.

"Looking for some action, friend?"

"Well, uh, yes . . ."

The Murphy Man makes a phone call: it's all set up. He leads the mark to the apartment building entrance.

"Go up one flight, first door on your left, 1A. Prime grade, friend, and she's ready and waiting on you. You pay me now, so there won't be any arguments."

Only a black man can have the real Murphy Man voice—cool, insinuating, familiar—and the real Murphy Man face—sincere, unflappable, untrustworthy.

And practitioners of the Hype or the Bill, a short-change routine. You start by paying for a two-bit item with a twenty-dollar bill. You get the change on the counter, then you tell the clerk, "I must have been dreaming—I don't mean to take all your small change. Here, give me ten for this" and count the ones back, minus the five. Or something like that. It's hard to get a conviction on the Bill, because nobody can explain exactly what happened.

The basic principle can be found in a sketch by Edgar Allan Poe on nineteenth-century hustlers who were known as Diddlers. The diddler walks into a tobacco store and asks for a plug of tobacco. When the plug is on the counter, he changes his mind.

"Give me a cigar instead." He takes the cigar and starts to walk out.

"Wait a minute. You didn't pay for the cigar."

"Of course not. I traded it against the tobacco plug."

"Don't recall you paid me for that either."

"Paid you for it! Why, there it is! None of your tricks on traveling men."

Unobtrusive and insistent, practitioners of the Bill are often addicts.

I wonder if there are any hype men left? Like Yellow Kid Weil and the Big Store: he would set up a prop brokerage office or bookmaking parlor and fleece his customers for several days before vanishing one night with the boodle. Also noteworthy is the sordid yachting swindle, practiced at one time by a certain well-known cult leader who shall be nameless. They're going to buy a boat together, sail the South Seas . . . this swindle requires that mark and swindler live in the same trailer, get drunk together every night and lay the same whore. Yellow Kid Weil would have been scandalized. "Never drink with a savage," was one of his rules.

The old-time bank robbers, the burglars who bought jewelry-store insurance inventories and knew exactly what they were looking for, the pickpockets trained from early childhood—they say the best ones come from Colombia—where are they now? The Murphy Men, the hype artists, the Big Store? Gone, all gone.

Ordinary outlaws specialize; so do the Natural Outlaws. Joe the Dead specializes in evolutionary biology. He dedicates his dearly bought knowledge of pain and death to cracking two biologic laws:

Rule One: Hybrids are permitted only between closely related species and then grudgingly, the hybrids produced being always sterile. The Biologic Police bluntly warn: "To break down the lines that Mother Nature, in her ripe wisdom, has established between species is to invite biologic and social chaos."

Joe says, "What do you think I'm doing here? Let it come down."

Rule Two: An evolutionary step that involves biologic mutation is irretrievable and irreversible. Newts start life in the water, breathing with gills. At the ordained time the newt sheds his gills and crawls up onto the land, now equipped with air-breathing lungs. Then he returns to the water, where he lives out his days. So it might be convenient to reclaim his gills and breathe underwater again?

"No glot, clom Fliday," says the Cosmic Uncle. It's the law.

So, for starters, Joe pulls a baby mule out of the cosmic manger. There is Mary—Mother Mule—and Joseph—the father—and the impossible child with a glowing, pulsing halo.

A Kansas vet known as Joe Lazarus was the instrument of

altered destiny. He had been kicked in the head by a mule and pronounced dead at Lawrence Memorial Hospital, but was returned to life. Like Saint Paul, knocked off his ass on the road to Damascus, after his miraculous recovery, Joe Laz knew what he had to do.

He set out to produce a fertile mule. He exposed horse and donkey sperm to orgone radiation in a magnetized pyramid, and inseminated the mare—didn't hack it. So Laz went further: he rigged a magnetized stall and bombarded the copulating animals with DOR—Deadly Orgone Radiation. He sewed himself into a goat skin and whipped his beasts to wild Pan music—any woman hit by the Goat God's whip will conceive—and finally he created a fertile mule.

Skeptics pronounced Joe Laz's mule the most colossal hoax since the Piltdown Man.

"I had it up my sleeve," Joe deadpanned.

A quiet, enigmatic former herpetologist residing in Florida challenges Rule Two. His name is Joe Sanford. Bitten by a king cobra, he recovered and devoted himself to the study of newts and salamanders. Sanford claims to have reinstituted gills in mature, air-breathing newts by injections of a lamb-placenta concentrate.

(The same preparation, in fact, was used by Doctor Niehaus of Geneva, Switzerland, to turn back the clock for his wealthy patients. To name a few: W. Somerset Maugham, Noel Coward, Pope Pius XII, President Eisenhower. I recall seeing Eisenhower waving a tiny American flag from his hospital bed, with a big stupid grin on his face, and wondering if he would ever die. Winston Churchill couldn't qualify, because he couldn't lay off the sauce for six weeks, a prerequisite for the Niehaus treatment, and no exceptions.)

Rule Two carries the implicit assumption that time is irreversible. Sanford makes a hole in time, and Joe sloshes through the hybrids.

It is not necessary to prove anything, simply to state. This is a biologic revolution, fought with new species and new ways of thinking and feeling, a war where the bullet may take millennia to hit. Like the old joke about the executioner makes a swipe with the samurai sword . . . well, missed me that time. But just try and shake your head three hundred years from now.

Let it come down . . . the ancient barrier between grass eaters and meat eaters. The old dichotomy of carnivore and herbivore has dissolved in primal hunger to spawn creatures who eat flesh or grass at will. Lions graze on the veldt. A herd of carnivorous man-eating wildebeests stalks the villages, creatures who are warm-blooded or cold-blooded according to altered surroundings. At the end of the human line everything is permitted.

All is in the not done, the diffidence that faltered.

Let others quaver out: "I dare do all that may become a man, who dares do more is none."

Not so, says Joe.

He who dares at all, must dare all.

When mules foal

Anything goes.

When mules glow

Anything foals.

Hybrids Unlimited . . . HU HU HU.

Doctor Whitehorn studied the man sitting opposite him. The man's skull looked as though it were made of a thin metal that had been shattered on the left side and rewelded together, a thin line of red-purple scar tissue tracing the joint.

As the doctor surmised, Joe's blind left eye was not blind. Joe had devised an artificial eye, wired into the optic center, that presented his mind with pictures, often quite at variance with the reports of the right eye. This was especially noticeable when he looked at human and animal subjects, and he came to realize to what extent that which we see is conditioned by what we expect to see—that is, by a habitual scanning pattern, whereas the artificial eye had no scanning pattern. The lens was fixed and Joe had to direct it by movements of his head. On the other hand, the lens could be adjusted to a wide angle, which greatly extended the range of his peripheral vision. He found that he could read motives and expressions with great precision by comparing the data of the good eye, which was picking up what someone wants to project, and the data of the synthetic eye. Sometimes the difference in expression was so grotesque that he was surprised it was not immediately apparent to anyone.

He knew now that Doctor Whitehorn, who was looking through his references with an amused smile, doubted their authenticity.

Doctor Whitehorn had come to research via psychiatry. Many doctors are drawn to this profession because they have an innate deficiency of insight into the motives, feelings and thoughts of others, a deficiency they hope to remedy by ingesting masses of data. Doctor Whitehorn was driven to abandon psychiatry because of his insight, which rendered contact with hopelessly damaged creatures extremely painful, and even more painful the brutish and insensitive treatment such patients often receive, because they are "insane" and therefore no one will believe their complaints.

It was not that Dr. Whitehorn was overly compassionate. He simply could not help feeling someone else's pain. And the man sitting opposite him radiated pain. Of course . . . the physical injuries . . . the prosthetic limb, the artificial eye, phantom limb pain and phantom eye pain. The doctor became aware of a strange odor, not coming from the man, but something he brought in with him. A reek of rotten citrus and burning plastic, like a burning amusement park.

"Well, Professor Hellbrandt. You have impressive credentials."

"I know my subject."

"Quite a few subjects, I'd say."

"My code name was Big Picture. You can spend your life fitting one piece in."

"Most people do less than that."

"Most people do nothing."

"Certainly there is work here for a man of your . . . uh . . . capabilities and qualifications, though I suspect some of these references to be forgeries."

Joe shrugged with his right shoulder, the human shoulder, and smiled with the right side of his face. The result was disconcerting.

Joe had a number of devices that he could fit into a socket just below the elbow of his severed arm. One was a shock unit, with two long, needle-sharp electrodes that could be jabbed into an opponent to deliver the shock inside. He had a cyanide syringe, for instant death, and an air-powered tranquilizer dart gun. He regarded these artifacts as toys, for which he would have less and less use as he pursued his research projects. Joe never allowed the real purpose of a project to be revealed or even suspected until he was in a position to use it. By then it would be too late for his enemies to profit from his work.

Having discovered the key to the money of others through research grants and scholarships and foundations, Joe was able to juggle a number of projects at once, all contributing to his overall objective of totally subverting the present natural order. He formed an ecological foundation called the Spreaders, ostensibly to study various useful species of plants and animals and introduce them into areas where they are at present unknown, taking into account the appropriate climatic conditions, disturbance of existing ecological systems, and potential usefulness as food source, control of pests, etc.

Actually he intended to carry out experiments in punctuational evolution by transporting small numbers of fish, animals and reptiles to unfamiliar environments and, also, by bringing into contact species that had never been in contact before, to open potentials for hybridization. It is interesting to note that one of the few existing hybrids is the "tiglon," a cross between the lion and the tiger—creatures who live in different habitats and do not come into contact in nature, except by Man's interventions.

Joe could come on buddy buddy good old boy with the other researchers and they accepted it. They had to accept it, because they were all afraid of Joe. His white eyes, his dead pale skin, his faint voice that nonetheless carried across the lab and into their heads . . . and his disquieting smile. When he wanted something done, they did it. He never saw any of them outside the lab.

No one but Joe and his team knew that a basic aim of his research was to sabotage the proposed highway through the Amazon basin. Coca-Cola, McDonald's and Hiltons waiting off-stage. He knows that if the highway goes through, it will mean the destruction of the last great rain forest left on the planet. Joe is a dedicated ecologist. It hurts him to see a tree cut down.

"They shall not pass," he decides.

He can see it already. The jungle Hiltons . . . "When Orchids Bloom in the Moonlight" on the Muzak . . . the bar, with orchids and a tank against one wall full of piranha fish. The management throws in live goldfish and pieces of raw meat.

The motels and souvenir shops and hamburger joints, drunken Indians, polluted rivers, the gritty bite of diesel fumes. In front of the Manaos Opera House, tourists pose with a boa constrictor.

Terrible scandal: a big pop star, in a jealous rage fueled by cocaine, grabbed his girlfriend's Yorkshire terrier and threw it into the piranha tank. As the piranhas attacked the floundering dog, the hysterical starlet threw a heavy bronze ashtray which shattered the tank, spilling snapping fish and bloody water across the patrons as the disemboweled, screaming dog dragged its intestines across the floor. Quite a scene it was, and of course there were plenty of cameras to freeze-dry this edifying spectacle for posterity and export. It's the little touches that make a future solid enough to be destroyed.

They had passed through the town of Esperanza and stopped for a beer . . . three Policia Nacionale, jackets unbuttoned, a pock-marked, rat-faced local youth, probably the professional brother-in-law of a cop, their lives and outlook as cramped and limited as the valley was vast and open.

Joe had seen the Rocky Mountains, the Alps, the Himalayas, but this was another dimension, a peephole through which he glimpsed a larger planet, much larger than the Saturn of his dreams. And the silence was proportionately heavier as he looked out across the vastness of that valley, very clearly seeing, as if through a telescope, the little town of crumbling stucco, the river and stone bridge, poplar trees, fields, grazing sheep and cattle, tiny patches in the wide canvas.

The Hiltons unbuilt, the highway choked with brush and vines as Joe pulls out the time rug, spilling motels and gas stations, Mr. Steaks and McDonald's, jukeboxes and pizza parlors back to jungle and howler monkeys and bird calls. A malignant strain of yellow fever unaffected by standard inoculation, horrible skin diseases, an accelerated leprosy that kills in months, the clock turning back to the Panama Canal, every foot of highway paved with skulls. Pull back. Pull out. And they can't get workers. The Indians lurk in remote areas, waiting like the jungle to reclaim invaded territory.

Joe eases over into transplant surgery. He soon excels, after an apprenticeship with Doctor Steincross, best 'plant man in the business. Joe is able to hide his potentials and act like any idiot surgeon, addicted to his operations and the adulation of patients, nurses and colleagues.

"Doctor Tod . . . Doctor Tod . . ." A respectful echo behind him in hospital corridors. He is written up in *Life*.

"Like Cato, give his little Senate laws / And sit attentive to his own applause."

It is, Joe decides, one of the most distasteful roles he has ever been called upon to play. But dead easy. Besides, transplant surgery ties in with his objectives of hybridization and mutation.

The problem is the rejection syndrome. If this obstacle can be removed, a biologic tidal wave will follow. But it is a formidable barrier. If the body rejects a life-saving organ from a fellow human, how much more immutably will it reject pieces of another species, or a biologic mutation within the species?

But there is light at the end of the incision: brain tissue does not reject. It is a different class of tissue. It feels no pain, and does not renew itself or heal after injury. Joe knows better than to start blabbing about brain transplants, but he knows the idea is there in the mind and brain of any transplant surgeon.

"Why not slip Einstein's brain into the body of a young biker whose brain has been destroyed in a collision?"

Many recoil in horror from such a concept. Why, it could lead to immortality! Just shift the old brain from one body to another. And sooner or later they won't be waiting for accident victims.

"Paging Doc Sibley . . ."—best scrambled egg man in the industry. He can switch brains in an alley.

This is of no interest to Joe. Clearly possible, but why do it? Interspecies transplants offer more enticing perspectives. Say, the brain of a chimp in a man's body. Unhampered by the crippling emotional blocks so carefully installed in humans by interested parties, the chimp might prove to be a super-genius; that is to say, he might realize a relatively larger segment of the human potential.

Why stop there? Why stop anywhere?

Joe *can't* stop. He has no place to stop in. He can't love a human being, because he has no human place to love from. But he can love certain animals, because he has animal places.

Grief is very painful for Joe—"iron tears down Pluto's

cheek." He feels it in the plates in his skull, in his artificial arms, in his artificial eye, in every wire and circuit of the tiny computer chips, down into his atoms and photons.

In setting up his project to research transplant rejection and immune response in animal subjects, instead of assembling a battery of immunologists and surgeons, Joe picked personnel without surgical training or specialized research experience. By the time a student gets through medical school his brain is so crammed with undigested, often misleading, data that there is no room left to think in. In addition to misinformation, the student has also absorbed a battery of crippling prejudices.

As a renowned transplant surgeon with an impressive array of degrees and titles, he has no difficulty in obtaining funds for his project. He has only to point out the financial advantages: the personnel he has selected will work for one-fourth the usual fees. So why bribe some prima donna immunologist away from some other project? Most competent surgeons would not be interested at any price:

"We are not veterinarians!"

In fact, any surgeon who would agree to work in the Zoo, as it was called, is probably incompetent or worse. Doctor Benway is the only MD on the program, and his license has been called into question.

Joe stresses mechanical aptitude, with particular emphasis on electrical and electronic expertise. Boys who from an early age took things apart and put them back together (more or less). Surgeons are nothing more than mechanics in any case, and many of them are piss-poor mechanics.

Here are some of the persons Joe recruited:

1. Electrician, inventor
2. Computer programmer, hobby is to tie his own trout flies
3. Mathematician, organic chemistry

4. Wood and ivory carver
5. Gunsmith, watch repairs
6. Veterinarian, lost his license for treating pet skunks
7. Gunsmith, inventor
8. Stage magician, hypnotist
9. Draftsman, makes model boats in bottles

"*Scrambles!*"

The Zoo Team plunges into an orgy of outlandish operations on the animal subjects . . . hearts, kidneys, lungs, livers, appendixes are exchanged in the operating room where often six operations are underway, the surgeons passing organs and instruments back and forth, slipping on the bloody floor. Brains are slopped from one pan to another like scrambled eggs.

"Move over! I got a pregnant wart hog here."

Each day, stretchers loaded with patched-together animal cadavers are carted off for autopsy, and some to Recovery. It is surprising that the animal subjects were able to exhibit any behavior for study after such surgery, but some of them were able to walk, bark, howl and snarl.

There were no meows, since Joe would have no cats in the Zoo, nor any raccoons, skunks, minks, foxes, lemurs or any creature with a high cuteness rating. He did not want even to contemplate or describe dubious surgery on these creatures, mute evidence that at one time a Creator with skilled, delicate and loving fingers drew breath on planet Earth, before the bad animal, Man, put an end to creation and so brought the evolutionary process to a halt.

For Man is indeed the final product. Not because homo sap is the apogee of perfection, before which God himself gasps in awe—"I can do nothing more!"—but because Man is an unsuccessful experiment, caught in a biologic dead end and inexorably headed for extinction.

"All right, boys, let's cut our way to freedom."

The hybrid concept underlies all relations between man and other animals, since only a being partaking of both man and animal can mediate between two species. These are blueprint hybrids, potentials rather than actual separate beings, capable of reproduction.

It is the task of the Guardian to nurture these half-formed creatures and to realize their potential. Some beings are bought with terrible suffering; others fail completely. All previous instructions, all guidelines, all past experience, count for nothing here. . . .

He holds the animal spirit gently to his chest, palms crossed. The first of its kind, the only one of its kind, turns to Him with total trust. There is no one else. And he must accept total responsibility. No one else is there. What does the creature need? He must find out and provide it, at any cost. The apprentice Guardian, apprenticed no longer.

Once you are in the field you are absolutely on your own. It is up to you to invoke the aid you need, by the intensity of your need. There has been much talk of love on this planet, and after all is said and done—and more is said than is done—few realize that there is a love more intense than any love of man for woman, or man for man, a love that is neither sexual nor religious. The love for a creature that you have created from your whole being transcends any other love.

And you do die of it, to lose the only thing your whole life means, every breath, every gesture, all the weariness and pain for this one act—such grief can kill. He begins to understand why people will do anything to avoid it. But he cannot avoid it. He has assumed the role of Guardian.

Outside a Palm Beach bungalow waiting for a taxi to the airport. My mother's kind, unhappy face, last time I ever saw her. Really a blessing. She had been ill for a long time. My father's dead face in the crematorium.

"Too late. Over from Cobblestone Gardens."

3

Neferti is eating breakfast at a long, wooden table with five members of an expedition: English, French, Russian, Austrian, Swedish. They are housed in a large utility shed, with filing cabinets, cots, footlockers, tool shelves and gun racks.

The Englishman addresses Neferti: "Look at you, a burnt-out astronaut. You are supposed to bring drastic change . . . to exhort!"

"It is difficult when my exhortations are shot down by enemy critics backed by computerized thought control."

"Critics? Stand up! Exhort!"

Neferti experiences a sudden surge of energy. He soars to the ceiling. The others continue eating. The Russian is studying graphs on the table between mouthfuls. Up through the ceiling. He encounters a blanket of compacted snow. He breaks through the snow into a crystalline cobalt sky over the ruins of Samarkand.

Below him he sees a Turkish shed on a rise above a deep blue lake. He alights and walks across an arm of the lake on pilings that protrude a few feet above the surface, to reach a spiral stairway with wide steps of tile in patterns of blue and red. He is willing to remain in this context and to accept whatever new dangers he may encounter. Anything is better than stasis. He is ready to leave his old body as he bounds up the steps, which curve toward a landing about twenty feet above the lake.

At the top he comes to a door of burnished silvery metal in which he can now see his face and garb. He is dressed in Tartar clothes . . . gold braid, red and blue silk threads with stiff shoulder pads and felt boots. There is a curved sword at his belt. His face is much younger, as is the lean, hard body. The teeth are yellow and hard as old ivory, his mouth set in a desperate grin. Clearly there is immediate danger and the need for drastic action.

The door has a protruding, circular lock. He twists the lock and the door opens. A small gray dog advances. He knows the dog and tells it to shut up. There are two more door dogs behind it, one black and one brown. He tries to lock the door behind him, but is not quite sure how the mechanism works.

He is in a small room with low divans around the walls, and pegs for clothes. There is another room of the same size, alongside the entrance hall, separated by a partition with an opening at the far end. In the second room are two men, one an elderly man in a gray djellaba, who presents Neferti to a fat middle-aged eunuch in a brown robe, with a toothless mouth and an unmistakable air of authority and silken cunning. The old eunuch is Master of the Door Dogs.

Neferti bows and says, "It is my honor."

The eunuch bows in return. Obviously they have serious and urgent business.

A servant brings mint tea and glasses. The three men confer. The door dogs sit immobile, looking from one face to the other.

The old eunuch takes from a leather bag a worn copy of *Officers and Gentlemen.* A gray dog sniffs and his lips curl back with a flash of yellow fangs.

Now he brings out a fork with the dry yellow skein of distant eggs. The brown dog sniffs and his eyes light up.

He brings forth a page of newsprint, a sweatshirt with the number 23, a knife with a hollow handle. The black dog sniffs . . . a panel slides open. The door dogs file out.

When Neferti told the door dog to shut up, it was a joke, because door dogs never make a sound. Silent and purposeful, they stray a few inches behind the heels of the target. No matter how quickly he turns, the door dog is always behind him. They are small creatures, not more than twenty pounds, with a long, pointed muzzle, something like a Schipperke. Door dogs are not guarders, but *crossers* of the threshold. They bring Death with them.

For a literary precedent, we turn to *The Unbearable Bassington*, by Saki (H. H. Munro):

Comus Bassington, having fumbled his prospect of marrying a fortune by asking the heiress for a loan of five pounds—nothing is better calculated to antagonize the wealthy than to ask for a small loan—must now accept a job in West Africa.

The farewell dinner is loaded with portents of doom:

"I did not know you kept a dog," said Lady Veula.

"We don't," said Comus. "There isn't one in the house."

"I could have sworn I saw one follow you across the hall this evening."

"A small black dog, something like a Schipperke?" asked Comus in a low voice.

"Yes, that was it."

"I saw it myself tonight. It ran from behind my chair just as I was sitting down."

"Have you ever seen it before?" Lady Veula asked quickly.

"Once when I was six years old. It followed my father downstairs."

Lady Veula said nothing. She knew that Comus had lost his father at the age of six.

Note that the little black dog followed Comus *into* the dining room. Here the door dog seems more a harbinger than a bearer of death. Who would put a door dog on Comus? He is already doomed as an embodiment of flawed, unbearable boyishness.

There is no clear line between harbinger and carrier, but rather one shades into the other.

A medieval chronicler called Gunther of Brandenburg wrote: "Never yet has the plague come but one has first seen a ragged stinking boy who drank like a dog from the village well and then passed on." The plague referred to is the Black Death.

And a harbinger can readily be converted into a bearer. The door dog is loaded with doom and misfortune, as a snake in spring is loaded with venom. The door dog is directed toward a specific target. It has been said that man makes dogs in his own worst image. Certainly your door dog is reciprocally fashioned as a vehicle for the worst image of the target. The door dog fits a target as a key fits a lock.

Black magic operates most effectively in preconscious, marginal areas. Casual curses are the most effective. If someone has reason to expect a psychic attack, an excellent move is to make oneself as visible as possible to the person or persons from whom the attack is anticipated, since *conscious* attacks on a target that engages one's attention are rarely effective and frequently backfire.

This strategy is especially indicated for critics. Leave your name in the phone book, attack writers on radio shows, anything to keep your image clearly in the *foreground* of enemy attention. Best of all, engage the writer in public refutation by outrageous misrepresentation and falsifications. For example, here is a critic on a writer who has spent six years on a book: "This slovenly potpourri, obviously thrown together in a few weeks."

A rule that is almost always valid: never refute or answer a critic, no matter how preposterous the criticism may be. Do not let the critic teach you the cloth, as they say in bullfighting circles. Never charge the cloth, even if the critic resorts to actual misquotation.

Writing prejudicial, off-putting reviews is a precise exercise in applied black magic. The reviewer can draw free-floating, disagreeable associations to a book by implying that the book is completely unimportant without saying exactly why, and carefully avoiding any clear images that could capture the reader's full attention.

This procedure is based on scientific evidence: Poetzel's Law states that dream imagery excludes conscious perception in favor of preconscious perceptions. And Freud's hypothesis that the neutral character of preconscious perception permits it to serve as a cover for material that would not otherwise escape the dream censor, so that unpleasant affect is attracted to preconscious perception. There is, in fact, a fifty-seven percent correlation between preconscious recall and peak unpleasantness. Charles Fischer says that dreams have a tendency to take up the *unimportant* details of waking life.

There are other tricks: the use of generalities like "the man in the street" and the editorial "we" to establish a rapport of disapproval with the reader and at the same time to create a mental lacuna under cover of an insubstantial and unspecified "we." And the technique of the misunderstood word: pack a review with obscure words that send the reader to the dictionary. Soon the reader will feel a vague, slightly queasy revulsion for whatever is under discussion.

Julian Chandler, book reviewer for a prestigious New York daily, knows all the tricks. He has chosen for his professional rancor the so-called Beat Movement, and perfected the art of antiwriting. Writers use words to evoke images. He uses words to obscure and destroy images.

This afternoon he has delivered his latest review to the office and made an appointment with the editor for three o'clock. Reading over a copy of the review, he feels a comfortable, cool-blue glow. A perfect job of demolition, and he knows it. And the editor will know it too. Two columns and not one visual image . . . word, pure word. The effect is depressing and disquieting, gathering to itself a muttering chorus of negation and antagonism.

"One starts on a mesa, a jump ahead of the posse, and soon finds oneself in the highlands of Yemen a hundred years later in quest of the Yacks, mysterious monkeys who have sex by rubbing larynxes, and this gives rise to a terrible (ho hum) plague. When the plague dies down one is back in the Old West, having lost track of time in a labyrinth of irrelevant incidents . . . like Theseus leaving a thread lest he be bored to death by the terrible Minotaur, and so finds his way back to the feeble and pointless ending . . . 'The sky darkened and went out.' Not nearly soon enough, was the feeling of this reviewer. Occasionally one glimpses flashes from the man who long ago wrote *Naked Lunch*, to show that he is not totally dead but simply sleeping, and putting his readers to sleep."

A sudden silence that can happen in big cities . . . traffic sounds cut off, a pause, a hiatus, and at the same moment the feeling that someone is at the door. This should not happen unannounced—that is what he is paying $3,500 a month for.

He steps to the peephole. The hall is empty down to the elevator. He slides the deadbolt and opens the door. A small black dog slithers in without a sound, its brush against his leg light as wind. He snatches a heavy cane he keeps by the door.

"Get out of here!"

But the dog is nowhere to be seen.

"It's gotten under something," he decides. But moving furniture and checking with a flashlight brings no dog to light.

"Well, it slipped out."

The following morning he complains to the doorman.

"A *dog*, sir?"

Clearly the Irish doorman resents the implication that he would allow an unauthorized dog to slink into the building. After all, he is the *doorman*.

"Yes, a small, black dog."

"A small, black dog, sir?" (Just a slight emphasis on *small* and *black*.)

Julian Chandler was short and slender. His family came from Trinidad, and he was inclined to boast of his black blood. This is outrageous insolence, but the doorman's face is impeccably bland, as he turns to smile at another tenant.

"Ah, good evening, Doctor Greenfield."

"Good evening, Grady."

Doctor Greenfield is an elderly WASP, trim despite his sixty years, with a pink complexion and a white mustache.

Suddenly the critic feels his carefully tended WASP connections falling about his feet like toilet paper. He considers sending a letter to the management to complain of the doorman's discourtesy, and decides against it. After all, a strange dog that comes into one's apartment, and then disappears—

"*Disappeared*, did it? Sniffed it up, more likely."

Arriving at his usual restaurant, Chandler sees the maître d' at the far end of the room seating a party, so he moves slowly toward his customary table. The maître d' turns and starts toward him with his practiced smile, which suddenly fades.

"I'm sorry, Mr. Chandler, but we do not permit pets in the dining room."

"Pets? What do you mean?"

"The dog that followed you in, sir."

"But I have no dog."

"I saw it distinctly, sir. A small black dog."

"Came in from the street most likely. It certainly isn't mine."

The maître d' looks unconvinced. . . . "Hummm, must be under something."

He calls a waiter, who peers resentfully under the table. "Nothing there . . ."

The sole isn't up to standard, and the critic's lunch is spoiled.

Chandler arrives at the office a little after three.

"Go right in, Mr. Allerton is expecting you."

New girl can't even get the editor's name right. He knocks lightly and steps in.

To his confusion a stranger comes out from behind the desk to shake hands, a youngish man with blond hair and brown eyes, who seems to float a few inches off the floor and then floats back to his seat.

"Shocking about Karl, isn't it?"

"What? I didn't know."

"Complete nervous breakdown."

"When did this happen?"

"Yesterday afternoon . . . became violent I understand . . . thought he was being followed by a black dog."

Chandler was profoundly shaken. Karl had always been known for his icy reserve.

"Where is he? We were close friends, you understand."

The new editor shrugged.

"Upstate somewhere, I believe." He leafed through some proofs on his desk. "Mr. Chandler . . . this review of W. S. Hall's latest book . . . you say categorically that it is a poor novel but you don't say why."

"But . . ." My God, didn't this punk know *anything?*

"But?" The young man raised a pencil-thin eyebrow inquiringly.

"Well . . . I *understood* . . ." Why, his orders had been crystal clear: trash it all the way.

"You understood?"

"I understood that an unfavorable review was indicated."

"Indicated? We are trying to maintain standards of impartial appraisal. After all, this is what criticism is all about. I suggest that you submit a rewrite for *consideration.*"

Short Eyes, known as See, and the House Dick, known as Prick, are unofficial operatives of Special Operations. Prick is a burly ex-policeman with a cop's florid face and a cop's mean, angry eyes. They are rarely used against enemy agents, but rather against civilian targets: writers, artists, filmmakers, intellectuals, inventors and researchers who are considered a danger to Big Picture.

Big Picture involves escape from the planet by a chosen few. The jumping-off place is Wellington, New Zealand. After that, an extermination program will be activated. Needless to say, Big Picture is a highly sensitive project. Even to suspect the existence of Big Picture is unwholesome. As the poet says: "After such knowledge, what forgiveness?"

Both operatives are trained in unarmed defense in the rather unlikely contingency of counterattack. Usually the target is too overwhelmed to consider immediate physical retaliation. And the attack occurs when the target is at his most vulnerable. The operatives have an unerring instinct for choosing the right time.

See is a more intricate artifact than Prick, an experiment in the creation of artificial character, computer-made for the target. He is the diametric opposite of the target in every way. In appearance he is completely undistinguished: not handsome, not ugly, not tall, not short, dark hair, gray eyes, thick ankles, and equipped with a dumpy, doughy, stupid wife.

The target has attended a literary conference in Harrowgate. It was a disaster. Fear seemed to blanket the hotel, the stunted garden behind the hotel, the conference hall. Holding the microphone, he found his hand shaking.

The first train back to London is jammed, and the writer takes a first-class seat. Every seat in his compartment is taken. Sitting opposite him is a youngish man, reading *Officers and Gentlemen*. As the train pulls into Victoria Station, the man looks at him, eyes contracted in spitting hate like a poison toad. The writer drops his box of matches. Later he glimpses the same man at the head of a long taxi line. The hate and loathing in

See's eyes is designed to key in all the worst moments of the target.

Prick is drinking heavily and putting on weight. Big Picture is moving into its final phase as they take over presidents, prime ministers, cabinet members and intelligence agencies. The few dissenting voices are no longer considered important. Prick finds his services less and less required. He is in fact a source of potential embarrassment to the department. Twice they have bailed him out of jail for assault and disorderly conduct charges.

"Next time you're on your own."

Feeling in need of a quick drink, he stops into a pub at World's End. There are two men halfway down the bar and a pub bulldog curled on the floor behind them. The bartender is wiping the bar. Prick is about to call the bartender and give his order, when the dog looks at him and growls. Its lips curl back from yellow fangs and the hair on its back stands up.

"What's wrong with your dog?"

"Nothing." The bartender goes on mopping his bar. "He just don't like those kind of noises."

"What noises?"

"The noises you were making."

"But . . ." The two men turn and regard him with stony disapproval. They are obvious hard cases. "Bloody Hell . . . you're crazy!" he says and walks out quickly.

It is then he notices that a small gray dog is following him. He whirls and kicks. The dog moves behind him. He tries several times but the dog is always behind him no matter how quickly he turns.

The dog soon becomes an obsession. It will follow him for several blocks and then disappear. At length he buys a heavy blackthorn cane. For several days the dog is absent. Then, as he is walking down Old Brompton Road, where the Empress

Hotel used to be, the dog is once again at his heels: a small gray dog with a strange, fishy odor. At the corner of Old Brompton and North End Road he whirls, sweeping the cane behind him. The cane encounters empty air. Prick stumbles and falls into the path of a laundry truck.

Prick's accidental death is small item on the back page. See reads it and he doesn't like it. He is a methodical man with a photographic memory. He rents a typewriter and chronicles a detailed account of the contracts he has fulfilled for British military intelligence: "I Was a Professional Evil Eye for MI-5." He deposits the envelope with a solicitor, to be dispatched to *The News of the World, People,* and the more conservative media, including the London *Times,* in the event of his demise, by accident or otherwise.

In MI-5 there are raised eyebrows. "I think Prick got drunk and fell in front of a car, period. And good riddance."

"Good riddance to be sure, but . . ."

Same office, five days later:

"See's got the wind up, threatening to go to the media. Wants money and a new identity in America."

"He should live so long."

The operative drops an envelope on the table. "That's the original, from his solicitor's safe. What we substituted is insane, paranoid ravings."

"Ah, very good. I think Henry can handle it."

See is having a beer at a corner table in a pub on North End Road.

"Who are you fucking staring at?" Four skinheads with bovver boots ranged along the bar.

"Look, I wasn't staring."

The boy contracts his eyes into a grimace of hate.

"You wasn't *staring?*" They spread out, moving forward.

See regained consciousness in the emergency room.

"You took quite a beating. Nothing broken, luckily. However, there may be a delayed concussion. We'd advise you to stay in the hospital forty-eight hours at least."

"No. I'm all right."

The intern shrugged.

A brown dog followed See out of the hospital. He couldn't shake it. It was, he decided, a tracking device. They are trying to find out where the envelope is. Well, he isn't such a fool as to go to his solicitor's office.

Arriving at his bed-sitting room, he opened the street door and shut it quickly. But when he opened the door of his room, the dog slid in ahead of him. He made a grab for it, and needle-sharp teeth slashed his hand.

"Bloody Hell." He bolted the door. "*Now* I've got the son of a bitch."

He went to the desk and took a .22 semiauto with a silencer from a hidden compartment. He started looking under chairs, poking in closets, his hand dripping blood.

"Must be in the bathroom." He looked behind the bathroom door, glanced into the mirror. It was all over in a few seconds.

A Spec Ops agent talks to the Medical Examiner: "Anything unusual about this one?"

"Hmmm, yes, several things. First, location of the wound, in the middle of the forehead . . . an awkward angle. Evidently he was standing in front of the bathroom mirror. Usual place is the temple, or, for those in the know, up through the roof of the mouth. Police call it 'eating the gun' or 'smoking it.' And the wounds on his hand, like a barracuda's bite."

"Couldn't it have been broken glass? He may have shoved

his fist through a window. We have reason to believe he was irrational."

"I don't think so. There were no glass splinters, and the scratches all slant one way."

"A cat perhaps?"

"Room was locked from the inside. Your man Henry, who had been tailing the target, summoned police. The officer who went in with your operative is sure that no animal slipped out."

Spec Ops doesn't like it: unknown perpetrator, unknown motive, unknown M.O. Assuming that the motive was retaliation instigated or carried out by a recipient of the special services of Prick and See, then the perp must realize that these operatives were simply paid servants. His next step would be to proceed against their employers. And how are they to protect themselves against an Unknown?

Bradbury, Spec Ops head, has heard rumors of Margaras, an international intelligence organization owing allegiance to no country or any known group. He has discounted the rumors as absurd—where does the money come from? Now he is having second thoughts, and he is not a man who likes to entertain second thoughts.

So why did they alert the masters by starting with the servants? Reluctantly, he recognizes a procedure frequently used by his own department, known as "shaking the tree." They *intended* to alert the masters, hoping to scare them into precipitate, ill-advised action.

"Get me the file on Prick and See all the way back."

The files go back to 1959, twenty-five years. Quite a few of the targets are now dead. It doesn't take him long to find his man: William Seward Hall, the writer, of course. Hall had opposed the use of Prick and See, and resigned in protest over the Spec Ops project.

"You don't understand this Hall character. He won't quit. He'll just come back harder. I say terminate."

"I think Prick and See will teach him a lesson, with just the right shade of show-you."

They taught him a lesson all right, Bradbury thinks: unrelenting hate and deadly persistence. Idiots! You have an enemy like that, you terminate. You don't leave the job half done.

The door dog is a limited artifact. Our most versatile agent is Margaras, the dreaded White Cat, the Tracker, the Hunter, the Killer, also known as the Stone Weasel. He is a total albino. All his body hair is snow-white, and his eyes are pearly white disks that can luminesce from within, a diffuse silver light, or can concentrate into a laser beam. Having no color, he can take all colors. He has a thousand names and a thousand faces. His skin is white and smooth as alabaster. His hair is dead white, and he can curl it around his head in a casque, he can ruffle it or stick it up in a crest, and he's got complete control of all the hairs on his body. His eyebrows and eyelashes flare out, feeling for the scent. His ass and genital hairs are wired for a stunning shock or a poison deadly as the tentacles of the Sea Wasp.

There are those who say we have violated the Articles by invoking Margaras. He is too dangerous. He can't be stopped once he gets the scent. He has not come justa smella you.

As Margaras closes in, the light waxes brighter and brighter with a musky smell flaring to ozone as the light reeks to a suppurating electric violet. Few can breathe the reeking, seeking light of Margaras. Nothing exists until it is observed, and Margaras is the best observer in the industry.

"Open up, Prick. You got a Venusian in there."

"I'll kill you, you filthy sod!"

LIGHTS—ACTION—CAMERA

The chase comes to a climax. All around him dogs howl and whimper and scream and moan as Margaras moves closer.

"What you want with me?"

"What you asking me for?"

Give him the light now, right in the face, enough to see the worn red upholstery of the first-class seat with a brass number through his transparent fading shell, fading with a stink of impacted mortality, a final reek of hate from shrieking silence, the pustules on his face swell and burst, spattering rotten venom in the breakfast room.

"Mrs. Hardy, help! He's gone bloody mad! Call the police! Call an ambulance!"

Margaras can follow a trail by the signs, the little signs any creature leaves behind by his passage, and he can follow a trail through a maze of computers. All top-secret files are open to him. The rich and powerful of the earth, those who move behind the scenes, stand in deadly fear of his light.

The dim silver light of Margaras can invade and wipe out other programs. He is the Call. The Challenge. The Confront. His opponents always try to evade his light, like the squid who disappears in a spray of ink.

Preferences in food and wines, evaluation of pictures, music, poetry and prose. An identikit picture emerges, charged with the energy of hundreds of preferences and evaluations. He can hide in snow and sunlight on white walls and clouds and rocks, he moves down windy streets with blown newspapers and shreds of music and silver paper in the wind.

Being albino, Margaras can put on any eye color, hair color, skin color, right up until he "whites" the target. "Push," "off," "grease," "blow away" are out: "White" is in. The White Purr: without color, he attracts all colors and all stains; without odor, he attracts all odors, the fouler the better, into smell swirls, whirlpools, tornados, the dreaded Smell Twisters, creating a low-pressure smell wake so that organic animals explode behind them, the inner smells sucked into the Stink Twister round and round faster faster throwing out a maelstrom of filth in all directions, sucking in more and more over a cemetery and the coffins all pop open and the dead do a grisly Exploding Polka. Privies are sucked out by the roots with old men screaming and waving shitty Montgomery Ward catalogues.

Odors can also be the most subtle and evocative agent for reaching past memories and feelings.

"The nuances, you understand."

The wise old queer Cardinal, oozing suave corruption, slowly slithers amber beads through his silky yellow fingers as the beads give off tiny encrusted odor layers. "Ah, a whiff of Egypt . . ."

Chlorine from the YMCA swimming pool, the clean smell of naked boys . . . and the differences, my dear. Just whiff this, from before World War I, when people traveled with steamer trunks and no passports. I mean, of course, the people who *mattered*. Comfortable, isn't it? And smell the Twenties . . . those dear dead days, hip flasks, raccoon coats.

Now sniff way back, to a time before homo sap made his perhaps ill-advised appearance. Notice the difference? Nobody out there. Nobody to talk to. Nobody to impress. Hollywood moguls simply drop dead, like divers with their air lines cut. Personally, I find it exhilarating. I can fancify how I would have done it all. Ah, well . . .

And you know the difference between the air before August 6, 1945, and after that date: a certain security. No one is going to explode the atoms you are made of . . . with a little strength and skill one could outlive himself . . . but now . . .

Margaras is on the Dead Dream case. If you intend to destroy an individual or a culture, destroy their dreams. This is happening now on a global scale.

The function of dreams, they tell us, is to unlearn or purge the brain of unneeded connections—according to this view what goes through the mind in a dream is merely the result of a sort of neural housecleaning. They also suggest that it may be damaging to recall dreams, because doing so might strengthen mental connections that should be discarded. "We dream in order to forget," they write.

But Joe knows that dreams are a biologic necessity, like sleep itself, without which you will die. Margaras is sure this is war to extermination. Sure, forget your biologic and spiritual destiny in space. Sure, forget the Western Lands. And make arrangements with a competent mortician.

But desperate struggle may alter the outcome. Joe is tracking down the Venusian agents of a conspiracy with very definite M.O. and objectives. It is antimagical, authoritarian, dogmatic, the deadly enemy of those who are committed to the magical universe, spontaneous, unpredictable, alive. The universe they are imposing is controlled, predictable, dead.

In 1959, a member of the scientific elite of England said to Brion Gysin: "How does it feel to know that you are one of the last human beings?"

Brion was noncommittal, and the Venusian added facetiously, "Well, life won't be so bad on the *reservation.*"

The program of the ruling elite in Orwell's *1984* was: "A foot stamping on a human face forever!" This is naïve and optimistic. No species could survive for even a generation under such a program. This is not a program of eternal, or even long-range dominance. It is clearly an *extermination program.*

Joe decided that people were too busy making money to foster a climate in which research could flourish. Joe didn't have ideas about rewriting history like Kim did. More of Kim's irresponsible faggotry: he's going to rewrite history while we wait. Well, let determined things to destiny hold unbewailed their way. DESTINY prances out in an atomic T-shirt—her glow in the dark.

Joe decides to go into deepfreeze for fifty years. With a million dollars judiciously distributed in bonds and savings accounts, the whole system set up with dummy companies and mail drops, Joe will be a rich man when he wakes up.

And what about Kim?

"Oh," Joe shrugs. "I guess that one can take care of himself in the Land of the Dead. At least he won't have any mail-order croaker pulling him out half-baked. Not with that 45-70 hollow point just under the left shoulder blade."

Joe puts out a hook baited with a blond Nordic *Übermensch* from the 1936 Olympics—Herr Hellbrandt. Yes, hell-burnt ...

Ah, a strike! Postmark is Medellín, Colombia. Honorarium of two hundred thousand dollars a year (or other currency of his choice) to take over a center devoted to genetic research. If interested he can contact our representative in Mexico City . . . Abogado Hernandez Desamparado, 23 avenida Cinco de Mayo, Mexico, D.F.

Joe has confided in no one. But they know. They are waiting for him. He decides to leave some future shock behind him: notarized clinical notes and X rays demonstrating the results of magnetic field therapy, citing cases of total remission of cancerous tumors that would, with conventional treatment, have been fatal in a few weeks or months. The cases cover many types of cancer, with instructions for building the therapeutic device from materials easily and cheaply obtained. The device is basically Reich's Orgone Accumulator, a construction of organic material lined with iron or steel wool. Joe has added a number of alterations, notably magnetized iron, which vastly potentiate the action.

Cancer seems as immutably real and exempt from intervention as a nuclear blast. The explosive replication of cells? Once it starts, it is like an atom bomb that has already detonated. Death is an end product of purpose, of destiny. Something to be done in a certain time, and once it is done there is no point in staying around. Like a bullfight. Destiny = Ren.

A cancer cell, a virus has no destiny, no human purpose beyond endless replication. It has no work to finish and no reason to die. Give it a reason to die and it will. The ultimate purpose of cancer and all virus, is to replace the host. So instead of trying to kill the cancer cells, help them to replicate and to replace host cells.

Produce the first all-virus rat, it's more efficient—instead of all these elaborate organs we have just cells, an undifferentiated structure. Instead of endeavoring to keep the rat alive, we will endeavor to keep the cancer cells alive. Instead of trying to keep the patient alive, we will keep his Death alive. If he can become Death, he cannot die.

Death is incidental to function. When function is accomplished, death occurs. So instead of joining the retarded medical profession and desperately trying to keep Death out, why not let Death all the way in?

Joe saw cancer as just another milepost. Cancer came into its own with the Industrial Revolution, a cancer model dedicated to producing identical replicas on an assembly line. The analogy carries over to human cells and replication, as solid as auto parts, tin cans, bottles and printed words. Joe didn't give a shit about cancer. He wasn't there to save human lives. He was there to alter the human equation.

The notes are published in the Alternative Press with detailed plans. Soon testimonials are pouring in from all over the country. *Life* does a "debunking" story. Warnings from the FDA, the AMA and the cancer institute quickly escalate to shrill hysteria. And mutiny in the ranks: Doctor X, a respected oncologist practicing in a midwestern city, asks that his name be withheld: "I have seen it with my own eyes . . . the remission and complete cure of hitherto incurably cancerous conditions."

All over America, people are making rechargers in various shapes, of pyramids, space suits and suits of armor, set on high towers and deserts and mountains, in undersea bubbles, built into hollow trees in deep forests overgrown with vines and orchids, in cliff dwellings and caves, in boats and dirigibles. There is no stopping it, and the medical bureaucracy would soon regret their ill-advised and futile attempt. Nurtured on self-deceit, accustomed to obedience and respect, they attempted to "reason" with the enraged patients, or worse, to overawe the mob by sheer presence, which was quickly revealed as a hollow fraud.

Hall has been reading a lot of these doctor books. His own Doctor Benway shines forth as a model of responsibility and competence by comparison. Perhaps the most distasteful book of this genre is entitled *A Pride of Healers*. To be remembered that it is Pathology who decides a patient got cancer or don't got it. The doctors open it up. Anything looks suspicious, cut off a hunk and send it down to Pathology. The doctors twiddle their scalpels and wait. A green light winks on.

"It's malignant, boys. Let's go. Gotta stay ahead of the Mets."

So in this pride of prowling healers, the runty, ugly, half-impotent pathologist finds a big surgeon humping his old lady. So he frames the adulterous surgeon for prostate cancer and everybody knows there is only one cure. The surgeon is castrated and his nuts sent down to Pathology. Holding the nuts of his enemy in his hand gets him hot and he surprises his wife with a real pimp fuck. He's got another surprise for her: as she comes, he shoves the severed nuts down her throat. As the Germans say, *unappetitlich*.

Most of them are not quite so lurid. Just ordinary no-good, greedy, callous, bigoted humans with grossly inflated self-images. Here is Mike Seddons from "Final Diagnosis": attractive, red-haired, empty as a waiting room. How can anyone believe in ESP or anything like that in the face of vast medical complexes, monuments to progress and science and rationality and healing? This wretched specimen has fallen for a nineteen-year-old nurse. They made it in a broom closet in a reek of Mr. Clean. He has proposed. She has accepted.

Then she comes down with bone cancer. They have to take off the left leg *stat*, scalpels crossed it hasn't spread. Does he still want her? She tells him to take five days to think it over. He does. With bleak clarity he sees the years to come. Oh yes, he *can* see, where his own interests are involved.

He is striding toward Surgery, Big Man On Complex now:

"It takes guts to practice surgery," he says. It certainly does. What would he do without guts? Striding toward Surgery, the

patient is clearly terminal—he would operate on a mummy—
and she is shambling along on her new prosthetic leg.

"Will you shake the lead out?"

"I'm doing the best I can, darling."

Why don't she go back to her crutches, he thinks irritably.
Aloud he says, "Why don't you jet-propel on your stinking
farts?"

Admittedly his words are somewhat unkind. But cancer does
stink. Of course it's not her fault she is in this loathsome
condition, or is it? His mother always said:

"Son, in this life everyone gets exactly what he wants and
exactly what he deserves." People tend to believe it, so long as
they are getting what they think they deserve.

Incongruously Mike thinks of an old joke. The eternal traveling salesman, protagonist of the eternal dirty joke, spots an
attractive woman in the club car. As fate would have it, she is
in the lower bunk just opposite his upper bunk. And he is
eyeballing her. She takes off her wig. She pops out a glass eye.
She spits out her false teeth. She unhooks her wooden legs,
looks up at him pertly, and says, "Is there anything you want?"

"You know what I want. Take it off and throw it up here."

He starts laughing. She demands why. Finally he tells her,
and she hits him with her prosthesis. Required five stitches.

So Joe has left a cloud of ink behind him like a retreating squid
in the form of his Orgone Cancer Cure, like a cure for death
itself, so closely is cancer linked with death. Exaltation sweeps
through cancer wards and cancer-ridden outpatients, and with
regained vitality comes anger: Why have doctors concealed this
cure? Why did the FDA burn Reich's books and suppress his
findings without a trial? (One judge refused to listen to *any*
testimonials.)

The medical profession has suffered a horrific loss of pres-
tige and credibility, compounded by frantic efforts to discredit
the cure in the face of mounting evidence of its effectiveness.

Time was when MD plates on a car afforded a measure of protection against vandalism. Now doctors are subject to find their tires slashed, MURDERING BASTARD written in soap on the windshield.

It stacked up and up. Unnecessary operations, patients dying in the emergency room. "We cannot accept medical admissions from emergency."

Woman with a heart attack. Her husband calls for an ambulance.

"I can't send an ambulance until I know what's wrong with her."

"I tell you she's having a HEART ATTACK!"

"I can't send an ambulance until I know what's wrong with her."

"SHE'S HAVING A CORONARY! A HEART ATTACK!"

"I can't send an ambulance until I know what's wrong with her."

Potentially beneficial and harmless products and treatments kept off the market . . . lethal products kept on the market. Recent example: the so-called nonsteroidal antiinflammatory drugs for arthritis. In England eight people died of liver failure caused by the drug Oraflex, and still they won't withdraw it—just change the trade name.

I saw a TV show where the company representative, the lies oozing and slithering out of him, tries to tell a woman her hepatitis could have been caused by something else.

"I know it was that medicine."

A vast bureaucratic conspiracy of mismanagement . . .

The Medical Riots of 1999: it all started in the Burn Unit of a midwestern hospital. It is policy in burn units to restrict the use of painkillers to the vanishing point, since burn cases may require weeks of healing and treatment. It was argued that to administer painkillers would frequently result in addiction. So the patient must endure baths in which the dead skin and flesh are scrubbed from the raw lesions with a stiff brush. You can hear them screaming all over the hospital and out into the parking lots.

A team of amateur astronauts who call themselves the Spacers landed in the Burn Unit when their homemade space rocket exploded, spattering them with burning rocket fuel and shards of white-hot metal.

Ten were admitted to the Burn Unit. They received 25 mg of Demerol on admission. After that, nothing but aspirin and Darvon. The Spacers didn't scream in the baths but they radiated such pain and rage that three nurses quit in one day. The only nurse left on duty was a tall, strikingly beautiful woman who was part black and part Chinese. "If I had my way, you boys would get all the junk you need. So what if you get a little habit? Boy your age can kick in five days."

After the first scrub they issued an ultimatum: "Morphine every four hours as long as we need it or we walk out."

"What is this nonsense? There will be no morphine and you are not going anywhere."

"Meet my brother, the lawyer-doctor."

"You propose to hold these people against their will?"

"It's for their own good. If they leave the hospital they will be dead in a few days from infections."

They set up a private clinic in a loft. When police raided the clinic to search for unauthorized drugs, two patients died from police bullets and one police officer died from injuries. It was all on TV. Soon a nationwide walkout was underway. With the threat of cancer removed, the medical centers appear as a vast waste.

"Fifty years the fucking croakers kept the cure from the people."

Joe had a kidney stone but they wouldn't believe him at the hospital. Got his X ray mixed up with someone else's. They say a kidney stone is the worst pain a man can experience. Not surprising that Joe was a ringleader in the Medical Riots of 1999.

The walkout spreads to other hospitals:

"MORPHINE OR WALK!"

"MOW! MOW! MOW!"

The doctors paw the ground uneasily, like cattle scenting danger.

"What are we waiting for, a hospital bed?"

"Kill all the fucking croakers!"

Security steps nimbly aside and the crowds rush in.

"Got a hotshot *cutting* doc here."

"I think he needs an operation."

"Hell yes, a Gutectomy . . . fetch my scalpel."

"Paging Doctor Friedenhof and Doctor von Streusschnitt."

Enter Professor von Streusschnitt, flanked by his scalpel bearers carrying saws and knives two feet long.

"We must perform—how you say—the Gutectomy. *Two* kidneys? Sure, von is a Jew. *Rauschmit!"*

It is estimated that ten thousand doctors, medical bureaucrats and directors of pharmaceutical companies were massacred in the week of the Long Scalpels. The killings were not by any means random. The rioters had lists: "There's the bastard let me pass a kidney stone in the emergency room."

And billions of dollars' worth of useless equipment was destroyed in great ether burnouts.

PANIC . . . MAYDAY . . . AMOK!

The day when the top came off. A time of incredible danger and ecstasy. Every wish, every dream, every nightmare is suddenly real as the grimy streets, the subways. A cop on the corner who clubs everyone in sight—smooth commuters with their briefcases, smart women from the pages of *Vogue*, dogs on leads—screaming, "I don't like you and I don't know you / And now by God I'm going to show you!"

Famished leopards and tigers, released from the Central Park Zoo, invade Lutèce. An alert survivor throws his venison steak to a leopard, who gulps it down. He leaps over the disemboweled gourmands and streaks to safety.

A pilot bails out of a burning plane and gives his passengers the finger: "See you in Church!"

Doctor Benway rides again. He surveys a ward full of intensive-care patients killed by a Swedish nurse who bathes twice a day. Her put household ammonia and Mr. Clean into the IVs.

"I thought it would clean them out, doctor."

"Hmmm, yes, straight thinking, nurse. It's all in the day's work. Get these stiffs out of here and let them bury each other. This world's for the living and we need the beds. Bring on the next shift!"

He turns into the Herr Professor. His eyes glint with crazed dedication and purpose.

"An die Arbeit!"

Avenida Cinco de Mayo in Mexico City has the enigmatic surface of an area where obsolete trades survive, like stagnant pools at the margins of a river. At No. 23, Joe finds the plaque, in tarnished gold letters: HERNANDEZ DESAMPARADO, ABOGADO. ASUNTOS DE DOCUMENTOS Y EMIGRACIÓN.

Three stories up in a creaky, open elevator, at the end of a long corridor. Joe knocks, one long, two short. The door immediately opens as if the man were waiting just behind it, like a jack-in-the-box. He is elegantly dressed in a dark suit, with polished ankle-high black boots and a pearl-gray tie with pearl stick pin.

"Señor Hellbrandt?"

Desamparado holds out a thin brown hand, smooth and cool to the touch, like the underside of a lizard that has emerged from beneath a stone. He motions Joe into a small room with an old roll-top desk and a swivel chair in front of it. By the desk is an oak chair with leather cushion and back. Joe sits down.

The *abogado* sits in the swivel chair, then neatly crosses his thin legs and pivots to face Joe. He is an old man in his seventies, with a disdainful expression that is obviously chronic. He picks up four pages of legal-sized paper held together with a copper paper clip. Joe notices that the clip has stained the paper with verdigris. The paper is old and thick, like parchment. Looking down at the pages through his gold-rimmed bifocals, as if what he reads is both wearisome and distasteful, finally Desamparado speaks, in a silky, sibilant whisper.

"Genetic research. When you have understood Race, you have understood everything."

He looked at Joe as if evaluating his ability to understand everything. Joe recognized a fellow corpse, a compendium of gestures, intonations and expressions painfully rehearsed and reenacted.

"You will have a free hand within the parameters of the project."

For a moment he seemed too weary to go on. His words hung like cold ashes in the air of the office, lit only by a grimy, barred window of wired glass that let in a dim gray-white light.

With an obvious effort, Hernandez Desamparado uncrossed his legs.

"There are papers to sign."

It took all of Joe's strength to get his pen out and glance through the various releases and agreement forms which the *abogado* placed in front of him. Then, taking a deep breath, he concentrated on the One Point, signed each document carefully and placed it face down on a blotting pad with leather corners. Desamparado retrieved the signed forms and filed them on a dark shelf deep in the old desk.

During this charade, which seemed to go on forever, Joe felt his carefully hoarded stash of vitality drain out of him into a cold gray fog. He shivered, recognizing a practitioner higher in the vampire hierarchy than himself. But Joe didn't have time to play politics.

There are many varieties of vampire. The old cloak-and-tomb vamps went out with Lugosi. Nowadays the vampires have got together and hired a good PR man to improve their public image. A chap named Winston has put forward the pregnant concept of benevolent vampirism: "enlightened interdependence" is the phrase he uses. Take a little, leave a little.

However, by the inexorable logistics of the vampiric process, they always take more than they leave. That's what vampires are about. And there are reverse vampires who give out energy, like fertilizer for a better long-term yield. At the top of the hierarchy are what might be called astronomical vampires, who approach the condition of black holes, sucking everything in and letting nothing back out. Joe hoped he wouldn't have to play his antimatter card.

Joe is alert, scanning the alley in front of him. Back in the front lines, back in Egypt. But this is a different time and place. He is breathing one-God poison here. The Muslim Arabs have taken over. The Pharaohs are dead, all their Gods crumbling to dust. Only the pyramids and temples and statues remain. . . .

This is Cairo, and he belongs to the forbidden Ismailian sect. A traveling merchant with his two bodyguards. Keeping the guide in sight, through labyrinthine alleys and bazaars and markets, the sour stench of poverty and a snarling, doglike hate. He is carrying a short sword, a short ebony club and a poisoned dagger. A very important and, I may add, dangerous, assignment.

The Far Assembly was simply a small teahouse with benches along the walls, in an isolated section of the market. Since all the seats were full, a stranger would pass on by. Now, as they approach, three men get up and pay and walk out. That is their signal to come in and sit down.

This was his first meeting with Hassan i Sabbah, who was sitting directly opposite, six feet away. He wrote in his diary:

I had an immediate impression of austerity and dedication, but it was a kind of dedication I had never seen before. There was nothing of the ordinary priest-fanatic here at all. A priest is a representative and, by the nature of his function, a conveyor of lies. Hassan i Sabbah is the Imam. It cannot be falsified. You notice his eyes, of a very pale blue, washing into white. His mind is clear and devious as underground water. You are not sure where it will emerge, but when it does, you realize it could only have been just there.

Questions raised: How did the Egyptian Gods and Demons set up and activate an elaborate bureaucracy governing and controlling immortality and assigning it, on arbitrary grounds, to a chosen few? The fact that few could qualify is evidence that there was something to qualify for.

Limited and precarious immortality actually existed. For this reason no one challenged the system. They wanted to become Gods themselves, under existing conditions. In other words, they prostrated themselves before the Pharaoh and the Gods that he represented and partook of. . . .

Then come the one-God religions: Judaism, Christianity, Islam, promising immortality to everyone simply for obeying a few simple rules. Just pray, and you can't go astray. Pray and believe—believe an obvious lie, and pray to a shameless swindler.

Immortality is purpose and function. Obviously, few can qualify. And does this Christian God stand with his worshippers? He does not. Like a cowardly officer, he keeps himself well out of the war zone, bathed in the sniveling prayers of his groveling, shit-eating worshippers—his dogs.

In Mexico City, Kim finds work in a weapon store and devises variations on the Maquahuitl. This is the only effective

Aztec weapon, consisting of obsidian chips set in wood, the usual shape being rather like a cricket bat. The sharp edges of broken glass with the weight of the hardwood handle, and an advanced warrior, a Blood Glutton or an Armed Scorpion, could cut both feet from under his opponent with a single swipe of his Maq. . . . Kim made Maquahuitls of many shapes, some in the form of long whips of flexible wood . . . or slotted into an arc of wood with a crosspiece to fit the hand . . . can be kept concealed . . . one blow to the throat . . . and flails with obsidian chips sewed into leather thongs that can be dipped in poison.

Kim liked to lose himself in the market, floating along with the crowd. The blood lust, evil and cruelty that rises from the poisoned soil is exhilarating . . . the smell of pulque and urine, open sewage ditches, peppers, tortillas and roasting meat, faces of a vast somber dream . . . faces of burnished copper, eyes blazing with fierce savage innocence . . . coffee-colored flesh smelling of vanilla, a gardenia behind his ear, faces vile and brutish, swollen with cold dead malevolence, an armless beggar catches a disdainfully flicked crust of bread in his teeth.

The young noble moves on, surrounded by his retinue of bodyguards and flute players . . . the crowd eddies into circles around performers and musicians . . . a juggler throws flint knives into the air . . . a mime troupe does a sacrifice act. They set up a pyramid of wooden boxes. Now the prisoner is brought in. He goes through a vile pantomime of abject fear. He is dragged to the altar. A priest plunges in the knife and blood gushes out. The onlookers snort and bray with laughter sharp as flint knives in sunlight.

As he walks Kim keeps his mind blank as a mirror with nothing to reflect. He gives no one reason to see him. Suddenly raw hot fear rises from the ground and flares out of booths. He knows what has happened. He has carried emptiness to the breaking point. He has been seen. A man stops directly in his path and stares. Others stop, pointing and shouting a word he does not understand: *"Dindin!"*

Eyes converge, flaring with red waves of hate and loathing.

With his hand Maquahuitl, Kim throws a straight punch at the man in front of him and cuts his throat to the spine. He sprints up an alley. A man grabs his arm. He lashes back, feeling the tendons snap under the glass . . . over a wall . . . into a garden . . . through a doorway. He can hear the pursuers fanning out on both sides. Kim pulls a shawl from his shoulderbag over his head and smears his hand in dog excrement. As pursuers round the corner he crouches by a mud wall, holding out his stained hands.

"Baksheesh! Baksheesh, Reverent Speakers!"

One man spits on him as they race by. Kim waits, holding out his stinking hand. The mob is trooping back, passes him muttering the Word. The Word he cannot understand . . . dark mindless faces pointing bray with laughter.

"Smell the roses, Dindin."

Faces flaring sulphurous malevolence . . . scorpion disease knowing staring his way now.

"Seen!"

A straight punch over a wall . . . stops under a cypress by the canal. He washes his dogshit hand first then the blood from his clothes and then his faithful Maq. He is pleased to find some throat gristle clinging to the black chips. They cut and break on bone and every break is a new cut, a new edge.

Kim, feeling eyes on his back like any old John Wayne cowboy, turns without haste, hand slipping into his obsidian glove.

A little green man is standing there. Smooth marbly green, his jade eyes slit sideways like a cat. He gives off a green smell of worn stone.

"Must leave at once. *Seen.* Follow."

Over a bridge smooth glide tilting the ground falling forward through maize fields frogs croaking reached a river high and muddy over the banks. The guide parts bushes at the water's edge to reveal a craft, a light raft lashed to two canoes. They get in the boat and push off into the muddy current.

4

Kim knows he is dead. But he isn't in the Western Lands or any approximation.

He receives a summons from the District Supervisor.

"So how come I'm not the Supervisor? After all, I *wrote* the Supervisor."

"No you didn't. You *discovered* the Supervisor. Or rather, you found out where the Supervisor is written and read it back. Writers don't write, they read and transcribe something already written. So you read orders, which are then conveyed through your spokesman, the Supervisor. The Imam. The Old Man."

"So I am the man for a very important and, you may add, very dangerous assignment?"

The D.S. permitted himself a narrow smile.

"I thought my last assignment was of the same category."

"It was, and a proper hash you made of it. Your job now is to find the Western Lands. Find out how the Western Lands are created. Where the Egyptians went wrong and bogged down in their stinking mummies. Why they needed to preserve the physical body."

Kim gives him the textbook answer: "Because they had not solved the equation imposed by a parasitic female Other Half who needs a physical body to exist, being parasitic on other bodies. So to maintain the Other Half in the style to which she has for a million years been accustomed, they turn to the reprehensible and ill-advised expedient of vampirism.

"If, on the other hand, the Western Lands are reached by

the contact of two males, the myth of duality is exploded and the initiates can realize their natural state. The Western Lands is the natural, uncorrupted state of all male humans. We have been seduced from our biologic and spiritual destiny by the Sex Enemy."

The D.S. turns to a Russian Commissar. "You see the man is well instructed."

"Straight thinking," grates a five-star general.

Tony Outwaite pokes at the fire with effeminate discontent. He picks up a pair of fire tongs, selects a coal no bigger than a walnut and moves it to another spot in the fire. "We are interested in very specific considerations—technical data, something that *works*—not these vague, vapid blatherings. We want the Western Land *blueprints*. Needless to say, they are closely guarded, perhaps the most closely guarded secret on the planet, the ultimate biologic and spiritual weapon that undercuts all other weapons. Paradise to the people . . . or at least to those who are capable of accepting paradise and paying the price. Have to pay the Piper, you know. Or you may find he'll pipe to another fashion."

The D.S. handed Kim a piece of deerskin with a picture on it. Kim felt the horror and disgust rising from the parchment.

"Fragment of an ancient Mayan codex. Much earlier than the Dresden."

The drawing was crudely done in reds and yellows that looked like a faded tattoo: a man strapped to a couch. A huge centipede, six feet in length, is curling over the bound figure.

"The Centipede God. At one time these monster centipedes existed and were fed on human flesh. Your job is to return to this period and—"

"Do a Moses in the bulrushes?"

"Yes. You see, the monsters were created by exposing normal-size centipedes to certain radiations. It could happen again . . . in fact will happen, unless your mission succeeds."

June 13, 1982. Sunday. At the Stone House. Looking out through the pane of glass by the front door at the weeds and trees and bushes, I can see quite clearly a high stone wall overgrown with vines, more green than white, and an ancient stone building, also overgrown. It is a simple structure of one story, about twenty feet wide, with a slanting roof.

It is physically painful to enter the medium where I can see this, a strain, a dislocation. The building looks the way this stone farmhouse could look after five hundred years without any human presence . . . a dead silent green, menacing and oppressive.

What happened here?

Well, I reckon it all started in Hill City. Population 173 . . . 172. Don't matter. It's the 173rd, Old Man Potter, that matters—not that he lived right in Hill City, God forbid. He lived about four miles out and another half mile off the county road in a little stone house he made himself, been out there twenty years they say. Nobody knows where he come from. He used to come into town once a month to get supplies and we all thought that was once a month too often.

Now Mars Hardy runs the general store and a nicer, kinder man never lived. He's nice to the black people, the Indians and the Chinese railroad workers, but he just couldn't be nice to old man Potter. Nobody could.

"Anything else, Mr. Potter?" he'd ask, and he'd be thinking, I just want him out of my store as quick as possible.

And Old Man Potter would just duck his head and *scuttle* out—that was another thing about him nobody could stand, the way he moved, very quick and silent. Winter and summer he wore a long black coat, it was like the coat just sort of scuttled along with him inside it.

Just what was so wrong about Old Man Potter? Well, none of us could say. I couldn't stand to have him near me, and the sheriff said, "I'd rather kill him than touch him."

We weren't even curious about him, that is, not until young Tim arrived with one small suitcase. His mother and father had died of scarlet fever and young Tim came to live with the Parkers, who were relatives, and that boy was into everything. So when Old Man Potter rode into town, Tim went out to the house and looked around inside.

"Funny house," he reported to the Parkers. "Niches instead of windows, must get cold in the winter. And there's another building, always locked, about eighteen by twenty, with windows in it, but the blinds are always drawn."

Tim could see no signs that Potter had ever done any farming, not even a vegetable garden. But Potter always paid in cash, so he must have brought a pot of money with him. Tim was not interested in theft. He was interested in data. He sent away for burglars' tools, and one day he picked the lock on the outbuilding and got in.

He couldn't see at first, because of the drawn blinds, so he went around and let them up. And what he saw then sent him running back down the hill.

"My God, you know what he's got up there? Cases full of *centipedes,* some of them two foot long like!"

"Well, when he finds the blinds up he'll know someone was in there and saw it," said Mr. Parker.

"So much the better," says the sheriff. "Maybe he'll just clear off."

"And leave all those critters up there to get loose?"

"What are we waiting for?"

We was on our horses and on the road in half an hour with cans of industrial alcohol and some dynamite. We intended to burn the place out, would have been glad to throw Old Man Potter into the fire 'cept none of us could bear to touch him, so we'll shoot him and then burn the carcass.

But we are too late. Old Man Potter must have sensed something, doubled back and turned his centipedes loose.

We get off our horses, advancing cautiously, guns at the ready, when Mr. Hardy lets out a yell.

"My God, somethin' bit me!"

And there on his leg is a six-inch centipede covered with hair, looked like it was growing into him. We had to pull it off in pieces and he is half out of his mind screaming he is burning and beating his head against the ground. Well, he dies, and we hightail it out of there. Gallagher got bitten too, and only the four of us made it back to town.

The centipedes spread throughout the area. There was no antidote for the poison, but one victim with a very light dose recovered and said it was like being in a white-hot oven, torn to pieces by giant centipedes. You could tell just by watching it was the most horrible death anyone could suffer. The 'pedes spread further and further, cases turning up in Michigan, Minnesota, Illinois, Ohio, Nebraska. Seemed it would never stop, but it did sorta level off in certain areas, which nobody could understand—maybe they are all dead in there.

And they finally built the Quarantine Wall, way ahead of the centipedes—they hope—after teams with protective clothing checked it out. The wall is considered impossible to get over. There are electrical barriers, toxic barriers, glue barriers. Of course they dropped tons of pesticide over the area, but you could never get them all.

Lots of talk now. Some say it's all a hoax to starve the poor and keep the best land for themselves. Yep, there's talk of moving in and building behind the Wall.

The island of Esmeraldas is known for its large centipedes, said to attain, on occasion, the incredible length of fifteen inches. There is considerable disagreement as to the danger to humans from a centipede bite, and to the best of my knowledge no precise analysis or classification of the venom has been carried out. We have all heard the story that centipedes carry venomous spines in each leg, leaving a trail of rotten, gangrenous flesh behind them. I think we can dismiss this as mythology. The bite of a centipede is inflicted by a pair of forcipules that grow from the first trunk segment, and not by the legs.

However, there is some factual basis for this lurid story. A doctor with a practice in Puerto Rico told me he had treated centipede bites. The bite produces a localized necrosis which, if untreated, can lead to gangrene. The remedy is surgical excision of the affected area, and washing out the cavity with a disinfectant solution. Then a light, porous dressing is applied. He surmised that the centipede venom may be related to the poison of the brown recluse spider, common throughout the midwestern and southern United States. Fatalities are rare, and usually occasioned by secondary infection of necrotic tissue.

Data on centipede venom is scattered and often contradictory. Tables showing the precise relative potencies of snake venoms, with lethal dosages, annual fatalities and percent of recoveries are readily available, and there is considerable information on scorpion and spider venoms. But one must scrabble about for centipede data. Fortunately, I number among my friends a young man named Dean Ripa, who could have stepped from the pages of a Joseph Conrad novel.

Dean is a snake-catcher by profession, selling his reptiles to zoos and private collectors. It is very dangerous and poorly paid work. He has been bitten three times and can barely recoup the expenses of his trips to far-off places in search of the venomous snakes. On one long journey to Ghana, the big chief of the tribe died the day that Dean arrived in the village, and Dean was lucky to escape with his life. It was around the time of this trip that he wrote the following letter in answer to my inquiries concerning the venom.

My dear Hall, in regard to your question about centipedes: there are about 3,000 species. They range from about 1cm in diameter up to about 30cm in length; from

15 pairs of legs to about 177 pairs. For predation they possess a pair of venom glands with forcipules at the first trunk segment. They are bilaterally symmetrical, of course, metamerically segmented animals with a double ventral nerve cord, typically with a ganglion in each segment and concentrations of nervous tissue above and below the gut at the ass-end of the body. Centipedes are sexually dimorphic. Also, the external genitalia of males are often concealed within the anal segment, so that the sex may not easily be determined. Slight pressure will, however, often cause them to evert, thus allowing the sex to be determined.

But you wanted to know about the venom. There is an extensive but scattered literature concerning the effects on Man. Instances of death from bites of scolopendrids were reported in the older literature, but recent authors are inclined not to credit the reports; since the aggressor was not actually seen, it may have been a scorpion or a snake. There is the tale of the large centipede that crawled across the abdomen and chest of a Confederate army officer, leaving a number of deep red spots forming a broad red streak. Violent, painful convulsions soon set in, accompanied by excessive swelling of the bitten areas. The man was dead two days later.

The bite of the European *Scolopendra cingulata* causes pain, and at worst inflammation, edema and superficial necrosis, but the pain goes quickly and the symptoms disappear in a few days. A fellow named Klingel was bitten some thirty times by this type. In twenty-six cases the only symptom was pain, which disappeared in about twenty minutes. In the other four cases the pain was more severe, like a wasp's sting, and the hand and arm became numb, with some pain in the neck and chest. These symptoms abated after a day or two. Sometimes the animal bit painlessly, especially an hour after killing mealworms.

The bite of *S. heros* is said to cause intense pain, and the animal also produces a red streak where it has crawled over the body. *S. subpinipes* produces intense pain, blistering, swelling, local inflammation, buboes and subcutaneous hemorrhage. *S. viridicornis* in South America causes pain for eight hours and small superficial necroses after twelve days. There are many more such accounts: vomiting, headache, swelling of a large area around the bite, which had a blackish center, subcutaneous bleeding, etc.

Apparently India, Burma and Ceylon have one of the worst species; the recovery from bites is slow, sometimes as long as three months. Every case seen developed acute lymphangitis with edema, as well as inflammation of the skin and subcutaneous tissues. In most cases a local necrotic process developed at the site of the bite, and in some cases this progressed to a condition not unlike phagedenic ulceration (a rapidly spreading and sloughing ulcer).

The most serious symptoms followed the bites of the Andaman Islands species, which can reach a length of about 33cm. Klingel found that animals that had not fed for several days could bite harmlessly and therefore the lack of poison could not be ascribed to lack of poison in the glands. Poor Klingel: I wonder if he used himself for that one too. The only well-authenticated fatality appears to be that of a child of seven years, bitten on the head by a *Scolopendra* in the Philippines.

The effects of the bite of the *Scolopendra* vary with the time of year. In winter the bite causes, at most, a small pimple that disappears in an hour. In spring, when centipedes are active, a bite causes inflammation which can last for up to three days, and a bite on the finger can cause the hand and lower half of the forearm to become swollen.

The effect of centipede venoms has also been investigated by injecting it into various animals. A man named Briot in about 1904 injected the venom of a French centipede into rabbits. Paralysis in the hind leg, edema, then an abcess and death seventeen days later were caused by 2cc of the venom. An injection of 3cc into a second rabbit caused death in one minute. Briot stated that the effect of the venom was like that of a viper's bite, causing almost immediate paralysis and necrosis.

I let a very large example of *Chilopoda* gnaw on my middle finger the other day. I caught it in a rotting stump and held it in my cupped hands, thinking it would not notice that I was a possible enemy. But it did notice, and I was envenomated, though only mildly.

I have been plagued by strange occurrences, which lead me to doubt my own mind. In the night I wake up and find some of the snakes crawling free about the quarters. A door locked the night before will certainly be found unlocked the next morning. Then there are the dreams: a grotesquely tall figure, thin as a bone and high as the ceiling, stands over my bed and watches me as I sleep. I try to wake up but I cannot. Malaria must be the cause of these visions, unless it's that damnable Atah. I don't know what he could be putting in the food. He seems such a friendly fellow, but you never know with them. He is bringing me some gruel this evening, and perhaps I shall ask him to *share* in my humble meal. Then we shall see what is the score!

> Yours most devotedly,
> Dean Ripa.

The town of Esmeraldas clusters around a small, deep lagoon reached by sea through a narrow channel. The lagoon is encircled by wooded mountains that reach, in places, an altitude of 3,000 feet.

During the six-hour crossing from Trinidad there was a fresh sea breeze, but as the boat turned into the lagoon the breeze died off and a heavy, oppressive heat enveloped the boat. The lagoon, shut in by surrounding hills, was dead calm and stagnant. I searched the hillsides for signs of habitation, but there were none. Certainly it must be cooler in the hills, and there would be a breeze.

The boat glided to a halt. Our luggage was dumped onto the pier. The sailors did not even wait for a tip. They rushed back to the boat, which reversed, turned in the lagoon, and headed out through the channel. I looked around from the rotting pier to the mud streets and the houses beyond, shacks that had been thatched at one time, with galvanized iron nailed on over rotting thatch giving the roofs a patchy, leprous look.

What I felt from my first contact with Esmeraldas was a feeling of depression and horror such as I have never experienced anywhere else.

I have been in high mountain towns in the Andes . . . thirteen, fourteen thousand feet, and bitter cold at midday. Everyone wears a gray felt hat, and after sundown, a scarf around the face, eyes red with smoke. The sod houses have no chimneys, just a drafty hole in the roof. There are strange skin diseases, sometimes confined to a single, desolate valley: great purple growths on the face, or hunchbacks with their soft humps like rotten melons. Guinea pigs scuttle across the earth floors— they eat them, and another source of food is frogs in the icy shallow ponds on the high plains.

I have traveled in villages in the Sahara, the desert flies thick as black cloth on the table at the only hotel. Flies . . . flies . . . you couldn't get a forkful to your mouth before the flies were on it. I have seen the cemeteries of the hairy Ainu . . . erect phalluses on the male graves, crudely carved in wood and painted with ochre, the phalluses split apart and covered with the drifting snow. Yes, I have seen many scenes of desolation, but nothing like the dead, inhuman fog of oppression and evil that covered Esmeraldas.

An official descended from a horsedrawn fiacre and slowly made his way toward us. He was a man of fifty, with a contrived slovenliness, like Peter Lorre impersonating a corrupt Chief of Police.

"*Pasaportes, señores . . . documentes.*" The Chief studied our papers suspiciously with his hooded reptilian eyes, of a glazed gray color like a carp's eyes.

"Purpose of visit, *señores!*" he suddenly barked out, glaring at us with insane hostility.

"We are here to study your centipedes. This island is known for its huge centipedes."

The official paled. "But why, *señores?*" His voice was pleading.

"Because we have been paid to do so. We represent the National Geographic Society, the Smithsonian Institution and the Peabody Museum of Harvard."

Overcome by these words of power, the official collapsed onto a cane seat. "Of course, of course, I should have known." He wiped his face with a dirty silk handkerchief.

"You should indeed. We have, incidentally, letters from Trinidad——"

Completely cowed, the official sat mopping his brow.

"——letters to the Mayor and the Governor of this island."

"I am both, *señor,* and the Chief of Police."

"Good. Then these letters of safe conduct are for you. Does this town boast a hotel?"

"We do not boast, but there is the Hotel Splendide."

"Can you find someone to carry our luggage?"

"That may be difficult. . . ."

Several men lounged nearby on the pier in the gathering twilight. The Chief beckoned and pointed to our luggage. The loiterers made a strange whispering, hissing noise and scuttled away. Suddenly a snaggle-toothed, wiry man with a bristling black mustache was there.

"I José!" He jabbed a thumb at his chest. "Plenty bad

people here." He spat at the retreating shadows, and piled our luggage onto a cart.

The Hotel Splendide is built around a courtyard where a few sickly banana palms and avocado trees grow. Since the patio is used to dispose of slops from the kitchen, there is the continual reek of stale garbage. Pigs and chickens forage noisily at dawn.

The manager is an old Chinese. He gestures to the room-key board. Obviously we are the only guests. We select a room on the front of the hotel, overlooking the street and the lagoon. There is a huge gray spider in one corner.

"Him velly good. Keep away centipedes and black widowers," the manager tells us.

We decide to settle in with Arachnid, as we have named our good gray spider.

It is a large room on the second floor, with hooks for our hammocks, the window screened with mosquito netting. Seated on our small trunks, for there is no place else to sit, we lighten our spirits with rum and a soft drink called Coca-Cola, which is said to contain a goodly quantity of cocaine, an ingredient devoutly to be wished. And it does go well with the light dry rum, which I prefer to the heavy black-molasses rum.

There are five in our party: Doctor Schindler, whose specialty is botany; Doctor Schoenberg, whose knowledge of spiders and scorpions is encyclopedic; Doctor Sanders, a wiry young sandy-haired English lad, is the chemist; and Chris Evans is our photographer.

And I? I am the chronicler of this expedition. I have also some knowledge of the others' specialties, superficial to be sure, but enabling me to see connections that might otherwise have gone unnoticed. We are here to collect centipede specimens, to obtain samples of the venom and carry out what analysis and breakdown we can with our limited facilities. We can, of course, easily obtain small animals for experimental purposes, to assess potency of the venom. That is no problem in such a wretched and poverty-stricken area.

Let me confess that I *hate* centipedes, above all other creatures on this horrid planet. And I am not alone in this aversion. Many others have confessed to me that they hold a special antipathy for this creature, which is so far removed from the mammalian mold. And certainly an important aspect of our mission is to ascertain to what extent the centipede merits the horror and loathing in which he is, so far as I know, universally held. There may be people who like centipedes. I have seen people handling tarantulas and scorpions, but never a centipede handler. Personally, I would regard such an individual with deep suspicion.

I have just petted my cat: "And how is this good little cat beast?" Now what sort of man or woman or monster would stroke a centipede on his underbelly? "And here is my good big centipede!" If such a man exists, I say kill him without more ado. He is a traitor to the human race.

Late that night we were awakened by scrabbling noises, and in the lantern light we saw Arachnid locked in mortal combat with the biggest centipede I have ever seen. Not knowing how to intervene without endangering our dubious ally, we cheered on the sidelines. We watched until Arachnid had overcome the centipede, which was writhing and twisting in the most atrocious manner, showing its awful, yellow underside—and this with the head severed from the body.

Arachnid then settled down to make a meal of his victory. Sleep after that was impossible.

We were up at first light. Obviously we must find more impenetrable quarters. In this we were fortunate.

It seems that some years ago (these people are vague about time), there was a workers' rebellion on the island. A revolutionary named Dolores, who had been educated in England, led the rebellion. It was, the Chief told us, very mysterious. Quite suddenly the peons took up arms, and would have seized the entire island, except for the intervention of British troops. The rebels dug in and occupied the southern area, where they exacted tribute and dug fortifications and tunnels that can be seen to this day. This stalemate went on for some two years. Finally the rebels were routed and their leader Dolores was publicly hanged.

The old jail was expanded to contain the prisoners brought in by the British, and a walled courtyard with watchtowers was added. Five of the ringleaders were tried and hanged. The others were deported to Trinidad and forced to work out long sentences on the plantations. The rank and file were held in prison for some months, and later relocated to different islands.

I learned from the Chief that ordinary crime is not possible. The island is a small place, and everybody knows everybody else. The Chief put a finger to his eye. This continual watching of everybody by everybody else is one of the specialties of Esmeraldas. Field glasses and telescopes are the most coveted luxuries, and your status is determined by the surveillance equipment you can afford. The whole town is steeped in a miasma of blackmail. All the children will inform, for pennies and sweets. The inference is obvious: the Chief is the head blackmailer of Esmeraldas.

It was during the revolution that every citizen became an informer, since no one knew how many revolutionary agents had infiltrated the coastal towns. The trial of the rebels turned into such a maze of contradictory testimony that the British transferred the proceedings to a military tribunal in Trinidad.

The jail was now ours for a moderate rent. The prison compound was built to accomodate the masses, and so was fairly commodious. Three of the watchtowers, which were wooden structures, had fallen down, but one was still in fair condition.

We reminded the Chief that we had come to study the centipedes.

"There is a man here who know much of these animals . . . too much," the Chief told us. "He lives inland." He made vague gestures indicating his low opinion of anyone who lived "inland."

A helpful scientist could be a real asset, and it couldn't be far. The island is only about eight miles wide. In a place like this everyone knows where everyone lives, and certainly where any foreigner lives. But the people we approached pretended they knew of no such person: It was too far—they had other business—he went away.

Finally José agreed to guide us to the house, for an outrageous fee.

"They have fear." He thumped his skinny chest. *"Muy macho,* not scared of centipede peoples. This all horseshit."

We took provisions for the day and armed ourselves with machetes and double-barreled 410 pistols, loaded with number six shot. This I have found to be a most effective load when the only danger one is likely to encounter is from snakes or humans, and quite sufficient for either one. In Malaya once I downed an amok in his tracks, firing both barrels directly into his neck at ten feet.

The mud street ended quite abruptly in weeds, scrub and jungle. This was not at all like the rain forests of South America, there being no large trees. Here were palmetto and scrub and coconut palms, banana plants, some hardwood. The path was hard to follow, and we had to clear the way with our machetes in some places.

I attempted to get some information out of our guide about the centipede cult.

"Who are these centipede people?"

He spat. "Bad people . . . plenty crazy . . . worship fucking bug."

I was reminded of the Egyptian scarabs, the scorpion Goddess and the frequent pictures of centipedes in Mayan pottery. One page of an ancient Mayan codex, of doubtful authenticity, shows a man tied to a couch, threatened by a huge centipede, six to eight feet in length.

"Do they hold meetings?"

His eyes narrowed with calculation. "Perhaps."

I decided to shelve this for the time being.

The path wound steeply uphill and the heat was suffocating. But I was even more fatigued than I would normally be in the course of such a walk. It was as though a heavy weight were pressing down on us with a persistent malevolence. Several times the guide lost his way, and we had to retrace our steps. His dog, an Airedale-terrier mix, ran ahead yelping.

It seemed as if we had been on the road for hours, but looking at my watch I saw it was only an hour. Suddenly we heard wild yelping from the dog, and thought he must have treed something. But when we reached the scene, I saw a hole with palm fronds around it and heard the dog's anguished screams. Looking down into the hole, which was about six feet deep, I saw that the dog was writhing, impaled on bamboo spikes. Obviously a trap set by the rebels.

"*Dios,*" said José, in a perfunctory manner. "*Pobrecito* . . . it is best you shoot him, *señor.*"

I drew the 410 pistol and killed the dog with a charge through the head. I reloaded and we pressed on.

The guide seemed entirely unmoved by the fate of his dog. He opened his mouth in an ugly gesture, jabbing with his finger.

"Him eat too much . . . here life is hard."

Toward midday we arrived at a clearing with a hut on stilts.

"*Aquí, señores.*"

A man came slowly down from an upper platform to meet us. Rarely have I ever felt such an immediate antipathy for anyone. He was quite tall and thin, with long, scraggly reddish-yellow hair and a dirty, ragged mustache. He made a grimace that was meant to be a smile, showing his rotten teeth, and released such a pestiferous breath that I stepped back a pace. I could not bring myself to shake his hand, but he seemed not to expect this. He simply stood there, barring the steps to his house.

His eyes were of an opaque, cataract gray, continually darting about in agitation, and never raised to our faces. He kept fidgeting in a very unpleasant, spastic manner, as if his hands and feet were moving of their own volition. I made the introductions, and at each name he simply nodded and said nothing.

"We are from the Peabody Museum, here to study the local centipedes and take specimens."

He started at the word "centipede," and his mustache twitched.

"We have been told that you can help us."

"I know nothing," he said, very rudely. "My study is butterflies. I think centipedes are to be found in another part of the island . . . to the west." He gestured with his fingers outstretched.

"Oh, well, in that case we will not take up any more of your time." I had at this moment a vivid picture of what his face would look like if hit by a charge of number six shot. I rather expected he would ooze some disgusting white fluid instead of blood.

We turned and walked away.

"Muy malo recibido," observed José.

The island of Esmeraldas fades in Hall's mind. For several nights he can go no further, until one morning he awakens from a dream of the Place of Dead Roads:

For days they have been floating down a wide river, a mile across and getting wider, the banks a distant green smudge, or invisible in the morning mist. The boat is an outrigger, with two covered dugout canoes as pontoons and a deck of split bamboo.

The two masts for sails to catch the little dawn wind also serve to support a tarpaulin cover to protect them from sun and rain. They usually tie up at night.

The Guide seeks out a faster current near the middle of the river, then picks up turn-off currents leading toward the shore, like exits from a freeway. Occasionally they pass farms, the buildings unfinished and already dilapidated, small areas cleared for banana and yucca, the ubiquitous tuber on every tin plate in the Amazon area.

Slowly the channel narrows and they pick up speed. The Guide is alert now, shifting from one current to another like a surfer, as trees and sand banks flash by.

"Coming to the pass!"

A silent rush of water as they skim through a narrow opening. Neferti can see grass just under the surface; must have flooded over recently. A solid wall of green ahead, but they make it through a narrow chute out into a vast lake, still riding the fast current. They are soon out of sight of land.

Suddenly the current dies and they are drifting in aimless calm, slower and slower, and finally motionless.

"As idle as a painted ship/Upon a painted ocean."

The water is clear as limpid air. They can see the tops of great boulders a hundred feet down, shading to the inky blackness that spreads beneath them like a velvet tapestry, shifting occasionally as forms move under it. No fish are visible in the clear areas near the surface, and their presence can be inferred only by movements and ripples of darkness at the margin of vision.

The lake spreads to the sky in every direction, a vast round blue mirror with a line of red as the sun touches the water. A light shock wave from the black depths, indicating the passage of some large creature, rocks the boat gently.

The Guide consults his map, which opens like an accordion. The map is brightly colored, depicting unusual beings. Some of them are growing upside down into the ground, shoots sprouting from their legs.

"Nearest current three hundred miles," he announces, the words sagging from his mouth. "We can row."

"We can row?" Neferti points to the sun, which hasn't moved in the past minute.

Wilson, the Guide, who lost his license as a White Hunter for shooting rhino with a bazooka, now turns on Neferti those cold blue eyes that always seem to be looking down a gun barrel.

"All we need is *push*, you know. No friction in the water." He passes his hand quickly through the water. A black shadow streaks up and teeth snap just behind his fingers. "See how long you'd last in the bloody water? No friction . . . the darkroom fish can move at a speed you'd better believe."

"Couldn't we just blow from the stern?"

"No good. No friction in the bloody air either. We have to get a push without the air or the water. Hmmm . . ." His eyes light up like burning sulphur. "We used to hold jack-off contests at Eton . . . you know, speed and distance. The speed boys all gravitated to small arms and shotguns, whereas the distance shooters went for long-range, kills at six hundred yards. Maybe if both of us stand in the stern and let fly, like . . . now, I make you for speed, right?"

"Right. About twenty seconds when I'm in the mood."

"Well, you bloody well better be moody and randy. Metabolism will start to freeze in an hour . . . fifty minutes now, so we have to look sharp. Differential pressure should jar us out of freeze coordinates. . . ."

Neferti nods as he sheds his loincloth and drops it absently behind him, as if to abandon it forever. His long green-yellow snake's eyes narrow, the way a snake freezes and gathers himself into silent intention as he feels the nearness of prey. His nipples and ears and nose turn a bright, pulsing red.

Wilson stands perfect and immobile as a statue, except for his seeking, throbbing phallus, his cold blue eyes searching the horizon for a distant target. There it is . . . sights lining up . . . his nuts tighten. He starts to squeeze the trigger. It is coming up from his long, prehensile toes and feet. His lean body glistens like fish scales. It gathers in a knot at Neferti's One Point, two inches below where his navel would be, if he had one. A raging, snarling animal, goat-cat-deer, is rearing out of him. He screams in exquisite agony as horns wrench through his skull and blood spurts from his nose.

Wilson squeezes it off. The target falls from his sights. The boat is moving, slowly at first, then faster and faster.

"Get forward!" Wilson yells.

Holding onto the seats, they can barely keep the boat from doing a tail-walk like a hooked marlin. They turn into a twenty-mile-an-hour current.

Wilson points: "Pede Island."

They smell it fifty yards out, a black insect stink that gets in your clothes and your hair. You feel like centipedes are crawling all over you.

"Easy, Laddy buck. Gets 'em all, at first."

As they step onto the limestone pier, a group of officials in filthy uniforms, the guns rusted into their rotting holsters, crowd around them like beggars, holding out their hands.

"*Documentes, señores. Por favor . . . pasaportes,*" they whine.

Wilson waves them aside with the back of his hand and they fall on their backs, struggling to right themselves, like overturned beetles.

"We'll head for the Explorers Club. Decent steak there and cold beer."

The streets are dark, lit only by kerosene lanterns here and there in the kiosks. No one stops to buy the merchandise: old post cards and magazines, moldy pork pies in cellophane wrappers, stale candy bars. No one stops.

All around them silent, milling crowds of half-naked people with the dead eyes of basic famine.

"Gotta keep moving, you understand. Blighters have no

place to kip. Once they stop, they fall down and they've bloody 'ad it, like that lot back there. Here we are."

The building seems to have been transplanted from St. James's Square and replanted in this area of vacant lots, garbage and open sewer ditches. The edges of the masonry are even and regular, but now grown over with moss and vines covered with yellow-green flowers that give off a horrible reek of excrement and whorehouse perfume. A dim, yellow light inside flickers ominously.

"Another power cut," Wilson explains over his shoulder.

A man in a moldy uniform with slugs crawling on it sidles out from the reception desk and blocks their way.

"Are you a member, sir?" He glares imperiously.

Wilson pushes him with one finger and the man falls to the floor, making galvanized movements with his back and waving his legs feebly in the air.

"Wouldn't step on him if I were you," Wilson cautions. "Bloody revolting." He leads the way up a marble staircase to the bar.

"What's this, George? A dead one at the door?"

"I'm sorry, sir. *Deeply* sorry. But we simply can't get live help these days . . . and he did keep out some riffraff from the *Delegations.* You know what I *mean,* sir."

"Scotch on the rocks, George, and . . . ?"

"Pernod."

"Pernod, it is, sir. Beauty of it is, few of them last till payday." He leans forward. "Why, only three days ago a drunken navvy knocked the head clean off our last one. Right shook up, 'e was."

"I daresay. You have rooms, George?"

"The Club is empty, sir. Take any room you want, but I'd appreciate it if you'd take a room on this floor. Save me going upstairs with me back, sir."

"Well, George, I'd hate to see you go upstairs without it. And can you have the kitchen send along two steaks with cold beer. We'll be in No. 18, just down the hall."

George laughs. "You will have your joke, Mr. Wilson. . . . I'll cook the steaks and bring them along."

The room smells of disuse, like a resort hotel off-season. George is laying out dirty, greasy plates for them on a table.

"George, this gentleman is from the *National Geographic,* here to study conditions."

George looks at Neferti grimly. "I can't imagine why, sir. The less said the better, is my way of looking at it."

"George, there was a Spanish professor, an authority on the subject . . . a member of the Club."

"Ah, yes, I remember him. A *foreigner,* sir. He hasn't been in for some time, but we do have an address for him."

"Good, you can leave it in Mr. Neferti's shoes in the morning. Tell me, is the University still operating?"

"I couldn't say, sir. If you ask me, that's where the trouble all started . . . with the student riots, sir."

"I think it runs a bit deeper than that, George."

"Yes, sir. Things often do, sir. Will that be all, sir? Good night, sir."

We set out next morning, after a good English breakfast. Bit of a walk. The only taxi in the Zone is requisitioned round the clock by the Delegations. It's an area of rubble and vacant lots and half-finished buildings, now falling in ruins. Some were obviously intended to be apartments, with ten stories of concrete and rusty iron girders. Arab families are camping in the levels with their goats and chickens.

"Is it true there's a monster centipede here?"

"It is. Seen it with my own eyes . . . bloody revolting. Stink will knock a man on his bloody arse."

"And it is fed by human sacrifice?"

"Well, yes, you could say that."

A solid line of buildings, none over three stories, made of

mud or concrete blocks, joined arbitrarily, in many cases blocking the roadway, which then goes over the buildings by ramps or tunnels under them. The whole thing looks like a giant nest spit out by insects deprived of their symmetry by some mind-altering drug.

"Have to pick your street . . . some of them is blocked solid. And God knows how many is stinking dead in their filthy warrens."

"What happened here?"

"Well, the stock market crashed." Wilson gestures to the milling crowds. He can calculate their shifts and move through them almost as fast as if he and Neferti had the streets to themselves.

"Put it like this, country simple, hayseed simple. A country is bankrupt. No gold whatsoever in the coffers, and they are issuing paper money without anything to back it up. So the bottom falls out and the money isn't even good shithouse paper. Same thing here. They were issuing fraudulent human stock. Nothing to back it up. No gold. The backup here is Sek Energy Units. They got no Sekem. At first they tried to spread it out, like—cut everybody down a few units, and they won't notice."

"How many are there, of the monster 'pedes?"

"Well, there was just one at first. Then he updated his tech. Must be thirty by now."

"Does the Sek shortage affect them?"

"Christ, no. They thrive on it. Most insects do, and some plants. It's a mammalian need. Notice there are no animals here? No cats, no squirrels?"

"I assumed they had been eaten."

"Oh, no. They all left. A Piper came and piped them all out."

Wilson turns back to contemplate the milling crowds. "Obvious solution is to dig a great bloody hole and prod them down into it. They still react to stock prods." He prods a man with the sharp prods at the tip of his electric cane. The man emits an inhuman scream and runs six feet.

"See what I mean? The rest could be up to the bulldozers. You want to see the 'pedes, do you? Well, slip on this mask."

There is a solid wall of emaciated people ahead, many of them completely naked, with hideously deformed genitals.

"Looks like we'll be needing our blasters."

These are .10-caliber revolvers with a cylinder holding thirty three-inch bullets. The bullet is sharp at the point, which is hard metal, with a base of hard metal and soft metal between, that mushrooms on impact to the size of a half-dollar.

"Wouldn't penetrate human flesh, just flatten. But it enters and spreads in insect mush. Well, might as well get on with it."

The guns make almost no noise, like popping the cork on a bottle of half-dead champagne, but the effect is dramatic. The bodies are flying apart like rotten melons.

"Slip on this disposable mac, Laddy buck."

Clad in ankle-length plastic macs, they walk through the cavity opened by their blasters, the dismembered larval claws and mandibles still twitching. They drop their macs gingerly into a trash receptacle.

Flying centipede varieties buzz about, laying eggs in the unfortunate,

"Rum go when they hatch out . . . look there."

A naked man tears at his flesh, screaming as centipede heads break through the skin in gushes of blood and pus. The silent crowds walk by, faces blank, catatonic. The stricken man kicks convulsively as a centipede head breaks through the crown of his penis. Another is eating its way through an eye socket. Wilson kills the man with a single shot from his H&K P-7.

An area of narrow passages between rows of wire-mesh cubicles, six feet long, four feet deep, five feet high, four tiers. The upper cubicles are half empty, because few can climb up to them on the rope ladders and notched logs. The lower cubicles are jammed with the dead and dying, who have barely enough energy to pour their buckets of sewage into the mud paths between the warrens. The cubicles dwindle out in barren hills and ruined buildings.

They come to a small amphitheater, with limestone seats around a circular space twenty feet in diameter, paved with smooth marble. In the middle of the circle is a stone stele, covered with tiny script composed from centipede hair and eyes and legs and claws, the signs moving in jerks and spasmodic patterns that intercross and overlap, stop and scrabble. The stone writhes with hideous life. Below the stele is a naked man, bound to a couch with leather straps. The couch is made of hardwood and the legs fit into ancient holes in the marble floor.

The spectators are completely naked, except for exquisite centipede necklaces and bracelets in segmented gold, with opal eyes, lips parted, pestilent breath in the air, faces squirming and crawling on the skull, eyes dilated to shiny black mirrors reflecting a vile idiot hunger.

"We feed with the 'pede."

La jeunesse dorée of Pedeville, obviously.

Neferti and Wilson push through to the front row. The timorous Pedes, as the natives are called, scramble out of their way.

There is the sound of running water. When the tank is full, it raises a bronze grid on one side of the theater. The head of a monster 'pede emerges, with a stink like a vulture shat out rotten land crabs. The man on the couch begins to scream as the centipede inches out. The 'pede lifts its head now, with a seeking movement.

Neferti stands at the head of the couch, one nonchalant hand on the stele, the other extended toward the monster 'pede, who now scuttles forward with hideous speed. Neferti's fingers are centipede legs in the air, ending in a smooth gesture of cancellation across the ancient writing that crumbles to dust under his fingers.

The centipede shrivels to a final spasm of reddish dust in the air, dust on the stone seats. The bound man pushes aside the leather straps, which shred into black powder.

Mission accomplished.

5

Neferti is moving through the alleys of a rural slum on the outskirts of Memphis. Dead eyes broken by poverty, disease and hunger follow his passage. People turn from him and the women cover their faces, for he is a Scribe, an elite class that is feared and hated.

Neferti had been born the son of a fisherman on the seacoast. His family was poor, but not starving like these inland people. There is a certain crustacean—sea scorpions they are called—highly prized by the rich, and Neferti knew where to find these creatures, just as he always knew if there was a scorpion or a centipede in the house. He can feel it, the way he can feel danger. Sea scorpions gave off the same emanations, much weaker but still detectable.

"Stop the boat. Sea scorpions here."

Delivering this delicacy to rich clients, he was often propositioned. And he had already decided whether the offer was to his advantage. It was not long before he received the proposition he was looking for: to become a Scribe, apprenticed to old Sesostris, the pederast.

Neferti learned the glyphs with breathtaking speed. Sesostris had never seen such a student. Neferti knew that it was dangerous to depart from the norm in any direction, and most particularly in the direction of excellence. But he didn't have much time.

Neferti wrote each day in advance, whom he would encounter and how he would deal with the encounter. He took pains, of course, to conceal these experiments from Sesostris. He can think in glyphs as he walks, writing from the pictures he passes: a horned owl, legs, eyes, a mouth, an empty road waiting. And he writes as he walks: coming forth, his legs and eyes waiting in the road; a sheaf of wheat in a field, his erect phallus under his loincloth. Coming forth waiting for thee from of old: legs, eyes, a mouth, a road, a hand pointing, an erect phallus, a sheaf of wheat.

Individual glyphs can be delineated in many different ways. They can be incorporated into a picture, and the pictures can move. Panels of glyphs can be shifted into various combinations. Neferti devised glyphs of his own to indicate whole panels and ways in which they can be fitted together. Where the horned owl lights, a connection is made.

Abata's official position was Assayer of Scribes, and since the number of Scribes was far in excess of the work available, he still exercised considerable influence, his position being more or less similar to that of a modern art critic.

The Scribes were divided into a number of schools: the Traditional, the Naturalistic, the Functional, the Situational, the Punctual, the Random, the Picture Puzzle. Abata invariably chose the most stilted, conventional and banal scripts, so that schools of this lifeless garbage flooded the art market. But his position was precarious. Brokers were consulting their own assayers. Even the most tasteless and vulgar parvenus of the emerging merchant class complained of his boring murals, that always looked the same from any angle or in any light.

"We want Picture Puzzle scripts."

In Picture Puzzle scripts, the glyphs are incorporated into the big picture: an eye, a phallus, water, birds, animals spell out the story. At first it is just a picture with a special look, then glyphs swim out of clouds and water, pop out of swift lizards, run with the hare of hours, sit with the toad of a million years, spatter out of excrement thrown by an angry ape, trickle out of streams, a boy masturbates in the shadow of an owl's wing, a weather vane whirls in the wind.

Abata's power depended on keeping the other assayers in line to support his judgments. This he found increasingly difficult. It was becoming obvious that his poor taste threatened the market. The other assayers began to shun him, catching the contagious reek of failure, and the Old Man had a contract out on him. A knife could streak out of an alley or doorway. He had bodyguards, but any one of his guards could be Alamout's man.

These were troubled times. There was war in the heavens, as the One God attempted to exterminate or neutralize the Many Gods and establish a seat of absolute power. The priests were aligning themselves on one side or the other. Revolution was spreading up from the South, moving in from the East and from the Western deserts. Not only had the rich monopolized the land and the wealth, they had monopolized the Western Lands. Only the members of certain families were allowed to mummify themselves, and so achieve immortality.

Neferti aligned himself with the rebels and the followers of Many Gods. There was a new edict against sodomy, issued by the One God priests. The penalty was impalement. His relation with the old pederast scribe Sesostris was now highly dangerous.

His patron was a kindly, ineffectual man of a vacillating disposition. He could not bring himself to take sides in the fierce controversy raging over the One God concept. Gently Neferti pointed out that a neutral position was untenable, especially in view of the new edict. His enemies had waited for this chance. In Sesostris's attempt to make no enemies, he would succeed only in making no friends he could trust.

Neferti intended to obtain the secret Western Land papyrus. Scribes at his level were not supposed to know even that such a papyrus existed. He carried at all times an alabaster tube of poison, in case of arrest, and a thin dagger with a grooved tip dipped in cobra venom.

The apprentice Scribes were housed in dormitories, under strict discipline. Neferti had hitherto bypassed these onerous conditions through his relation with Sesostris. This exemption, together with his brilliance, made him a target for hate and envy, solid as the blow of a fist and sharp as an ax.

The glyph of the spitting cobra gives protection. He knows just where to spit his poison and what poison to use, and he has allies who think as he does. But now his position was extremely precarious. To continue his relationship with Sesostris, he set up rotating places to meet: a room in the village one day, hidden coves and caves another.

All Scribes study the Egyptian pantheon: Ra, Bast, Set, Osiris, Amen, Horus, Isis, Nut, Hathor. Many Gods are known only to a few initiates, like the Shrieking Scorpion: half cat and half scorpion, said to have been conceived by a union between Bast and the Scorpion Goddess. With her lashing tail loaded with deadly venom, her rending cat claws and insect mandibles, she is evoked only by the most terrible curses. And the Centipede God, with a centipede's body, the poison fangs sprouting from the glands of his neck, and a man's translucent head in which the brain glows white-hot behind red, faceted eyes. His bite causes death in terrible agony, the victim roasted alive. The Centipede God lives in red sandstone caves in the blistering Hot Lands of the South.

Neferti fashions little blocks of clay and hardwoods on which glyphs are delineated in raised outline, so that he has only to press the block into ink and then imprint the glyphs on papyrus. Demons and Helpers can be drawn into being and assigned functions and contexts. They have their special abilities, their weapons and means of access, their enemies and friends, their masters and servants.

One of the Helpers is characterized by an indentation on the upper tip of his member where the Creator left his thumbprint. It was a small thumb, no bigger than a finger but much longer, with three articulations. This Helper leaves behind him a smell of musk and thunder and the blue smell of the sea wind. Giver of Winds is his name. Fleet and light-boned, he can skim over swamps and quicksand, climb a sheer cliff or a palace wall. His long thin fingers can crush a man's neck or tear off an arm. He can parry the quickest sword slash and dodge an arrow. He is the Helper on perilous journeys and impossible escapes. He knows the Bang-utot cord of sperm that strangles a sleeping enemy, the smells of valor and danger, of ferrets and spiced lace stained by radiant journeys.

His Mayan counterpart is Ah Pook, patron of street boys, wanderers and outcasts: a face of green marble, thick round lips, flaring eyes like jade slits. He knows the slums of Tenochtitlán, the warrens and reeking alleys of the Centipede City. His phallus is a smooth, translucent green, and he gives off a smell of fungus and toadstools, of jungles and untamed wild cats and orchids, of moss and stone.

Another helper is the adolescent Ka of the god Amsu. Of a shining, dazzling beauty, he knows every nuance of sex and courtship. He is the only defender against the female goddesses of sexual destruction and orgasm death, the vampire Lilith, and Ixtab, the goddess of ropes and snares and sexual hanging. His phallus is a pulsing tube of opalescent pink light. His smell, sweet and heavy, burns through the body with prickles and shivers of delight. His hair is a brilliant blazing red. Even the goddess Bast quails before him, reduced to a lovesick drab.

The Healing Helper is a calm gray presence with a kind, unhappy face, for he has taken on much pain. But he is deft and quick. Pain dissolves beneath his fingers, and sickness loosens its hold. He brings a smell of clean bandages, dawn wind in fever dreams, sleep after sleepless nights.

For every Helper, there is a corresponding demon or adversary. Many play both roles. There are old demons wracked with the pain of toothless, impotent hate, who live only to injure, occupying evil old caretakers and doormen.

The Pharaoh is a One God believer, but he does not have the support of his Palace staff. Obviously he will be assassinated sooner or later. Neferti does not wish to associate himself with a lost cause which he opposes in any case, but he is still under the Pharaoh and his secret police. They are everywhere, watching and listening. One moves in stylized pantomimes of innocence.

At any hour of the day or night, the Pharaoh summons everyone in the Palace to an audience.

"The Pharaoh awaits! Come!"

No time to get dressed, just a hasty robe and here we go again.

They form ranks in front of the Pharaoh. His Palace guards, a caste of genetic eunuchs, move up and down the line, carefully searching for weapons. When the word is given, the Palace retinue parades past the throne very slowly.

"Stop!"

Each one stops at the Pharaoh's feet for the Examination. The Pharaoh, with his alabaster white face and black snake eyes, looks at you, around you, through you, looking for a dagger in your mind, listening for the whispered furtive words, smelling for the sweat of guilty fear. His guards stand ready, massed on both sides of the throne. Motioned on by a twitch of his staff, you try not to look too relieved. Now he points with the staff, and the guards move forward. Someone is dragged away.

Neferti knows the arts of telepathic blocking and misdirection. You can't make your mind a blank, for that would be detected at once. You must present a cover mind which the Pharaoh can tune into, and which is completely harmless: "For me the Pharaoh is a God." You can't lay it on too thick.

Needless to say, one's enemies attempt to take advantage of the occasion. There are telepathic ventriloquists who can throw disloyal thoughts: "How long must we endure this vile pig Pharaoh? Our time will come . . . soon, very soon."

And there are the Smell Throwers, who can throw smells

onto the target in a crowded street. People hiss and start away, leaving him in a circle of eyes burning with hate and loathing. Sometimes a Smell Thrower will take advantage of the Examination to discredit a rival, causing him to appear before the Pharaoh reeking of excrement. It is a dangerous expedient, however, as a skilled practitioner can throw it back with double stink.

The sin of Secret Painting is rife, though punished by impalement on a white-hot bronze phallus. Secret Painters are divided into tribes. Neferti belongs to the Cobra Tribe. They keep with them at all times the means of suicide, and gather in their secret haunts to compare suicide and murder weapons. They are not averse to taking as many with them as possible.

Their haunts are not secret in the sense of being hidden. To the outsider they would appear as a perfectly ordinary house or inn. Should an unwanted stranger happen in, he will see nothing noteworthy, but rather an emptiness, a lack of anything that can engage his interest or pleasure. The food isn't exactly bad, but it is exactly the kind of food he doesn't like. If he ventures on a sexual encounter, it will end in a grating climax, at once painful and disgusting. The sheets are not dirty, but they feel dirty and smell dirty.

One of the wise palates from the Good Guide Book came in here, and went out with his buds switched over—he moans and rolls his eyes like Crazy Horse impersonated by Jimmy Durante over the most appalling junk food for starters, and sardines eaten from the can with a shoehorn, washed down with Green River. The meat course is second-run rejects from premises closed by the Board of Health, doused in stale ketchup and anchored down with cherry milkshakes laced with gritty undissolved granules of cheaper-by-the-ton synthetic malt, then a canned pineapple and marshmallow salad with Postum.

They don't come back. And usually they can't get out quick enough.

A certain species of vampire which can take male or female

form sneaks into the rooms of youths. The pleasures they offer are irresistible, and the victim is hopelessly captivated by these nightly visits which no lock or charm can forestall. The victim loses all interest in human contact. He lives only for the visits of the vampire, which leave him always weaker and more wasted. In the end he is little more than a living mummy.

These visitations have decimated rural areas, and the large estates are deserted. It has long been suspected that these vampires are the ghosts of mummies who immortalize themselves in this way and convert the energy required to maintain the Western Lands.

Revolution is spreading, and many of the large estates are deserted and have been taken over by partisans.

The Partisan Leader Mementot has uttered a terrible threat: "I am going to destroy every fucking mummy I get my hands on. The Western Lands of the rich are watered by *fellaheen* blood, built of *fellaheen* flesh and bones, lighted by *fellaheen* spirit."

Terrorized, the rich have brought in mercenaries from the South, filthy Ethiopians who delight in the torture of prisoners. A common practice is death by fire in muslin. The victim is wrapped in strips of muslin soaked in beeswax, to the semblance of a mummy, then set alight to divert his captors with the Mummy Dance, accompanied by flute music . . . hideous shrill mimicry of burning screams.

"Go! Go! Go!" they chant, pissing all over themselves with laughter.

A sibilant quivering hiss, and the partisans attack like silent hungry ghosts. One dispatches the dancing mummy with a sword slice that severs the charred head. Grimacing hideously, it bounces among the mercenaries. Sagging like unstrung puppets, their vile torture lust steamingly exposed to sharp steel, deserted by their employers who have shut themselves into fortified citadels, the mercenaries either join the partisans or retreat and disband to the Hot Lands of the South.

In the Hot Lands there are seven artesian wells, and the settlements cluster around the precious waters. The houses are completely sealed, except for ventilating screens impregnated with oils that kill insect invaders. The oil must also be worn on all exposed surfaces when venturing into the open, and suits with many layers of silk to cover the body, and boots to the knees. No one goes out except at night, when the temperature plummets to 120 degrees. The houses are cooled by layers of burlap and a constant drip of water, the evaporation giving off more coolness as the outside heat increases.

The wells are fed by underground rivers which sometimes change course. In Japan they get into baths so hot you have to stay absolutely still until the water cools. One movement and you would scald to death. Here it's the same with the air, and it doesn't cool. One quick movement and you start roasting. Takes an hour to cross a room. Talking will roast your lips and strangle you with your bursting tongue. Three months of that, and then the faint stirring of coolness around the edges, cool blue on your burning flesh, the winds of God bringing rain.

Certain highly prized minerals are found only in this area: a metal which can be molded like clay but will harden to the consistency of bronze, and the burning metal that glows with a soft cold fire, giving off a steady, silent rain of death. One exposure means death in a few weeks, as flesh and entrails wither and the brittle bones snap like dry reeds. A metal unguent gives protection from the deadly emanations of the Burning Silver.

Some Secret Painters of the Cobra Tribe have gathered in a squalid inn. They sip excellent wine served in earthen mugs. A "wrong one" would get the wine suitable to the vessel, a sour grit that sticks to his teeth and coats his mouth. They do not regard all strangers as undesirable, to be gotten rid of as soon as possible. But certain categories are definitely bad news they don't want around: informers, Palace spies, purveyors of gossip and rumors, lunatics and religious sons of bitches.

As usual, they are comparing weapons for suicide and murder, poison pins and rings and clasps and earrings and teeth, poison sewn under the skin, articles of clothing soaked in poison. For suicide, cobra and mamba venoms are quite quick and painless, rather pleasant in fact, and some of them are also cobra venom addicts.

The venom of the cobra, dried and administered in a carefully adjusted dose by blowing the dissolved venom into the flesh through a sharpened tube, produces a feeling of serene euphoria which lasts up to three hours. Repeated exposure leads to dependence, which confers upon the addict immunity to the venom. This is advantageous when using cobra as a weapon.

Cobra venom is now restricted to initiation ceremonies and the use of a few advanced adepts, who converse in sibilant hisses, reptilian purrs and sometimes the icy cold shriek of reptile hysteria. They slowly become cold-blooded, and cease to dream. The withdrawal symptoms are excruciating, the cold blood as low as 75° F heated back to 98.6° in a few hours. Patients must be restrained from suicide by any means at hand. Industrial doses of heroin are the only remedy if no venom is available and, since cobras are not always handy, few choose to contract this perilous addiction. Fortunately, dependence is not quickly established.

Turning now to some of the more deplorable files: hmm, yes, Reggie Carlton . . . anonymous features that are somehow very displeasing. In fact, one feels definitely queasy . . . a hideous member straining out from just below the navel, wrinkled purple black at the end. The shaft juts up, flat on top, with little nodules of purple-pink flesh around the crown oozing with deadly venom. The dead empty eyes, the hideous cock. Deformed children beg behind him. Every cock is deformed, some swollen and bulbous, some thin as pencils, two-pronged penises with tiny fangs strike at each other spurting venom, a rectum where the penis was, the penis now grows slowly from the navel.

These demons from Bosch are familiars of the Gaboon Viper, a bloated snake with symmetrical patterns of brown, white and black, thick as an average thigh, tapering to a blunt tail. The head is like a small shovel, translucent gray-pink poison glands on each side and on the snout, two little purple-pink horns that writhe and smell toward the target (replicas of the Gaboon's cock). Instead of wriggling along like a decent snake, your Gaboon Viper crawls along on his ribs, straight ahead, like a purposeful caterpillar.

Despite their bloated and torpid appearance, they can move with great rapidity to catch a rat in the air, or a horrified hand. The venom is both hemotoxic and neurotoxic, often leading to severe neural damage. The blood venom holds the nerve venom in place, and the nerve venom renders the victim liable to gangrene and other infections. If one does not die from the Gaboon's huge dripping fangs, he is often left a permanent invalid. One case is paralyzed from the neck down, another is slowly dying of encroaching infections. His arm has already been amputated, the infection is spreading to the brain.

To top it all, the Gaboon growls like a dog would, if a dog were cold-blooded. It's a growl dates back to some models that appeared at the end of the Reptile Age, about the size of a wolf, part reptile and part emergent mammal. May have been cold-blooded, with fur and reptile teeth. Looked quite promising. Others were warm-blooded with scales and wolf teeth. What happened? Trouble with the thermostat most likely.

The Bras cultivate an alert, malevolent somnolence that can shift to the cold hysteria of deadly rage. The cult embraces many venomous snakes who chew and eat and live on death: the mamba, dropping from trees in a green streak, his little jaws open, for this long slender delicate snake, no thicker than a heavy walking cane, is six feet in length. "Very fast. Very good," as Hemingway said about General Omar Bradley. The fangs are small, and there is no local irritation or swelling. One may not even know he has been mamba bit, until his speech begins to slur and slobber, his gait to lurch and stagger and fall. DOA an hour later, if there is a hospital to be DOA at. No pain.

The Bras find the Boons rather common.

A group of languid Bras have gathered in a Cheney Walk flat that attempts to capture the effect of an Egyptian garden in the drowsy noon heat. Unfortunately the storage heaters aren't working. The man from London Electric, who alone are authorized to repair a storage heater, muttered something about "the element" three weeks ago, and hasn't been seen since.

Sandun has them all spreading and hissing with his account of how three Boons emptied a gay bar in Chelsea:

"There they are at the bar, in full white tie like a 1920s Arrow Collar ad by E. C. Leyendecker, and without a frame's transition they are starkers from the shirt down, still being nonchalant with a Murad and sipping champagne while the hideous Boons growl and spurt deadly venom all over them. They trap fifty screamers stuck in the exit.

"The Boons are looking for a Receptacle that will fertilize their deadly sperm, so now and then they do a spot search like this. But the faggots is dropping like poisoned pigeons. The venom is corrosive, eats its own hole. The Boons draw themselves up:

" 'Unworthy vessels. Let's toddle along and leave these chappies to stew in our juice. They're filthy.'

"Good show, that. Good enough to steal."

The area controlled by the Pharaoh's troops is dwindling. Beyond that line is a power vacuum, empty lands and palaces and villas that are anyone's for the taking.

'"For the rich became poor and the poor became rich. This

state of things continued for a hundred years," a chronicler states.

The landed aristocrats who fled to the city joined the ranks of the new poor, supporting themselves by menial work and charity from the Palace. And their estates fell to the partisans who, having no means to merchandise large-scale produce, turned to subsistence farming, fishing and hunting. . . .

Thirty men and boys are gathered in the room, their bows and spears stacked against a wall, sitting at a long table drinking distilled wine. They are discussing the various demons they can expect to encounter after their physical deaths, which they can meet at any time. Feuding tribes, disgruntled mercenaries and ex-soldiers roam the countryside like dog packs. They are referring to the Book of the Dead and other texts and maps laid out on the table.

The demon guards have made mummification a prerequisite for immortality in the Western Lands. Why, exactly? Obviously the mummies serve as receptacles to collect and store the plasma of the fellaheen needed to preserve their masters. In return, the sucking mummies are given conditional immortality, as vampires to be milked like aphids.

So the One God, backed by secular power, is forced on the masses in the name of Islam, Christianity, the State, for all secular leaders want to be the One. To be intelligent or observant under such a blanket of oppression is to be "subversive":

"What are *you* looking at?"

And the old gods will eke out a wretched, degraded existence as folklore for the tourists.

"Ju-Ju doll, meester? Shrunked-down head? Pointy bone? Velly feelthy! Velly stlong!"

The One God can wait. The One God is *Time*. And in Time, any being that is spontaneous and alive will wither and die like an old joke. And what makes an old joke old and dead? Verbal repetition.

So who made all the beautiful creatures, the cats and lemurs and minks, the tiny delicate antelopes, the deadly blue krait, the trees and lakes, the seas and mountains? Those who can *create*. No scientist could think it up. They have turned their backs on creation.

Ju-Ju doll, meester?
Fill with nails
Got good Ju-Ju
Never fails
Shrunked-down head?
Hair will grow
Pointy bone?
Velly feelthy
Velly stlong

It is of course assumed by Western savants that the Egyptian animal Gods are the fantasies of a primitive and backward people, who did not have the advantage of the glorious gains of the Industrial Revolution, a revolution in which a standardized human product overthrows himself and replaces his own kind with machines (they are so much more efficient).

However, all fantasy has a basis in fact. I venture to suggest that at some time and place the animal Gods actually existed, and that their existence gave rise to belief in them. At this point the monolithic One God concept set out to crush a biologic revolution that could have broken down the lines established between the species, thus precipitating unimaginable chaos, horror, joy and terror, unknown fears and ecstasies, wild vertigos of extreme experience, immeasurable gain and loss, hideous dead ends.

They who have not at birth sniffed such embers, what have they to do with us?

The Hawk cults, blue eyes harsh and pitiless as the sun; the

Owl cults, with huge yellow night eyes and wrenching needle talons; flying weasels and reptiles. . . .

But the One God has time and weight. Heavy as the pyramids, immeasurably impacted, the One God can wait. The Many Gods may have no more time than the butterfly, fragile and sad as a boat of dead leaves, or the transparent bats who emerge once every seven years to fill the air with impossible riots of perfume.

Consider the One God Universe: OGU. The spirit recoils in horror from such a deadly impasse. He is all-powerful and all-knowing. Because He can do everything, He can do nothing, since the act of doing demands opposition. He knows everything, so there is nothing for him to learn. He can't go anywhere, since He is already fucking everywhere, like cowshit in Calcutta.

The OGU is a pre-recorded universe of which He is the recorder. It's a flat, thermodynamic universe, since it has no friction by definition. So He invents friction and conflict, pain, fear, sickness, famine, war, old age and Death.

His OGU is running down like an old clock. Takes more and more to make fewer and fewer Energy Units of Sek, as we call it in the trade.

The Magical Universe, MU, is a universe of many gods, often in conflict. So the paradox of an all-powerful, all-knowing God who permits suffering, evil and death, does not arise.

"What happened, Osiris? We got a famine here."

"Well, you can't win 'em all. Hustling myself."

"Can't you give us immortality?"

"I can get you an extension, maybe. Take you as far as the Duad. You'll have to make it from there on your own. Most of them don't. Figure about one in a million. And, biologically speaking, that's very good odds."

We have notice of knives, rebirth and singing. All human thought flattened to a dry husk behind a divided pen. He walks in the glyphs and flattens man and nature onto stone and papyrus, eliminating, except in stone and bronze, the dimension of depth. We were not ignorant of perspective. We deliberately ignored it. A flat world was ours and everything in it had a name once and all the names were ours once. With perspective, names escape from the paper and scatter into the minds of men so they can never be held down again.

The means of suicide haunts their position. We are not averse to a king had a name and had once stone statues to be sure secret in the usual sense and bronze perspective . . . rage of animated dust that growls like a dog . . . barks and snarls of black granite serene crystal converse in sunlight . . . relive in boats a slough to the sky dotted with rafts, the smoke of cooking fire in dawn mist. All human thought flattened there in present time . . . flashes of innocence . . . birth and singing in the marshes.

God of the Long Chance, the impossible odds, the punch-drunk fighter who comes up off the floor to win by a knockout, blind Samson pulling down the temple, the horse that comes from last to win in the stretch, God of perilous journeys, Helper in the voyage between death and rebirth, the road to the Western Lands.

To be reborn at all makes your condition almost hopeless. He is the God of Almost, the God of If Only, the God of Miracles, and he demands more of his followers than any other god. Do not evoke him unless you are ready to take the impossible chances, the longest odds. Chance demands total courage and dedication. He has no time for welchers and pikers and vacillators.

He is the God of the Second Chance and the Last Chance, God of single combat, of the knife fighter, the swordsman, the gunfighter, God of the explorer, the first traveler on unknown roads, the first to use an untried craft or weapon, to take a blind step in the dark, to stand alone where no man has ever stood before . . . God of Mutation and Change, God of hope in hope-less conditions, he brings a smell of the sea, of vast open places, a smell of courage and purpose . . . a smell of silence confront-ing the outcome.

The Great Awakening arose from the horror of a dead, soulless universe. All the old answers have failed: the Church, the State. All the hundreds of cults with their answers, all seen as lies in the inexorably gentle white light of the White Cat, lies with nothing but terror and emptiness behind the lies.

It started in the sensational press, *The Enquirer, People, The World:* ANCIENT EGYPTIAN PAPYRUS DEMONSTRATES THAT LIFE AFTER DEATH IS WITHIN THE REACH OF EVERYMAN.

One of those life-after-death flutters in every issue: some housewife got a tip on the stock market from her dead husband. However, soon the Papyrus starts unrolling very precise instruc-tions for reaching the Land of the Dead. The message falls on summer golf courses waiting for rain, on the parched deserts of mid-America, dead hopeless wastes of despair, a glimmer of light and hope on a darkening earth. The great mushroom-shaped cloud always closer.

Just as the Old World mariners suddenly glimpsed a round Earth to be circumnavigated and mapped, so awakened pilgrims catch hungry flashes of vast areas beyond Death to be created and discovered and charted, open to anyone ready to take a step into the unknown, a step as drastic and irretrievable as the transition from water to land. That step is from word into si-lence. From Time into Space.

The Pilgrimage to the Western Lands has started, the voy-age through the Land of the Dead. Waves of exhilaration sweep the planet, awash in seas of silence. There is hope and purpose in these faces, and total alertness, for this is the most dangerous of all roads, for every pilgrim must meet and overcome his own death.

Governments fall from sheer indifference. Authority figures, deprived of the vampiric energy they suck off their constituents, are seen for what they are: dead empty masks manipulated by computers. And what is behind the computers? Remote control. Of course. Don't intend to be there when this shithouse goes up. Nothing here now but the recordings. Shut them off, they are as radioactive as an old joke.

Look at the prison you are in, we are all in. This is a penal colony that is now a Death Camp. Place of the Second and Final Death.

Desperation is the raw material of drastic change. Only those who can leave behind everything they have ever believed in can hope to escape.

Neferti lived at this time in the Trains beside a river. This was in what used to be the Kansas City yards, a maze of switchbacks and passenger cars and freight trains. New tracks are constantly being built and the cars shifted around by various motors and pulley devices. More or less a thousand people live here.

Train whistles outside. We amuse each other with train whistle arrangements passed through echo chambers, ruined warehouses, broken windows, empty railroad stations, cheap hotel rooms, lonely sidings, misty, muffled foghorns, the cries of lost cats, farm ponds at twilight, croaking frogs, fireflies, music across the golf course. Some with old steam engines make trips to Denver and St. Louis. Others on abandoned, rusty, weed-grown switchbacks aren't going anywhere, and there is some sense in that.

Now these young fellers so hellbent to get to the Western Lands wouldn't know if they was there already. Gotta keep moving and moving and moving ; . . . where? The faster you move, the more it looks the same. Corn and grass grow between the cars, many of them covered with vines.

Neferti parts some rose vines and enters the dining car. Boys in white suits and blackface rush forward.

"Good evening, white boss man, got catfish boiled alive in asparagus piss . . . it's piquant."

They pull off their masks and sit down wearily.

"I wonder if we could ever get this thing moving?"

"You want moving trains, they got 'em. Got an itch for St. Louis, the Valley maybe? Go to the House of David and watch the girls eat shit? Dayumn! Makes you feel good all over. Or find yourself a drowned whore, cured two weeks in the River des Peres, and roll and snort and wallow in her? Peoria and Pantapon Rose's cathouse? Denver and Salt Chunk Mary?"

The boys are frying catfish on an alcohol stove. So why not just set here and look. Look at that old river down yonder.

The boys serve each other martinis.

"Here you are, Jones." He hands him a shiny dime.

"You sure is a fair white man, boss, a fine old whitey. When I die I want to be buried right on top of you with your prick up my ass."

"Your attitude is commendable, Jones. How does 'Head Porter' sound to you?"

"Like the music of the queers . . . I mean the spheres, boss."

But this waiter–white-man act is wearing thin and we know it. Just let these things run on and on until they stop. Your death is always with you. You don't have to run around looking for it.

He looks out across the river at the setting sun.

"Where are my smudge pots, Nigger? I want a smoky sunset."

"Got used up as smoke bombs in the Last Riot."

The Last Riot was a confrontation between the old tired way, Church and State, rule of the unfit for the unfit, biologic suicide. When the smoke cleared away, wasn't much left . . . just empty buildings and Sekhu, human remains.

Neferti strolls down to the market after dinner. The merchandise is laid out in houseboats and stalls along the river.

He picks up a revolving blowgun. Six darts can be loaded into a cylinder, which revolves by hand and blows them out one after the other. The gun is two feet in length and looks like a flute. He buys two extra cylinders, darts and a selection of poisons: blue-ringed octopus, sea snake, stonefish, cyanide. He chooses a functional model of ebony, the cylinder of aluminum.

Single-shot tubes, no thicker than a pen, made of ebony, teak, bone and ivory. They fit into a Scribe's kit, the little ink pots containing the poisons to be blended as a painter blends his colors. A smooth-bore revolver, each bullet shooting six nail-size darts that spread out a foot wide at ten feet. You can't miss, and you can take out a roomful of assholes or a pursuing crowd, falling all over each other.

Rested from his sojourn in the trains, cleansed by emptiness, Neferti is ready now to resume the endless journey over the hills and far away. His clothes are an intricate arrangement of pockets to accomodate tools, drugs and weapons.

He has studied at the Sleight-of-Hand Academy. Disguised as a nude dancing boy, he once pulled a hog castrator from the crotch of a rival sheik, who subsequently pined away and died of shame. With his painted eyes, his lithe, slim figure and his deadly hands, he looks more like a beautiful evil woman than a man—which is to say he has incorporated his female component into a deadly concentration of incandescent purpose.

Neferti moves on, his purchases discreetly distributed about his person. He wears a light backpack. In his hands is a cane of whip steel, with a crook at the end. He can hook an ankle or a throat, an extension of his arms to touch, to move aside. There is reason for caution here—from the corner of his eye, he catches the deadly silent rush of an assailant from a down-slanting side street. Neferti whirls and gives him cyanide darts right across his chest. The man turns blue in the air, and his knife clatters ahead of him as he falls.

As he walks along, a boy pads in beside him.

"What you look for, meester?"

"Clothes, young man, rather special clothes."

"You mean maybe clothes from El Hombre Invisible?"

"Precisely."

"It is expensive, meester, you will see. I will guide you to my commission."

"Neferti! You honor my humble shop."

The old man stands up, in all his courtly insolence. "But how could I"—he rubs his hands—"be of service to you?"

"I have need of a cloak."

The old man's face goes blank and cold.

"What you ask is illegal."

"Is not anything of value illegal?"

The old man's face relaxes into contented depravity.

"Of course, one must always take the Big Picture. . . . Yes, I have what you need. See for yourself."

They move into a vault. Suspended on elaborate frameworks to simulate the client, in this case lithe and thin and six feet in height, are the Cloaks of Darkness and Invisibility. Like thick black velvet, gathering always more darkness, they can suck the light out of a room or a street.

Neferti slips into a tight sweater. He fingers a djellaba of a blue-black color. There are boots from ankle to hip.

"The clothes of darkness, señor. Yes, come in many sizes. Here is a cloak to be worn at dusk and dawn, gray-black as you see, always the thick velvet feel, with gray-white velvet in the morning light, the black velvet lingering in corners like a fog of underexposed film, a path of darkness. Capes . . . yes, to be whipped about one, throwing swirls of darkness, and slim-fitting invisibles, tight pants, turtleneck and Russian hat. It's terribly dashing. But the old-time capes are still popular, how you can *swish* them around . . . a great swish of velvety darkness knocks the stupid words out of a redneck mouth with his bloody teeth."

Neferti adjusts the cloak about his shoulders. Soft and light as air, it settles around his body, molding to every contour. The hat is like a wig, fitting across the forehead and down the back of the neck below the cloak, and the ankle-high boots walk on layers and cushions of darkness.

He steps out into the arcade of the market. It is late afternoon. Many of the stalls are empty. The palpable silence of an empty market, the heavy absence of many voices, all manner of men on their way to buy and sell, all absent, not even the shrug of negation or a ripple of water.

Those who have been raised in the market can distinguish what manner of merchant is there by the particular silence in his empty stall or shop or the accustomed place under the colonnades where he spreads out his wares. For a man is delineated more clearly by what he is not than by what he is, as if cut from stone by the mason's chisel. A moving tunnel of silence left by the water seller, a cool silence that is not thirst.

Here is the silence of a loud-mouthed cripple selling worthless merchandise. A faint whiff of incense, a calm, a dispersal, and the little people have cleaned up after him. The compound silence of the partisans of silence. Many turn aside, for few can breathe here in the absence of words.

Neferti is careful to hug the shadows, lest someone see a patch of darkness where there is no shadow. Under the arcades there are always shadows, and besides, the market is empty, or almost empty.

He passes a small café with benches along the side where men sit drinking mint tea and passing around kief pipes . . . laughter behind him.

He comes now to an open space of rubble and sand, where the merchandise is unloaded. A smell of horses and manure, oxen and leather, the rank reek of camel drivers. He looks up: a scattering of clouds. He will have to cross on cloud shadows.

Almost through, a path with trees ahead and the sound of water. Then, a sudden shift of wind and he is caught in a spot of blazing sunlight. He hurries on.

A cry goes up. He has been seen. Four men are rushing

toward him, pulling out knives and snatching up stones and lengths of rusty iron. Neferti whips out his revolving blowgun, *sput sput sput*, spitting out little puffs of death.

He catches the lead man, a paunchy brute with a round pig face and bristling eyelashes, with a cobra load. The barbed dart thunks an inch into the hard, fat, hairy stomach. The man's mouth flies open. He stumbles and falls to his knees. A pile-up like a football scrimmage. Stonefish dart, the pain like acid through the blood. A man in front of him with an adze . . . henbane and cobra venom right in his open mouth. He tries to raise the adze, his hands like blocks of wood.

The man hit with the stonefish dart is still screaming. A crowd gathers suddenly, as if they had sprung from the ground, cruising and snapping like aroused sharks. The moment is coming when they will all look at Neferti. He speaks sharply.

"Can't you see, the man is having a fit. Go fetch the Healer at once!"

They look back at the screaming man, just long enough for Neferti to slip into the cool shade of a tree.

6

Whan that Aprille with his shoures sote
The droghte of Marche hath perced to the rote,

Than longen folk to goon on pilgrimages . . .

There is something exhilarating about the concept of a pilgrimage, stirring dull roots with spring rain, sudden smell of the sea, vast empty lands, at once festive and purposeful, and any such occasion will attract a cruising school of swindlers, steerers, fixers, guides and outright killers for profit.

The Thuggees, the Deceivers, are in business again, bound together in the brotherhood of murder, waiting for the moment when the glad cry goes up:

"Beeeetho!" (Outsider)

Whereupon travelers who have passed themselves off as Accountant, Hippy, Survivalist, Farmer, Artist, Academic, Hard Hat, Pop Group, CIA, KGB, as one man cast off their roles and strangle the Beethos.

How can one protect his caravan against the Deceivers? Of course you can give them a flutter on the E-Meter, but you don't need that. Self-evident spiritual truth cannot be faked, any more than you can fake a poem, a painting or a good meal, and the lack of truth in fraud is immediately apparent to the eye that can see truth. So why do so many receive the venerable lies of the con man, clearly out to get their money by trickery or violence? Answer is, the mark *fears* the con man, fears his stronger will, his glittering eye. He listens like a three-year-old child.

> The Swindler has his will.
> I fear thee, Ancient Swindler.
> I fear thy skinny hand.
> Fear not, fear not, convention guest
> This body dropped not down

It was the fake murder scene with a bladder of pig's blood, where the Swindler pretends to kill his accomplice, who has bungled the deal they were all going to clean up on, into which the mark put his life's savings. Now the mark is an accessory to murder. They spirit him out of town and go on bleeding him.

"Afraid I have bad news. The relatives are screaming for an autopsy."

"I thought that was all settled."

"So did we."

First they have to pay off a doctor to sign a "natural causes" death certificate. Next thing, the doctor has been indicted for faking death certificates, all his certificates are under investigation. Fortunately, we've been able to shake hands with someone in the record department to pull our file. A surprise witness bobs up, a scrub woman passed out in a broom closet was awakened by the shot. All these people need to be "paid off."

The mark fears the con man, and he wants desperately to be part of the dangerous, glamorous world of Yellow Kid Weil and the High Ass Kid. This carrot is ruthlessly dangled, and the mark comes back moaning for more. And sometimes the mark comes out ahead.

"I tell you, Henry, I just can't stand it. He keeps calling me up. 'Any action?' I change my address, he gets a private ass hole to find me. He's even got marks lined up. Good ones, too. I don't want his marks. I don't want his money."

"Didn't you say once you were looking for the perfect mark?

Well, it figures, you found what you was looking for. I think your phone is ringing."

The road to Waghdas, the City of Knowledge, is a long, circuitous detour through labyrinths of ignorance, stupidity and error. Like the Thuggees, the pilgrims, each with a cover story of some trade or profession, pretend not to know each other but present a united front in the face of dangers and emergencies.

Custom checks are frequent, and we must find ways of concealing drugs and weapons from a search. The drugs are disguised as food and preserves and ointments, the weapons as canes and pens, disassembled into seemingly unrelated parts, concealed in shoes and the hems of garments, strapped to our animals. In some cases it is necessary to force animals to swallow pellets of drugs and ammunition, which are subsequently recovered from their dung, or if time is short and we are in need of meat, the animals are killed and slit open.

The party to which we had attached ourselves numbered several hundred, and a sorrier, seedier bunch of scavengers I have seldom seen. They were all seeking their fortunes, lured by tales of fabulous gold and gems, precious woods and rare herbs that would make them rich so they might live out their lives in sloth and luxury. There was a wide variety of conveyances and pack animals, some of them drawing wagons and buckboards, which were continually getting mired down in the river crossings and swamps on the road.

The road to the Western Lands is by definition the most dangerous road in the world, for it is a journey beyond Death, beyond the basic God standard of Fear and Danger. It is the most heavily guarded road in the world, for it gives access to the gift that supercedes all other gifts: Immortality.

Every man starts the course. One in a million finishes.

However, biologically speaking, one in a million is very good odds indeed. The Egyptians and the Tibetans made this journey after Death, and their Books of the Dead set forth very precise instructions—as precise as they are arbitrary.

Who makes the rules? In Waghdas, jumping-off place for the Western Pilgrims, it is considered by most schools extremely disadvantageous to wait for death. If you wait for death, you are subject to death conditions. You are playing against house odds. Failure is almost certain. The best anyone can reasonably hope for is a favorable rebirth.

"Don't wait, kid. Leave now!"

"Leave how?"

Waghdas teems with people who will tell you how. Here is The Pilgrim Market in Waghdas, the City of Knowledge. It stretches as far as the eye can see in all directions. There are underground sections, sections in orbit, vast, intricate structures tower a thousand feet in the air.

Knowledge takes many forms and contexts. Cloistered ivy-covered halls, serious youths in academic garb . . . the typical is so often *not* where it's at, deliberately avoided like a cliché, that it becomes in time atypical, and by the inexorable logic of fashion, is once again where it's at.

Knowledge can be as explosive as Matter into Energy, as deadly as the virus for which the only cure is Death. Knowledge can bind men together in secret brotherhood, the knowledge of some unspeakable deed or rite so foul that an outsider could not conceive of it. So the brothers are safe if they stay together and keep silence.

The Market is honeycombed with secret societies, and new ones are constantly taking form. Most of them are oriented toward the pilgrimage, and involve a rigorous course of training, which is considered essential for a bare fighting chance of survival . . . training in a wide gamut of weapons and disciplines, meditation, Vipassana, Zen and synthesized disciplines incorporating old teachings with the latest advances in brain and neurological research.

Other societies prey on the pilgrims, for the area is infected with every variety of faker and swindler selling spurious Western Land plots and villas and condominiums. There you are in your beautiful villa, straight out of Disneyland, on a clear blue lake that drains away, while you sit, with a last derisive gurgle . . . *"suuuuugggger."*

Hustlers, guides, fixers, travel agents cruise the market like sharks. Messiahs on every street corner transfix one with a confront stare:

"Your life is a ruin."

"We have the only road to personal immortality."

Swamis, Rinpoches, practitioners of IS: "That's all there is to it, folks, what *is* right here, right now in front of you, and once you grasp the IS, you got the WILL BE."

Uncouth survivalists, bristling with weapons, scent deadly contagion on all sides.

"God damn perverts and dope fiends."

"Sex across the state line and injections of Marijuana."

Communist partisans preach Immortality to the People.

Don't wait. Leave now. How?

There are electromagnetic booths that guarantee immediate exteriorization from the body. Be careful: Are you really getting out, or is it one of those fake trips like Mission Impossible where someone thinks he is home in Russia and he is actually in a CIA Ops room?

A dangerous road. Every pitfall, every error, every snare to which Everyman has been liable since the beginning, you are sure to meet on the road to the Western Lands.

Waghdas is the *most* fashioned-minded city, the most factious and the most sensitively attuned to any nuance of change. The fact is that most pilgrims don't even have a clue. So they are constantly cruising around, and any new trend will attract a frantic school of pilgrims, snapping and sniffing for the new thing. Waghdas is swept by fads, like the tornados of Kansas or the hurricanes of Miami.

A new weapon? Oh, not new at all. Old as Egypt: the flail.

But suddenly everybody who is anybody is flail-crazy: flails with live snakes woven in, centipedes and scorpions in thin, glass containers, poisoned porcupine tails, a sea wasp whipped from an aquarium holster.

"Ah, *madame,* I have often wondered what jewel I could offer you worthy of your incomparable beauty . . . and now, quite suddenly, I know."

He deftly extracts a tiny blue-ringed octopus from a cigarette-case tank and places it around her horrified neck. The octopus lights up and glows bright blue, a blue that spreads to her face as she weaves in her chair and topples face down in the Baked Alaska.

Then blowguns take over, and blowpens, like an artist's pencils, in bamboo and thinnest teakwood, ivory and ebony.

"But it isn't the gun, darling, it's the way you *blow* it."

There are magnificent old red-faced English-colonel types can throw one of those fake English coughing fits . . . *hurumph* . . . coughing out a gaboon-viper dart with every *huumph hah hoh.* It's like the Masque of the Red Death. The clubroom is littered with stricken agents, bleeding through every pore and orifice. . . .

Elegant young Oxonian with an ivory blowgun held between thumb and index finger with impeccable elegance as he puffs out a dart . . . *shput* . . . that simply blows his opponent away as a nothing and a nobody. Uncouth types who belch out the darts like a machine gun . . . *Burp Burp Burp!* (Ugly frog-faced CIA operative belched out the Parade Bar.) Singing blow artists . . . *zinng* . . . the dart's out . . . flute blowguns and blunderbuss clarinets . . . and horns that can blast out ten darts to Dead Man Blues. Irish tenors trickle out the darts, snuffboxes and the deadly Sneezers . . . *"Choo at you,"* and he sneezes the dart out like a bullet.

Many pilgrims hope to simply *style* their way in by doing the chic thing, the hip thing, the trendy thing, the righteous jumping swinging thing. They dislocate limbs and slip disks in a frantic effort to assume fashionable postures, which constantly change with bewildering speed . . . the bumbling, sloppy, awkward thing is *out* . . . the tense, purposeful, graceful thing is *in* . . . the nonchalant, jaunty thing is *out* . . . the interested, earnest thing is *in* . . . sex is out, sex is in . . . in out . . . right left. You'll never make a style queen, Brad, unless you straighten up, stoop a bit, loosen up, tighten up . . . keep your eye on the ball . . . learn to look *away* . . . learn to look *at* . . . stop . . . go . . . the style trap.

The styles change faster and faster as the Ultimate Arbiter issues directives weekly, daily, hourly. People strip off unsuitable garments in the street, sneering at less agile contenders who have not taken the Alexander course in smooth, quick undressing and re-dressing. Everyone carries toilet kits, in case hair styles should suddenly change, and they are to be seen shaving off untrendy long hair or beards in restaurants, in the streets or in subways, their hairs drifting about and sifting into food like fine herbs. They learn to whip around like boomerangs. You come in leather and get the "sorry, sir" treatment, or you come in a tux and get the same from a leather bar.

The Arbiter's face is like gray wax, his lips very red, his eyes sparkling with dazzling malice. He is going mad: loincloths to full dress, skinheads, eighteenth-century dandies, togas, djellabas. Everyone now carries huge suitcases about.

Waghdas, City of Knowledge, is a center for outfitting pilgrims to the Western Lands. Since the dangers are manifold and different for each pilgrim, what equipment and provisions he will need is conjectural. However arcane, recherché, rarified, outré, Alexandrian your requirements, the Waghs can meet them.

Sharp practice and purveyors of the deadly illusion drugs abound: The Western Bubble gives a vista of lake and valley, vast cities and temples and avenues through which the pilgrim moves without effort, free of his body to roam at will without hunger or fatigue or thirst. All this fades in a few hours, leaving the traveler with his hunger, his thirst, his carnal needs, his awkward, bungling body, abrasive, dreary, dead-end surfaces where everything is exactly what it seems to be. There is no mystery, no magic. Death is as prosaic as the daily paper to flattened minds, a bedpan to a terminal cancer patient. There can be nothing beyond, since there is nothing in front or to the sides in this dead empty place without purpose or meaning. The unfortunate traveler, having poured all his magic into the bubble . . . POP . . . gritty surface with nothing behind . . . a smell of burnt plastic and rotten oranges.

The traveler stops by a concrete wall painted in pyramids of pastel blue and pale pink, a broken box, some lathes, an empty concrete sack. A framework in front of the wall supports a roof of tattered plastic broken into jagged patterns. You can see stick people frozen on the wall, like the shadows of human figures left on the walls of Hiroshima. The shadows don't move. There are windows, used to be a store . . . list of prices on a slab of white wood.

You know no one is behind the wall. Nothing is there but the photograph. Look at the shadows that should dance with the wind. They don't move. Look at the big dark-gray window: on the left side, what could be a man's stick-thin leg with a brace. His head is on the right side of the window, mouth open, a mustache.

The Thuggees operated in India during the early years of the nineteenth century, before the railroads. At that time travelers and pilgrims moved in groups, and it might be weeks or even months before they were missed. The Deceivers would join a caravan of travelers separately and seemingly unknown to each other. Each Deceiver had his cover: some were merchants, some druggists or soldiers or smiths, and they were all competent in their cover trade. Their word for their victims was Beethos, "outsiders."

At a given signal, the Stranglers would dispose of the travelers and rob them. Then the bodies would be perforated with pickaxes so that the gases would not attract dogs, hyenas and jackals, and buried under campfires lit over the graves. It is estimated that the Deceivers killed a million Beethos in about twenty years. It has been called one of the greatest criminal conspiracies in history. The Thuggees were all servants of Kali, goddess of destruction.

Pilgrims to the Western Lands travel in groups, and latter-day Deceivers operate in the area, equipped with modern weapons. At encampments a number of soap opera scenes are enacted:

Here is the young couple in a lean-to. She is a liberal Vassar girl, he is the aging ingénue Deceiver. Deceiving keeps him young.

She: "You and I are going to have to talk about our relationship."

He: "Well, darling, I think we have a beautiful thing really."

She: "Is that all it is to you, Jerry? A thing?"

He: "Don't move, Wendy!"

He shoots a black mamba in the air as it slithers down toward her pearly throat.

He (looking down at the dead snake): "You see, Wendy, that's what it is. One human being knowing he can depend on another in the face of death."

She: "I think I understand, Jerry. No matter what happens we'll always have that."

Beetho!

Her eyes widen in horrified comprehension, and her face goes slack and blank. She sinks to the floor. He wipes off his knife, his face blank, empty, serene.

An ex-cop and two hoodlums drink on supply boxes in an improvised bar.

"We cruise around in the car, spot some shine . . . call to him really friendly, 'Hey, come over here a minute,' and he comes over all grins."

The man shows his awful yellow teeth in a hideous grimace. "Then bust him right in the teeth." He goes through the smile act again. "Then bust him right in the teeth."

The cop says, "Just jab them in the nuts with your stick. Then they are dead meat. Do anything you want with it."

"Bust him right in the teeth . . ."

BEETHO!

The third hoodlum takes out a silenced gun and shoots the raconteur in the mouth. Shoots the cop in the crotch.

The Beetho Caller is a skilled operator since he must decide on the precise moment of action. Some specialize in these relationship things, and have been known to fall in love with a Beetho and escape with him or her. But the call of the Beetho runs deep. There can be heartrending scenes between a man and his ordained Beetho, but we got a simple job to do for Kali.

Encampment of pilgrims. They have been delayed for some weeks by floods. They sit around at campfires or fidget aimlessly. There is a smog of duplicity and vague fear that dampens conversation. People throw out remarks, hoping they will mean something. People have nothing to say, but they are afraid of saying nothing, so what they do say comes out flat and vapid and meaningless. The shadow of death is on every face. Everyman fears his neighbor, and with good reason, for the Deceivers are paid in death.

Horus Neferti is a bit tired of being the perpetual ingénue, the eternal reflection of unbearable radiant boyishness. But then radiance is a potent weapon that has served him in a number of awful engagements, a light weapon. You have to conserve and pace your kilowatts. Otherwise you can blow a fuse in a tight spot.

Dusk in a Necropolis slum. The streets are so deep that some are in darkness at the bottom. Light is the most precious commodity here. And always the streets are worn deeper by the mindless, gibbering dead . . . stratum after stratum of tombs, down into darkness. The rich live in the Light Streets on the sunny side, where there is light for an hour each day. The others are sinking deeper and deeper into the lightless depths.

Neferti was outside on the rubbly outskirts of the Necropolis, in a deep valley but still above ground. Dusk comes early and in the gray dusk, with the smell of death heavy in the still air, about ten huge scavenger dogs were closing in around him, behind them a ragged pack of snarling grave robbers.

He looks at them and smiles and turns on his radiance. He emits at first a pale glow like a firefly's, just enough to guide the dogs right to his crotch and his throat and the backs of his legs. When you don't know what to do, do nothing. Can feel it now, a ball of fire just below the navel, sweeping up and out his eyes in a brilliant flash of light. The dogs and the grave robbers are thrown back. They turn and run, yelping, whimpering, snarling.

Horus Neferti turned aside into a Jump Joint, where your dreams come true. Yeah, sometimes. They work like this: you got a scenario in your mind, usually made up of dreams. Sophisticated electronic equipment makes the dream solid. Or rather there are infinite nuances of solidity. There is Death Solid. It can kill you. Or maybe just knock you down with brass knucks, like the ghost of Joe Varland in "A Short Trip Home." Wavering, ebbing strength gathered for one last solid punch.

Death Solid is more or less the Gold Standard around here. Some people are pikers, darling. And there are plenty that order something and then try to dodge the check. Got news for you welchers: it can't be done. Because it's *your check*.

People out for a lark, don't want to go too far, that's all right. They got the shallow end of the pool if that's what you want. We never lose a dreamer—unless he slips into deep water, that is.

How does the machine work? Largely, by concentrating what is already there. A dream amplifier.

Neferti strolls around languidly with heavy-lidded, bored disdain . . . guides, steerers, pushers, whores of every persuasion. A pusher pads in beside him. The pusher's face is shriveled and stained.

"Plenty good Jump Junk!"

Jump Junk is the worst habit a man can contract. You get out for eight hours at first. When you come back down, it's like a coke letdown with an alcohol and barbiturate hangover and acute junk yen. Takes more and more to stay out for less and less time.

He dismisses the pusher with a backhanded gesture.

Health Food Stores guarantee natural products . . . snake venom, insect, fish and mollusk. Unexplored territory for the most part. Stonefish poison, which is contained in barbed spines that break off in the flesh, is perhaps the most excruciating pain a man can experience. The pleasure of junk is relief from pain, so how about stonefish poison cooled out with King Cobra or blue octopus? You can smell it going in and coming out. The urine reeks of rotten fish.

A technician engaged in packaging dried cobra venom inadvertently inhaled a small quantity. He described a state of serene euphoria. Cobra venom, under the title of Cobraxine, was even used in the 1930s as a painkiller in terminal cancer. It was discontinued because of the high cost of production and . . . "We don't want another addiction in our laps," said a highly placed narcotics official. "They'll be raiding the zoos."

An old snake man in Florida has been taking a King Cobra shot every day for forty years and he looks very young for his age, which God only knows, and He has forgotten. The only man who can take a full load of King and survive.

The neurotoxic venoms like the cobras, sea snakes, kraits, tiger snakes, mambas and blue-ringed octopus are painless and may even be pleasant in correct dosage. Hemotoxic venoms like rattlesnakes, water moccasins, centipedes and most vipers produce extremely painful swelling at the entry point. And there is always the possibility of gangrene and other lingering infections. Many snakes, like the Gaboon Viper, possess both hemotoxic and neurotoxic poison. The animal extracts can be rendered down into injectable or sniffable preparations.

Dandies in eighteenth-century garb have reverted to snuffboxes. Bufotenine, extracted from a poisonous toad, brings one out in a strawberry rash, *so* becoming with pink lace. Some looners have a creepy thing about anal administration. They are being fucked by the Mamba Spirit, turn green in the face, and green spit hangs down off the chin in streamers.

Neferti runs into some old Red Night buddies and they turn aside into a snakepit just for jolly, wouldn't you? Two frantic young fags got up as Cupid with little wings and bows and quivers shoot at each other with darts of tiger snake venom. Chances are about fifty-fifty, and what could be fairer than that? The decor is tasteful, all ancient Greek faggot, backdrop of marble couples and glades and colonnades where naked youths lounge.

A hit! The stricken youth drops to his knees, face slack with idiot lust, his lips and tongue swell, blood sings in his ears, the painted blue sky fades to black, he is dying, ejaculating . . . the other youth cradles him in his arms, looking down with a smile of hideous complicity, naked comprehension stripping his lover down to the last bone-wrenching spasm. The dying youth squirts a great jet of blood from his phallus with a scream of ecstasy.

"What idiot games are here!"

A clutch of centipede freaks, naked, on top of each other's

faces, sit with idiot grins, covered with erogenous perforations to the bone, slowly scratching iridescent sores that burst under caressing fingers, yielding gushes of foul-smelling yellow ichor streaked with blood as the addicts twist in galvanic spasms.

This is under the head of sideshow so far as we are concerned. Not about to get involved in these animal drugs. Many purists prefer to administer the venom straight from the living animal, like Cleopatra applying the asp, and they swear they have such an affinity with a snake or even a spider that it will inject exactly the correct dosage.

Two Boons each take a graze of the fangs of a huge Gaboon viper, thirty pounds, he growls like a dog. They are making it, blood coming out of their eyes and prick and ass and all the pores of their skin, slower and slower as the neurotoxic venom takes effect. Now they lie in a coma, covered with blood, and their medic steps forward with the antivenin and symptomatic treatment. They will make it, just a brush with death. The viper emits a somnolent moan and settles down to digest a rabbit.

And of course the inevitable faggot in Cleopatra drag, my dear, he's ninety if he's a day, billed seventy years ago as the most beautiful man in the world, comes out with an asp which he applies histrionically to his breast as a medic shoots him in the ass with antivenin.

"Cleopatra, is this well done?"

"It is well done and fitting for a *queen* . . . ah, soldier . . ."

He advances wantonly, then falls on his face shit dead. A heart attack. Or maybe it was the antivenin killed him. Anyhoo, he died like a true queen.

And frantics who want to be repulsive go about with scorpions and centipedes crawling over them—"Oh my dear, I'm terribly down. I need a lift from my Pede!" and right there in Ma Maison he pulls down his pants and applies a foot-long centipede to his erect member. The diners were electrified.

"You see, it's all replaced by special scar tissue."

Hollywood moguls are pelted with blue-ringed octopuses as

they disport themselves by the swimming pool. A drunken script writer suddenly stands there weaving back and forth.

"What's your problem, Joe?" The words slither out. Joe is pulling what look like tiny blue Frisbees out of a handbag, his hands in rubber gloves.

"You think you can buy talent and throw it out when you've wrung it dry? I'm going to show you some *natural* talent."

He sails a blue-ring out. . . . Slop, on a sagging bosom . . . Plop, on a fat cold face.

They float like great dead carp, white hairy stomachs sticking up to the sky in the still gray smog.

Sound can act as a painkiller. To date we do not have music sufficiently powerful to act as a practical weapon.

Remember an English-gentleman-in-India story: an encounter with a rude native youth who didn't know enough to move out of his path. When his servant moved forward to administer the indicated correction, the boy's hand flew to the flute at his belt as if reaching for a weapon. Then he darted away.

In the government rest house, despite six stiff whiskies, the narrator still had difficulty getting to sleep and was disturbed by foul dreams. "At three in the morning I was awakened by what I can only describe as a corpse blowing into my ears, the most loathsome, filthy sound I have ever heard. I am not ashamed to admit that I grabbed my pants and fled in blind terror.

"Next day, I found that my dog and my faithful native boy had not escaped in time . . . eyes starting out from the sockets, faces frozen in a terror so hideous that I could not look on those faces. I ordered them immediately sealed into coffins. That cursed music communicated some secret so loathsome that no decent man may hear it and live."

Must have been a decent dog.

Everybody wants a sure-thing weapon . . . a ray, an artifact. There is nothing more terrifying than to stand in front of a deadly, snarling enemy with nothing but a psychic weapon that may or may not work. That is when you reach all the way down and come up with a *Stopper*.

The Hindus teach that the Heaven World is more dangerous for the soul than the Hell World, since it is more deceptive and conduces to the fatal error of overconfidence and assumption of immunity. Like a fighter the soul must be constantly in training lest it grow soft on an ephemeral throne. So the splendor of the palace, the constant parades, the state barges, the gold and lapis lazuli, the chariots and bowmen, eat away one's awareness of the ultimate reality of conflict. . . .

"Security, the friendly mask of change / At which we smile, not seeing what smiles behind." Like the Family Album of the Romanovs. From morning till night, ceremonies. Every meal a state occasion. How could anyone preserve a modicum of intelligence and character under such a barrage of meaningless and banal masquerades? The answer is they did not. They became as empty and banal as the parts they played in the crumbling dream of Imperial Russia . . . the summer palaces, the yachts, the sailors and troops in review, state banquets and shoots, distraction for the soul and very little sustenance. No wonder they cannot see the gathering shadows, obvious to the impartial eye of the camera.

Of course ancient Egypt is incomparably more splendid. Gold everywhere and jewels, slaves and soldiers, all the heady trappings of absolute power. Severed hand bleeds on a post in the garden. He was Master of the Hounds and robbers poisoned five choice mastiffs brought down from the North. Few things are more dangerous to the soul than absolute power. Remember, it's granted for a purpose, to achieve certain definite objectives. The objective is SPACE.

In Waghdas the objective is agreed upon or they wouldn't be there at all. As to the means of realizing the objective, there is much divergence of thought and method, so much disagreement that another area of concurrence is imposed. All agree that a single authoritarian system would be fatal to the objective, and could only lead to the old frauds, the old lies, the old hierarchical structures.

Taking advantage of the freedom so gained and held, there are parties who work indefatigably to overthrow freedom and impose a One-God, One-Party order. They are dying out. Occasionally we put out a PNO on some group—Public Nuisance Order—and they are disposed of in one way or another, like cows with the aftosa.

Film sequentially presented . . . now, imagine that you are dead and see your whole life spread out in a spatial panorama, a vast maze of rooms, streets, landscapes, not sequential but arranged in shifting associational patterns. Your attic room in St. Louis opens into a New York loft, from which you step into a Tangier street. Everyone you have ever known is there. This happens in dreams of course. Now when dealing with an adversary the strategy is to inveigle him or her into your territory. Instead of crossing the river, bring the people on the other side to your side, where you know the country and can marshal your allies.

City like Tangier on a tidal river which runs along the front of the town where the Avenida de España used to be. I am staying with Waring and his manservant, Targuisti, at the Riverfront Pension. There's a balcony over the river, with cane chairs, and we sit there in the evening watching shark fins in the iridescent green water as the boats go by. A smell of mudflats and stagnant seawater. It's a nice lazy scene, sitting there sipping a planter's punch or a gin sling or sometimes rum and coconut milk, but there is a wrong note.

At this same pension this old religious nut comes to eat every night since his wife is too religious to cook, reads the Bible all her waking hours, and there are about thirty of these pestilent characters, who call themselves the Selected of Jehovah.

Waring and I are laying our plans to be rid of them once and for all by registering a complaint with Targuisti's brother-in-law, who is a captain of police. When dealing with creeps like that, anything goes.

As often happens, fate jogs my arm. One late afternoon I am standing in back of the pension when this Selected bastard sidles up to me like a vicious old crab and says, "You think Missouri is a *lump?* Well, I'm from Missouri," and he goes into the lounge of the pension to read the Bible. I can see his wife in front of their 1910-type frame house about seventy feet away, talking to another evil old Venusian piece of shit named Sister Willoughby. So I levitate fifty feet in the air just for jolly, wouldn't you? She sees me and starts screaming, *"Satan! Satan! Satan!"* and scampers inside and comes out with a shotgun.

My universe is less stable than Don Juan's, sometimes I am an impeccable warrior and at other times I act like a timid suburbanite in a *New Yorker* cartoon. The present emergency finds me in warrior valence, so I swoop down on an invisible slide, get the gun away from her and carry her off kicking and screaming to a nearby hillside where I turn her into a rabbit and blast her with the shotgun and take the remains back and give it to the pension cook to fix for dinner.

At dinner there is this mealy-assed Bible fart with his hunched-over fat lump of a son, looks like he is sculpted out of rancid lard, and he is moaning, "Lord, Lord, where is my helpmeet?" And he glares at me, not suspicious, just the way he would look at anybody drinking a glass of beer all nasty and intemperate. I'd forgotten he is a vegetarian and I won't have the pleasure of watching him eat his other half. Any case, there is no time to lose. We must get to the *Comisaría* before he reports his wife missing and before Sister Willoughby starts talking in tongues.

"Sorry to bother you with neighborhood business, but that old Willoughby woman is going crazy and screaming at American schoolteachers with good American Express credit cards that they are Whores of Babylon, and the Riverfront Pension is losing its trade because the Reverend Norton preaches temperance sermons in the bar . . . they are *bothering tourists.* "

The Captain looks up gravely, his face clouding over.

"But what brings us here is the fact that his wife has been missing for some time now. We strongly suspect . . . everything points to . . . witnesses heard a shot . . ."

"His gun is registered, of course." (Your Moroccan police do think of everything.)

"Captain, he has probably *eaten* the remains. It is only one of their vile customs. And the Willoughby woman . . . highly dangerous. Why, she might well physically attack a tourist on his way to the bank. Moroccans are enlightened and civilized people. Benemakada is famous even in America for *promptness* in dealing with the mentally ill before they commit some atrocious act."

(The sooner they get some heavy sedation into Sister Willoughby the better, I figure.)

So we all pile into a police car and whisk the Willoughby woman to Benemakada . . . right this way for the pearly gates. A young English intern comes out, peeling off his white coat.

"Just pumped enough Thorazine into her to sedate a rabid horse. Before she went under, she was screaming some rot about you swooped out of the sky like a Satanous vulture, carried off her sister and turned her into a rabbit." He cocked a quizzical eyebrow at me. "Did you actually, old boy? Good job and all. Aha, I think she needs another jolt. She just took the Lord's name in vain."

Now for the Reverend Norton.

"But my wife is only missing since this afternoon. I went back and she wasn't in the house, nor could I find Sister Willoughby, who was to have shared our evening prayers."

"Your neighbors tell a different story. They say Mrs. Norton has been missing for almost a fortnight." The Captain pulls out a paper. "Mr. Norton, I have here the certificate of registration for a shotgun. Where is this weapon?"

"Well, now, I don't rightly know. Usually I keep it over in

that corner by the door. Maybe it was stolen by the Arabics."

A policeman stands there with the gun. "I found this buried under the house, Captain."

"Mr. Norton, it is my duty to arrest you on suspicion of murder. We are a civilized people. There is no capital punishment here. You may even get off with twenty years, pleading a crime of passion." He nudges the Reverend with a horrible leer. "She was fucking some Arab. You go crazy. Before you know what's happened, you've killed her. Must have been Satan took over your hands when you did it. Confess, man, and ease your soul."

"Killed my sainted Mary? You must be mad, or in the pay of the Communists!"

"Such talk will do you no good." He gestures to another policeman, who stands there with a skeleton in his arms. "How will you explain *that?*"

"It is a custom of our sect."

I look significantly at the Captain, who nods grimly.

"Like some folks just keep the ash . . . we have the whole skeleton preserved, since it sayeth in the Good Book: 'Cleave ye to the bones.' Cost me a lump of money too, all dried out and sanitary. Now that there is Aunt Clara."

"That is the skeleton of your wife, Mr. Norton. You not only killed her, you *ate* her."

Well, the others was rounded up and summarily deported in the hold of a cattle boat, and that took care of that nest of vipers.

Few pilgrims reach the town of Last Chance. Sloth, self-indulgence, alcohol, addictions, old age, stupidity, all are obstacles. But lack of a special courage is the only insuperable barrier—the courage to confront *your* opponent, *your* final enemy. If you lack this courage, you will never reach Last Chance. Any pilgrim who has in life solved problems with violence must go through Last Chance or back to square one.

No one leaves Last Chance without mortal combat. To be tested in this combat is to risk the second and final death. In Last Chance you play for keeps.

Some heavies ride in with atomic bullets, will take out the target and immediate environs like a saloon or half a hotel. These "A-boys" get a wide berth. This is an Old West section, false fronts, smell of tumbleweed in the wind, saloons, hotels, Chinese laundries and opium drops, cathouses and gambling joints. For pilgrims who prefer to shoot it out, the shooting kind . . .

"Come out from behind that A-shit and shoot it out like a man. What kind of a Honey Badger are you, endangering whores and schoolteachers and cute freckle-faced kids?"

"I'ma sorry. You're simply not ME."

And there is the Rule of the Duel can be adapted to eliminate knowed varmints no good from the day they was borned till the day they die and let it be today.

During the five Duel Days, corresponding to the Mayan week of Ouayeb, any challenge must be accepted. Sensible citizens cower in gun towers or cyclone cellars armed to the tits, but lunatics walk around screaming, "I know you're in there, you candy-assed richies. . . . *Come out and fight!*"

A distant crack from a gun tower. A 45-70 catches him square in his big mouth and takes out the back of his neck in a spray of blood and vertebrae.

And there are Open Seasons that spring up like tornados, and they are out in the street slapping every passerby. Duelists with their seconds and their surgeons strut through the streets, elbow into bars.

"Did you say something?"

"No, not me."

"Oh, I thought you said something. . . ."

"Warning to all residents of Douglas County . . . Open Season approaching. Residents are urged to take cover immediately."

The Rule of the Duel is considered to be an indispensable safety valve to abort mass riots and political revolutions. The intention is to keep the wars *small*, and *individual*. . . . Man to man, creature to creature. So anyone who feels disgusted can head for the nearest Duelin' Honky-Tonk and work it off one way or another. So folks stop bottling it up inside and the heart attack rate drops and drops, and by Pasteur and Lister and Doc Halsted! the cancer rate is dropping too.

You can take your pick here. Deadly correct duels with seconds and surgeons standing by . . .

" 'Zounds, sire, what a gash is here. Why, a man could drive a coach and four into your guts."

Eighteenth-century dandies: "Ah yes." He looks at the challenger as if trying to focus his image through a telescope. "As challenged, I have the right." He strokes the other's cheek and clicks his tongue.

"Such a pretty face, and I don't find saber scars at all fetching. Your rapier, now, makes only a small hole but . . . it suffices." He sniffs some snuff.

"And shall we say a civilized hour . . . around noon? It will give me an appetite for *déjeuner*. "

As swordsmen they are equally matched. A second consults the sundial. "I'll miss lunch with the Duchess," he wails.

The surgeon is drunk already. A hurried conference. The contestants retire into changing booths and emerge with push daggers in both hands, half-moons of scalpel-sharp steel projecting from the toes of their flexible boots and a little ridge of steel up the instep for crotch kicks. They explode in a blur of fists and feet and spurting blood. One, disemboweled by a crotch kick up to the navel, spitting hate like a dying weasel, throws his push dagger. Right through ribs into the heart.

It's a draw. There will be a return engagement.

A handsome Mexican boy faces an older opponent. Blade-to-blade machetes, eighteen-inch blades sharp enough to shave the hair off your arms or chest. The *chico* is quick. He catches the other across the back of the hand, severing tendons and veins. The other drops his machete without any change of expression, catches it with his bare foot, kicks it up into his left hand and splits the kid's head like a coconut.

A Junker student duel has gone wrong somehow. Starts off with the tall Saxon sweeping a cut into the face of the Student Prince. The seconds nod and smile . . .

"*Ach ja, ach ja . . .*"

But the Prince doesn't like it. He crouches slightly and swings from the hip, and cuts the Saxon's head clean off. It rolls across the grass snarling incredulously. The seconds look on appalled.

"*Unerhört! Unerhört!*"

"*Mein Gott, Er hat den Kopf ganz abgeschutten!*"

Many of these encounters involve *almost* certain death for both contestants, but any duel where both duelists are *sure* to be killed is ruled out, not by any formal decree, but by deep biologic disgust. To take a long chance is good. To kill yourself is a revolting act, like self-castration.

Two boys stripped to the waist face each other with flails, thin strips of perforated steel dipped in stonefish venom. One cut will cause death in a few seconds of hideous agony. Their eyes blaze with total hate. They are much alike. More and more alike. One boy utters a piercing scream and leaps forward—*swish*, a miss.

He jumps back. They circle, eyes narrowed to slits of calculation. (The flails have handles of flexible steel or springs. The exact degree of flex is a fine point of flail fighting.)

A feint to the face, then drop to a low crouch for a sweeping leg swipe . . . just a graze, but enough. The onlookers nudge each other.

"This is tasty!"

The boy is *riding* the pain. The ground undulates under his feet. *Whack* . . . a solid hit across the arms and chest. *Swack* . . . He gets one back across the face and neck. Both are dead before they hit the ground, faces swollen out of human semblance.

The flail lends itself admirably to the administration of poison, since instead of one dart or arrow you have only the question of choice: which poison?

Neferti is flail shopping . . . fountain pen and swagger stick flails . . . little curved talon knives in this umbrella model. The hollow undersides can be packed with goodnesses . . . ten centipedes and a cup of crushed brown recluse . . . the gangrenous sores rot to the bone in seconds . . . built-in poison dips . . . or you can spray it on from a tasteful atomizer . . . bits of sawblade sewn into leather. Or, if you prefer something folkloric, obsidian chips with deerskin thongs marinated in black widows, datura, aconite and blue krait venom . . . two-handed flails with scalpel blades and lead weights can take off a leg . . . ten-foot bullwhips with six-inch tips of double-edged steel tapered to needle points.

Neferti picks a cane with bamboo-strip flails steeped in curare and blue-ringed octopus.

Last Chance is a town where a high premium is placed on courtesy. Since the challenged has the choice of weapons, a barroom bully doesn't know what he might be getting into . . . a dogfight with World War I biplanes, a medieval joust or a motorcycle duel with bicycle chains. A contestant with no special skills may insist on the deadly 50-50: one gun loaded, one with blanks, the choice by lot. Both contestants fire simultaneously at point-blank range. Or two pills, one milk sugar, one cyanide. Both contestants swallow and wait.

The 50-50 is the most dreaded of all duels, since the factor of skill in combat is ruled out. Quite ordinary courage can sustain a duelist in a pistol or sword encounter; 50-50 is something else.

The antagonists face each other across a table. On the table are two cups of tea and two white capsules on a silver tray. The first choice is decided by a throw of dice or other random procedure. He selects one of the tablets and washes it down with tea. The other swallows the other tablet. Then they wait . . . it's the waiting that makes the difference. How long? You can rig the capsules to dissolve in a certain length of time. Can be anywhere from sixty seconds to twelve hours.

Here is a cigarette duel. Dissolving time is the time it takes to smoke a cigarette. They light up and look at each other.

"I aim to finish smoking mine!"

The other laughs, a dry, rustling sound like a scorpion eating its mate. "You know how it hits? Like a bolt of lightning . . . throws you right out of your chair."

"Throws me?"

"Who else? I'm a blessed cat."

"Famous last words."

The survivor pissed in his pants from the relief.

Most people back off from a 50-50. A 50-50 can empty any bar.

"You say something?"

"Not me, mister. Gotta get home to my aged mother with an opium suppository."

Whether it's skill or 50-50 depends on who gives the challenge. And what constitutes a challenge?

"Why you 50-50 stumblebum, come out from behind that cyanide tablet and act like a man."

"Can't take a straight chance can you, pistol boy?"

"Fuck you, kamikaze kook."

Then suddenly a pistol man will challenge a 50-50, or a 50-50 will challenge a pistol. He is allowed ten days training. How many good pistol shots have had the experience of taking someone to the range who never fired a gun before and the novice does better than he does?

And sooner or later a 50-50 knows his luck will run out.

The atmosphere of Last Chance is polite, deadly, purposeful. For Everyman comes here to find *his* enemies, and Everyman who gets this far has deadly enemies to whom he can never become reconciled and who can never be reconciled to him. You will meet your enemies in Last Chance sooner or later. Meanwhile there are hotels and restaurants for every taste and pocket-book.

If certain rules prevail, they prevail only sporadically and in certain areas. There are fair-game slums where anything goes and the whole place teems with assassins, since a lot of richies don't want to meet their enemies on fair terms. Much easier to hire someone to grease him from ambush or call him out. But these professional duelists do not last long.

Right now Kim is looking for this Deputy Sheriff known as Zed Barnes. He was a crotch shooter, so they called him the Honey

Badger. According to legend the Honey Badger always goes for the crotch in a fight.

Once Kim was out pissing in the early morning sunlight. *Zummmmmm* . . . he felt the wind of Zed's 30-06 miss by half an inch from three hundred yards.

"I'm going to get you, Honey," Kim vowed.

He gets out his short-barreled .44 Special and his double-barreled 20-gauge shotgun pistol, gets on his strawberry roan and starts looking.

And he puts on a steel jockstrap comes to a point in front.

Honey has fled to Mexico with twelve assholes like him. Some of them had worked in the Belgian Congo, where they turned in severed black genitals and collected the bounty, and there were Putumayo rubber-boom guards and foremen. He occupies a small Mexican town in Chihuahua, extending his territory by enlisting all the creeps from the area—boys who set cats on fire . . . now there's a likely lad to work for Honey.

He prospers and plants his informers everywhere. Those suspected of treachery were tortured to death for the pleasure of Honey and his sycophants who, if they fell from favor, provided future entertainment.

Now, when Honey finds out Kim is in Last Chance shaking the tree, he can't pass up this chance to rid himself of his most dangerous enemy. Zed knows he don't have a chance on equal terms. He plans a long-range shot with his telescope-sighted 30-06.

Honey comes into town disguised as a dirty old prospector and walks over to the counter in Scranton's Saloon and General Store.

"Ham and eggs!"

He eats it.

"A pint of whiskey!"

He drinks it and rolls up in his filthy sleeping bag.

Got himself hid good.

Now Kim knew Zed would come out of his *queréncia* and try it, because Kim was becoming an obsession with Zed. Every time anything happened, like he gets the shits, Kim must have hired the kitchen staff to poison him. He had a loyal cook boiled alive in lard. His closest associates are moving back from him.

See, he *has* to try it, just as the opponents of Hassan i Sabbah had to try it. The Sultan can't get it up? *It's the Old Man.* And the Sultan threw all his good concubines to the crocodiles.

Zed has to come. And Kim will know him when he comes by the most distinct thing about a man: his smell.

Bloodhounds can trace a man through a city, through millions of other human smells. But Kim has a Pharaoh Hound. He can sniff through the centuries. He gives the hound a sniff of Zed's dirty underwear he got from Zed's houseboy, the only one Zed thinks he can trust at this point.

Pharaoh Hounds don't bark or whine. When they get the scent the ears and muzzle flush red. The redder they flush, the closer the quarry.

Kim walks into Scranton's with his Pharaoh Hound and it just so happens the Old Prospector wakes up and the hound takes one sniff of the prospector and his ears turn a bright rich red and so does his muzzle, and Kim says, "All right, Barnes, come out from behind that Old Prospector."

Zed's face is a thing to see: abject panic. His lips crawl back from his teeth and his eyes bug out and he makes a galvanic snatch for his Sidewinder, the .45 bullets loaded with diamond-back venom, enough to kill five men in each bullet. But he misses and hits a passing cow that gives one despairing *mooooo* and drops dead in its tracks. Kim disintegrates him with one shot that takes out a wall of the store.

Now, Mr. Scranton, the storekeep, has runned to the cyclone and vegetable cellar when he seen the dog's ears turn red. He asks Kim to pay for his store, plumb ruint and about two hundred in canned goods vaporized right off the shelf, smells like beans and tomatoes right down into the timbers, he has to tear the whole place down and start over, and worst of all it stinked like vaporized Zed Barnes, the vilest stench a man could gag on.

So that was it with Zed Barnes, not really a worthy opponent, but that 30-06 whistling by Kim's prick, that had to be leveled out and evened up.

They say Adam was made out of clay. Well, Zed Barnes was made out of vulture shit. Ain't nothing too dirty for God to put his hands in it to make more creatures to buy his shit and produce it. "Increase and multiply."

They need *more more more* to fill factories and offices and *more more more* to consume the shit produced.

So he starts faking it. He is putting out human stock without the names. Literally Nameless Assholes, NAs. Their name is mud. Their name is shit. Without Angel, Heart, Double or Shadow. Nothing but Remains, kept operational by borrowed power overdrawn on the Energy Bank . . . physical bodies animated by bum life checks.

Knocking Zed out could start a panic, as the human stock drops off the board. They are selling short at gorilla level. It has already dropped to pigs and is going down fast.

7

The Road to the Western Lands is devious, unpredictable. Today's easy passage may be tomorrow's death trap. The obvious road is almost always a fool's road, and beware the Middle Roads, the roads of moderation, common sense and careful planning. However, there is a time for planning, moderation and common sense.

Neferti is inclined to extreme experience, so he gravitates toward the vast underworld of the Pariah Quarter, the quarter of outcasts, of the diseased, the insane, the drug addicts, the followers of forbidden trades, unlicensed embalmers, abortionists, surgeons who will perform dubious transplant operations. Old brain, young body? Old fool has a young body but not the sensibilities of youth. He has sold his soul for a strap-on.

It may be said that any immortality blueprint depending on prolonging the physical body, patching it together, replacing a part here and there like an old car, is the worst plan possible, like betting on the favorites and doubling up when you lose. Instead of separating yourself from the body, you are immersing yourself in the body, making yourself more and more dependent on the body with every stolen breath through transplanted lungs, with every ejaculation of a young phallus, with every excretion from youthful intestines. But the transplant route attracts many fools, and the practitioners are to be found in this quarter.

London, Paris, Rome, New York . . . you know where the streets and squares and bridges are. To reach a certain quarter, you have only to consult a map and lo, a string of lights will show you how to reach your objective on the subway.

In Waghdas, however, quarters and streets, squares, markets and bridges change form, shift location from day to day like traveling carnivals. Comfortable, expensive houses arranged around a neat square (all residents have a key to the gate) can change, even as you find your way there, into a murderous ghetto. Oh, there are maps enough. But they are outmoded as soon as they can be printed.

Neferti uses this method to orient himself and find the Pariah Quarter: place yourself in a scene from your past, preferably a scene that no longer exists. The buildings have been torn down, streets altered. What was once a vacant lot where one could find snakes under sheets of rusty iron is now a parking lot or an apartment building. It is not always essential to start from a set that no longer exists. There are no rigid rules, only indications in this area. Do you pick just any place? Some work better than others. You will know by certain signs whether the place you have chosen is functional. Now, get up and leave the place. With skill and luck you will find the location that you seek in Waghdas.

Neferti seeks out the vilest slums of the Pariah Quarter. He is dressed in the inconspicuous garb of a traveling merchant with a single bodyguard. They encounter an obstacle course of beggars. Neferti tosses a coin to an armless leper, who catches it in the suppurating hole where his nose used to be and hawks it out into a clay pot in a gob of pus and blood. Other beggars squirm forward, exhibiting their sores. The bodyguard lashes out with a flail of copper weights and the beggars shrink back, spitting and drooling hideous curses. One turns and raises his robe and jets out a stream of shit, smirking over his shoulder.

They turn into a wine shop where Insult Contests are held. These contests are illegal by order of the Board of Health on the grounds they pollute the atmosphere. But in this quarter anything and anybody goes. It's an art rather like flamenco.

One of the creatures who lounge about in female apparel is seized by the Insult Spirit. He leaps up and focuses on a target, imitating every movement and mannerism with vile hate and inspired empathy, thrusting his face within inches of his victim.

An English Major is reduced to hysteria as his monocled, frozen face cracks and a stream of filth pours from his mouth, words that stink like vaporized excrement. He screams and rushes out, followed by cackling laughter.

The victorious insult queen stands in the middle of the floor like a ballerina. He turns and looks at Neferti, feeling for a point of entry, like a questing centipede. Neferti hurls him back with such force that he flattens against the wall and sinks to the floor, his neck broken.

The others spread out in a semicircle. Neferti lashes out with his poison sponge flail. Faces and arms swell and turn black and burst open. He holsters his flail. (Flails are holstered by pushing the handle up through the bottom of the holster like an octopus retreating into its lair and pulling its tentacles after it.)

Neferti adjusts an imaginary monocle. "Let's toddle along and leave these rotters to stew in their own juice. They're filthy."

He stops in a cosmetic shop to rub perfumed unguents on his face and hands, and dusts his clothes with shredded incense.

They proceed to the Encounter Inn . . . bar along one wall, a few tables. The Bartender is a beast man, a baboon cross with long, yellow canines. When Mandrill vaults over the bar, prudent patrons take cover. Now he fixes his baleful little red eyes on Neferti. His glare glazes with reluctant respect. He becomes obsequious.

"How can I serve you, noble sir?"

Neferti orders an opium absinthe. His bodyguard tosses

down a double mango brandy. Neferti sips his drink and looks around: some young courtiers from the Palace on a slumming expedition, a table of the dreaded Breathers. By taking certain herbs mixed with centipede excrement, they nurture a breath so foul that it can double a man over at six feet like a kick to the crotch. At point-blank range the breath can kill.

Every Breather has a different formula. Some swear by bat dung, others by vulture vomit smoothed by rotten land crabs, or the accumulated body fluids of an imperfectly embalmed mummy. There are specialty shops catering to Breathers where such mixtures can be obtained. They vie with each other for the foulest breath. The breath mixtures slowly eat away the gums and lips and palate.

Now a Breather exhales into the air above the courtiers' table and dead flies rain down into their drinks. The Breather lisps through a cleft palate, "Noble sirs, I beg your forgiveness. I simply wish to prevent the flies from annoying your revered persons."

Neferti shudders to remember his encounter with an old Breather. . . .

The Breather bars his path. His lips are gone and there are maggots at the corners of his mouth.

"A pittance, noble sir."

"Out of my path, offal."

The old Breather stands his ground. He smiles, and a maggot drops from his mouth.

"Please, kind sir."

Neferti shoots him in the stomach with his .44 Special. The Breather doubles forward and such a foul stink jets from his mouth in a hail of rotten teeth and maggots that Neferti loses consciousness.

He came to in a chamber of the Palace, attended by the royal physicians. He shuddered at the memory and vomited until he brought up green bile. Worst of all was knowing that his Ka had been defiled. Three months of rigorous purification, during which he ate only fruits and drank the purest spring water, restored him to health.

A beautiful young Breather with smooth purple skin like an overripe tropical fruit glides over to Neferti.

"Honored sir," he purrs, "I can breathe many smells." He exhales a heavy, clinging musk that sends blood tingling to Neferti's groin.

"I can show you how to pass through the Duad."

The Duad is a river of excrement, one of the deadliest obstacles on the road to the Western Lands. To transcend life you must transcend the conditions of life, the shit and farts and piss and sweat and snot of life. A frozen disgust is as fatal as prurient fixation, two sides of the same counterfeit coin. It is necessary to achieve a gentle and precise detachment, then the Duad opens like an intricate puzzle. Since Neferti had been exposed to the deadly poison of Christianity, it was doubly difficult for him to deal with the Duad.

So he nods and the Breather, Giver of Strong Smells and Tainted Winds, guides them through a maze of alleys, paths, ladders, bridges and catwalks, through inns and squares, patios and houses where people are eating, sleeping, defecating, making love. This is a poor quarter and few can afford the luxury of a private house with no rights of passage. There are many degrees of privacy. In some houses there is a public passage only through the garden. Others live in open stalls on heavily traveled streets, or in the maze of tunnels under the city, or on roofs where the neighbors hang clothes to dry and tether their sheep and goats and fowl. Some are entitled to exact a toll. And some routes are the exclusive prerogative of a club, a secret society, a sect, a tong, a profession or trade. Fights over passage rights are frequent and bloody. There are no public services in this quarter, no police, fire, sanitation, water, power or medical service. These are provided by families and clubs, if at all.

Neph is letting his far-seer scouts get too far ahead. Some call them spirit guides or helpers. It is their function to reconnoiter an area so that one knows what to expect, and to alert headquarters with regard to dangers, conditions, enemies and allies to be contacted or avoided. They are bringing him instead general considerations on the area . . . valuable and interesting, but not precisely applicable in present time.

Neferti is in The Golden Sphincter, an ultra-sleazy gay bar at the end of a long, crooked alley, no doubt hollowed out by generations of people sidestepping the human and animal waste that litters the worn stone, stained brown from years of urine and excrement. This bar is on the outskirts of Waghdas and jackals are as common as the feral cats. He sips his drink and looks around: three old queens at the end of the bar, pathic vultures writhing in carrion hunger and the frightful frivolity of the species.

"Do it to me, Death!"

Poisonous puppets . . . Neph recognizes a thin, red-haired man at the bar as a hit man he knows slightly. Good, too . . . does work for the Vatican.

As he walks by the three queens he breathes out, almost subliminally, "The animal doctor should put you to sleep."

A reproduction of the Belgian boy urinating and a seashell of pink papier-mâché stained by dirty years. As Neph was urinating a water closet flew open and a man popped out, a lean Turk with a goatee. From his fly protruded a steel-blue erection.

"You like?"

Back in The Golden Sphincter, he nodded to the Breather.

"There is a rear entrance."

The door opened on what looked like a museum corridor in a blast of stale, cool air. As he stepped into the corridor the door shut behind him. Neph felt a blast of black hate, utterly repulsive and at the same time sad and hopeless.

What hates him? That which is not him and can never

become him. They hate him for what he is, because they must become what he is or die. A man is delineated by what he is not. So let their hate be the chisel to form a statue of dazzling beauty. With every curse, every spitting, drooling snarl, every apoplectic sputter, every poisonous snide-queen screech, his marble is polished, the blemishes cleared away, that little twitch of the mouth smoothes out as the worry wrinkles relax into smooth white stone. Shrieking, the attack subsides and withers away, like bacilli caught in the antibiotic dead end.

A dedicated Lesbian denigrator slinks back to vomit her stomach acids on my impeccable marble.

"It would be well, my Short Rib," I tell her, "to kiss my big toe . . . there is a slight imperfection, a protuberance . . . a little of your acid *just there*. . . . Thank you, you can go now."

She spits out green bile.

"Self-contained heel. I hope you choke on yourself."

Neph experiences a cool, stony relief. They are gone . . . for the moment.

Neferti and the beautiful Breather are strolling through a flower market. An old hag rushes out and screams at the Breather, "You have sucked all the smell from my flowers. *Voleur!*"

"Only to give it back tenfold," and he breathes out such a smell of flowers that the market is covered by a smog of cloying sweetness.

They pass the Restaurant Notre Dame. *"Voleur!* My food tastes like beaverboard. You have sucked all the flavor out!"

The Breather turns and exhales, delicious garlicky cooking smells permeate the quarter. Everywhere people with the spit hanging down off their chins storm the Notre Dame.

"I can jet my way about like an octopus. You see, I'm a *reverse* vampire. Take a little, give back a lot. More than they can use, in fact. Keep moving is my motto. Only way to live. Now, one-way grounded vampirism, worst thing can happen to a man. I mean maintaining a permanent image with stolen energy. Some run it into the ground hot and heavy, moaning in a bloodless desert. Others take a little, leave a little, live and let live—but by the terms of the vampiric process they always take more than they leave. The error here is a *fixed image*.

"In fact, a fixed image is the basic mortality error, a ME that cannot be allowed to change, certainly not to change color. Remember the white man in Johannesburg was stung nigger-black by a swarm of bees? They take him to the nigger hospital and he wakes up screaming, 'Where am I, you black bastards?'

" 'You is with yo' mummy and daddy, chile.' "

Neferti is dropping his Ego, his Me, his face to meet the faces that he meets. There is nothing here to protect himself from. He can feel the old defenses falling, dropping away like muttering burlap, dripping from crystal bone, burning out like a Coleman mantle . . . the black mantle shreds in the night wind.

In the 1920s, everyone had a farm where they would spend the weekends. I remember the Coleman lanterns that made a roaring noise, and the smell of the chemical toilets. . . . Khaibit, my shadow, my memory, is shredding away in the wind.

THE HONEY DOOR

Stoneworkers uncovered a stratum of fossilized honeycombs. The congealed sweetness sealed in over the centuries wafted out and the Pharaoh, Great Outhouse 8, whiffed it fifty miles away in his palace. It was said of Great 8 that he could tell when any of his subjects defecated and differentiate among them by the smell.

He dispatched his most skilled stonecutters to the spot. The stratum of stone combs was cut free from the surrounding rock and carried to the palace. Of an irregular shape, it measured ten by eight feet and in some places was two feet in depth.

Great 8 was very old, and he gave orders for his embalming. After the preliminary procedures of extracting the internal organs and the brain and drying and curing the mummy, instead of being wrapped in linen, he would be placed naked into a sarcophagus cut from the combs, the sarcophagus to be filled with honey.

It is known that sugar does not spoil, and soon others are following in the sweet steps of Great Outhouse 8, having their mummies preserved in orange and strawberry, rose and lotus syrups, glycerine with opal chips . . . the sarcophagus swings on a pivot so that the chips float about, and there is a little crystal window to observe the deceased in his final habitat.

The priests are disquieted and paw the ground like cattle scenting danger. A flood of unorthodox embalming methods could sweep away the fundamentals of our *Thing*, they wail. And their fears are not without foundation.

The embalmer, Gold Skin, has discovered a method by which a thin sheet of metal can be applied to a mummy by coating the mummy with charcoal and immersing it in a vat of gold, copper or silver salts activated by a device which was his closely guarded secret. Wrapped in the Golden Skin, one need not fear the encroachment of extraneous insects or scavengers, of time or water. However, the initial mummification must be doubly rigorous, lest one be sealed forever in the vilest corruption of liquefied flesh and bones and maggots.

Gold Skin leaves a small orifice capped by an airtight seal. Every year, on the conception date of the deceased, the Breathing is observed: the seal is broken, and the assembled dignitaries advance and sniff. If there is evidence of mortification, the embalmer is cut into small pieces, which are consumed in a very hot fire with ten Nubian slaves at the bellows so that every fiber of his being is utterly vaporized, until nothing nothing nothing remains as the ashes blow away with the afternoon wind to mix with sand and dust. It's the worst thing that can happen to an embalmer with mummy aspirations . . . got his condominium in the Western Lands all picked out and paid for.

It sometimes happens that a business rival, a disgruntled former employee or a malicious prankster may gain access to the tomb, make an opening in the gold skin, and squirt in an enema bag of liquid shit and rotten blood and carrion with a goodly culture of maggots selected from a dead vulture. He then seals the opening and polishes the metal so that his intervention is undetectable.

This is the Fifth Breathing, and a goodly crowd is there. On previous occasions a sweet, spicy smell wafted out and there was an appreciative sigh from the guests. This time, as he unscrews the cap, it is torn from his hands and a geyser of stinking filth cascades out, spattering the dignitaries with shit and writhing maggots.

Gold Skin was saved from execution, since the Pharaoh and the High Priest recognized the handiwork of the dreaded demon Fuku, also known as the Mummy Basher for his vicious attacks on helpless mummies.

Fuku is the God of Insolence. He respects nothing and nobody. He once screamed at the Pharaoh, Great Two House 9, "Give me any lip and I'll jerk the living prick offen your mummy!"

Creature of Chaos, God of pranksters and poltergeists, dreaded by the pompous, the fraudulent, the hypocritical, the boastful . . . wild, riderless, he knows no master but Pan, God of Panic. Wherever Pan rides screaming crowds to the shrilling pipes, you will find Fuku.

Cut-rate embalmers offer pay-as-you-go plans, so much a month for mummy insurance. If you live fifty years or die tomorrow, your future in the Western Lands is assured. (An old couple with their arms around each other's shoulders stand in front of their modest little villa.)

The Western Lands are now open to the middle class of merchants and artisans, speculators and adventurers, pimps, grave robbers and courtesans. The Priests wring their hands and warn of a hideous soul glut. But Egypt is threatened by invasion from without and rebellion from within. So the Pharaoh decides to throw the biggest sop he's got to the middle classes, to ensure their loyalty. He will give them Immortality.

"If we alienate the middle classes, they will take their skills to the partisans and the rebels."

"It is true what you say, Great Outhouse. But I likes the old ways."

"I too. It was a good tight club in those days. If things get rough, we can always liquidate the excess mummies."

The Embalming Conclaves are able to offer cheap rates because the embalming is done on a moving belt, each team of embalmers performing one operation: remove brains, remove internal organs, wind the wrappings. They become extremely dexterous and quick. What used to take a month can now be done in a day.

"These changes are too fast for Khepera," moans the High Priest. (Khepera, the Dung Beetle of Becoming, is seen rushing frantically about, faster and faster. He throws himself on his back in despair, feebly kicking his legs in the air.)

Three hours and twenty-three minutes from Death to Mummification: an hour to gut it out good, an hour in the drying vats, an hour in the lime-cure vats, internal organs stashed in tasteful vases, wrap it up and store it in the communal vaults, which are carefully controlled for humidity and temperature and patrolled by armed guards at all times.

"You see, Great Outhouse, things have gotten out of hand."

"True. Things always do, sooner or later."

Even the lowly *fellaheen* carry out home embalmings in their fish-drying sheds and smokehouses. Practically *anybody* can get into the Western Lands.

The young question the mummy concept:

"To keep the same asshole forever? Is this a clarion call to youth?"

"It stinks like petrified shit."

"Have you something better to offer?" says a serious young

Scribe. "We know that mummification can ensure a measure of immortality." He turns to Neferti. "And what can you offer that is better than such precarious survival?"

"I can offer the refusal to accept survival on such terms, the disastrous terms of birth. I can offer the determination to seek survival elsewhere. Who dictates all this mummy shit?"

"The Gods."

"And who are they to impose such conditions?"

"They are those who succeed in imposing such conditions."

"To reach the Western Lands is to achieve freedom from fear. Do you free yourself from fear by cowering in your physical body for eternity? Your body is a boat to lay aside when you reach the far shore, or sell it if you can find a fool . . . it's full of holes . . . it's full of holes."

Neferti and the Breather stand before a door of fossilized honeycombs.

"This," says the Breather, "is the top of His sarcophagus."

"What did you do with the Pharaoh Great Outhouse 8?"

"We ate him. He was unspeakably toothsome."

The Breather breathes on the door, a heavy, cloying sweetness. Neph steps back quickly, lest he be candied on the spot, for a sweet breathing can be as lethal as the foul breathings.

The door swings open on an oiled pivot. A Breathing festival is in full swing. Singing Breathers give out the appropriate scents, mariachis belch fried beans and chili. There are bread ovens and tortillas.

The patron Saint of the Breathers is Humwawa, Lord of Abominations, who rides on a whispering south wind, whose face is a mass of entrails, whose breath is the stench of death. No incense or perfume can remove the stink of Humwawa. Lord of all that sours and decays and, in consequence, Lord of the Future. And Pazuzu, Lord of Fevers and Plagues . . . on his breath, hospitals and gangrene, leprous flesh, suppurating glands, black vomit, the diarrhea of cholera, stink of burnt plastic and rotten oranges.

He will teach Neph to *ride* the smells.

"Stand there." The Breather stands six feet in front of Neph and gives him a full breath of carrion. As instructed, he lets the smell come in. The feeling is like eating a very hot pepper or breathing smelling salts, a violent clearing and purging of the head, a lightness, a lift as you breathe death and confront his smell, his corruption, without flinching, for you are breathing in *your death.*

Breathe in your death.
Death you're in. Breathe.
You're in. Breathe death.
In breath. You are death.

It is essential for immortalists to remember, do not take anything too seriously. And remember also that frivolity is even more fatal . . . so, what now?

We leave The Golden Sphincter. Out the back way . . . steps going down . . . a thousand feet of stone steps through rubble, down down down into the distance, we are moving down sideways like a slipping plane. You lean over on the stick and slide down through the air to lose altitude, so we are sliding down the steps. On either side is brush and cactus . . . it looks like Gibraltar. Are we the famous Rock apes skipping down a slope? Down into compounds where women hang out their wash and gossip. Boys with their bicycles. British we are, British we stay—dead fingers in smoke pointing to Gibraltar.

At the bottom of the steps is a little concrete platform by the highway, and across the way is another little landing platform, if you can reach it. Nothing in sight in any direction. A feeling of complete desolation . . . nothing, nothing here.

I sit down on the little concrete shelf and lean against the grassy hillside. I look at the grass under my cheek and stretch out my legs over the stone steps leading up to a road. In front of me is the highway. But there is no traffic, no movement on the highway. Why go on? I look back up the steps. The sky is dark with rain. I seem to be stuck here . . . waiting.

Board a train. It is night, and I can see water outside, glittering points of light sliding by, now green rocky slopes, train whistles rocking shifting clickety clack gathering speed . . . Raton Pass . . . ruined warehouses windows broken flash by . . . swaying from side to side as I walk down the aisle to the toilet . . . smell of stale cigar smoke, steam and iron and soot and excrement encrusted in the cracked leather seats. I can't see my face in the mirror opposite, on the door of the toilet . . . just the blank empty mirror . . . *whooooooooooooooooo* . . . fading. . . . The train is now moving along an inlet or wide river. . . .

Look at their Western Lands. What do they look like? The houses and gardens of a rich man. Is this all the Gods can offer? Well, I say then it is time for new Gods who do not offer such paltry bribes. It is dangerous even to think such things. It is very dangerous to live, my friend, and few survive it. And one does not survive by shunning danger, when we have a universe to win and absolutely nothing to lose. It is already lost. After what we know, there can be no forgiveness. Remember, to them we are a nightmare. Can you trust the peace offers, the treaties and agreements of an adversary who considers you in the dark? Of course not.

We can make our own Western Lands.

We know that the Western Lands are made solid by *fellaheen* blood and energy, siphoned off by vampire mummies, just as water is siphoned off to create an oasis. Such an oasis lasts only so long as the water lasts, and the technology for its diversion. However, an oasis that is self-sustaining, recreated by the inhabitants, does not need such an inglorious vampiric life-line.

We can create a land of dreams.

"But how can we make it solid?"

"We don't. That is precisely the error of the mummies. They made spirit solid. When you do this, it ceases to be spirit. We will make ourselves less solid."

Well, that's what art is all about, isn't it? All creative thought, actually. A bid for immortality. So long as sloppy, stupid, so-called democracies live, the ghosts of various boring people who escape my mind still stalk about in the mess they have made.

We poets and writers are tidier, fade out in firefly evenings, a Prom and a distant train whistle, we live in a maid opening a boiled egg for a long-ago convalescent, we live in the snow on Michael's grave falling softly like the descent of their last end on all the living and the dead, we live in the green light at the end of Daisy's dock, in the last and greatest of human dreams. . . .

I spit on the Christian God. When the White God arrived with the Spaniards, the Indians brought down fruit and corn-cakes and chocolate. The White Christian God proceeded to cut their hands off. He was not responsible for the Christian con-quistadors? Yes, he was. Any God is responsible for his wor-shippers.

What am I doing in Gibraltar with my sulky Ba? Waiting, of course. What does anyone do in Gibraltar? Waiting for a boat, a bank draft, a letter, waiting for a suit to be finished, waiting for a car to be fixed, waiting to see an English doctor.

The first night Hall spends at the Rock Hotel. He finds the English colonial fog unbearable, the room small and uncomfortable, workmen banging in the afternoon when he wanted to sleep. So he checked out and found a room on Main Street, up a flight of dingy stairs, the dark reception desk, a room in the back opening on an airwell. What is the special stink of this place? A smell of greasy french fries and stale fish, of old mattresses never touched by the sun, of the constant 80° heat. He recalls the same smell about cheap hotels in Panama City.

He has made arrangements to pick up his mail at Lloyd's, where he has an account.

"Sorry, sir. There is nothing for you."

He cashes a check and walks along Main Street in the shadow of the Rock. You can see it from anywhere, this great mass of rock and brush and fortifications and radio towers.

British we are, British we stay.

A tearoom with tiled floor and potted plants stretching fifty feet back from the street, mirrors on both sides reflect Halifax, Malta, military and civil service personnel, talk of leaves and allowances and servants. He can hardly breathe here. He pays and walks out, feeling disapproving eyes. *"Not* overseas personnel."

Clothing stores with Irish tweed, cameras, field glasses, music boxes, and the Indian shops, replicas of the same shops in Panama, Malta, Madagascar . . . ivory balls, one inside the other, tapestries with tigers and bearded horsemen with scimitars. Who buys this junk? He thinks it must be a cover for some monstrous conspiracy. Of course, many Indians are money changers.

A soldier-sailor bar with swinging doors, some old Tangier hands over for a day's shopping. Earl Grey's Tea, Fortnum & Mason's marmalade, brown sugar, a special cream biscuit. The suit isn't quite ready. The tailor promises it for tomorrow. Shall they stay over at the Rock?

Back to his hotel room, a heavy key you leave on the rack. Bed not made . . . the sheets look dirty and smell dirty, not white but gray, the color of orphanage sugar, and damp, they cling to his skin like a sweaty shroud. At five-thirty he gets up and drinks two stiff whiskeys in his room, sitting in a straight chair of black, stained wood, a picture of Edward VII on the wall, no doubt a complimentary gift from the company who installed the water closets with copper pipes and the tank up by the ceiling, with its constant drip.

The dining room almost empty . . . an old-fashioned commercial traveler with a consignment of Hong Kong music boxes, cheap transistors and pen flashlights. The waiter is ugly, fattish, with frizzy black hair and gold teeth, in a filthy black jacket and a white shirt black at the neck.

He orders steak and french fries resignedly, with a half bottle of red wine. "Oh, yes, and bring me a double whiskey first."

"We don't have a spirit license."

"You certainly don't."

The steak is thin and crinkled and cooked to leather. The french fries drip with grease, and the waiter has brought some sweet white wine.

"Bring me red wine, you hairy-assed Rock ape, or I drink it from your throat!!" he grates at the threshold of hearing without opening his lips. The waiter recoils with a puzzled snarl. Hall points to the menu.

"This . . . take that away and bring me this." The waiter snatches the bottle and walks away muttering. The tablecloths are the same damp gray as the sheets, stained with food and wine and beer and cigarette ashes. Quite intolerable. He remembers seeing a hotel sign from the airport out by the East Beach: Hotel Panama.

He checks out of the hotel and finds a cab rack on a small square under trees filled with sparrows.

"That would be out East Beach way. . . ."

GUINNESS IS GOOD FOR YOU

Concrete and barbed wire overgrown with weeds and vines, radio towers, compounds where Spanish women hang out clothes and gossip in yacking parrot voices . . . Spanish boys with their bicycles.

The Hotel Panama people are polite in contrast to other Rock hotels. They show him to a room on the back overlooking a workers' compound and the radio towers and the Rock. Clean, with a large, comfortable bed, a closet and a writing desk, a bathroom with a large bathtub in pink porcelain and plenty of hot water.

The next day he checks at Lloyd's.

"Sorry, sir. Nothing for you."

My God, my ship leaves in three days. If the books aren't here by then . . .

In front of the hotel a road runs along the beach to the fence around the airport, about five hundred yards from the hotel. In the other direction, East Beach Road joins the main road that runs around the Rock about forty feet above the shoreline. Where the East Beach joins the main road is a municipal incinerator, with a towering smokestack smudging the sky with greasy black smoke.

Again to Lloyd's.

"Here we are, sir. Sign here please. . . ."

Just in time. The boat leaves at 9 P.M. tomorrow. He buys a webbed shopping bag for the book package. He will not open it until he is on board. He buys a stock of liquor, some biscuits and cheese. On impulse, he turns into a steep side street. A doorway, dark steps. DOCTOR HENLEY, PHYSICIAN AND SURGEON. Well, why not give it a shot?

The office is shabby, like the doctor's flashy clothes. The doctor is in his early sixties, tall and thin with quick darting blue eyes, like a crow looking for a bright object to carry away.

"So, what can I do for you, young man?"

"Doctor, I have a medical problem. I'm a morphine addict and I'm taking a boat for Venezuela tomorrow . . . fifteen days."

"Hmmm, well . . . you *do* have a problem."

"I can get by on a grain a day, doctor." He slides a twenty-pound note from his wallet. The doctor looks at the note.

"I can write for ten grains and that's stretching it, or I can give you five grains of Dilaudid."

"I'll take the Dilaudid."

The doctor writes. Hall glimpses a spotty past. Spot of bother here and there. Hong Kong, Singapore, Aden, Alexandria. How did he ever wash up on the Rock?

The doctor speaks into the phone and hangs up.

"Take this to the English chemist on Main Street . . . ask for Señor Ramirez."

He hurries to the chemist's without due delay. Señor Ramirez looks at the prescription briefly.

"Two minutes, sir."

He returns with a dark brown vial. "That will be ten pounds, sir." The chemist knows there will be no argument.

He is the only passenger on the tender. They hoist anchor as soon as he is aboard. His room is perfect: a bed, a writing desk, a chair and dresser. He shoots an eighth of a grain and goes to sleep.

He wakes to the movement of the ship and the smell of the sea. After breakfast he unpacks his books. Where else but in London could he have acquired exactly the books he needs? In Paris perhaps, and many of the sources are French, but then the books would never have arrived in time. It's all here . . . analysis of the centipede venom, case histories, illustrations of the three thousand varieties. He opens his portable typewriter case. . . .

8

Thanksgiving Day, Tuesday, November 24, 1985. A future city called Leukan, a compacted complex of red brick tenements with balconies and fire escape ladders. On a cot covered by a cheap army blanket I am cuddling a white baby. It is white all over. Even the eyes are white. I can't see the face clearly. The child has long white claws. The eyes are glittering white like diamonds or snow, a musky hot animal smell, nitrous film scraps lighting up little theaters of incident before they burn out like Coleman lantern mantles.

A street like a float, corner of Pershing and Walton . . . the corner floats away through the trees, anglers fishing from sidewalks, mild jerk of leaves, a squirrel shifts to freeze into a still, the old sets are brittle, falling off the page, waves dash against sea walls, old photos curl and shred. The Veiled Prophet Parade floats in the hot summer night . . . yellow glow of lights, giant leaves, eating pink cake, the cardboard around the edges blowing away in the rising wind, piers crumbling into the sea's waves, wrecked house, rain, gray sky.

Take a look at this craft, like a secondhand car or plane riddled with hidden miles and tragic flaws. Good for a one-way trip, you hope. HOPE IT GETS ME THERE is its name.

"Joe, I think the wing is coming off."

"Both wings, boss."

"Well, fix it!"

(He used to be some kinda tycoon can't adjust to a precarious spacecraft, and precarious isn't the word for this horse's ass.)

"Fix it? What with, Boss Man, a Band-Aid and chewing gum? Why'ncha strip to the waist and pitch in with the men? Get out there and fix it yourself."

"*Me?* Uuuhh . . ." It begins to sink in. These old power-and-finance models is the worst, worse than KGB Colonels.

Kim is camping around, doing a parody in a yachting cap. He is already in Space, very far out there in icy blackness and at the same time here in this prop town. The whole town of Lawrence is for sale, perhaps the Russians or someone is buying up the town. His only link with the living Earth is now the cats, as scenes from his past life explode like soap bubbles, little random flashes glimpsed through a Cat Door. It leads out and it leads back in again. Touch the controls gently for serene magic moments, the little green reindeer in Forest Park, the little gray men who played in my blockhouse and whisked away through a disappearing cat door.

The doors are all around you . . . a pond at twilight, a fish jumps, the cat snuggles against me and raises his paw to touch my stomach. . . .

This heath, this calm, this quiet scene . . .

Did Wordsworth drink at all? Was he a closet opium addict? Shingles, you know. We are men of the world, we understand these things. Was he in plain English a child molester, a short-eyes?

"And here's a farthing for you, Lucy."

"Cooooooo . . . a farthing, sir, and all for me?"

"Yes, my little honey duck, all for you."

(All for you if you let me in.)

"What's the matter with my little sugar bun?"

"Oh, well, winter coming on and I need a new coat, you know."

"But I bought you one last year."

January 4, 1986. Dream that I was sharing a room with Joe Stalin. The room was an alcove off a corridor leading to a restaurant. This is in Chicago. It don't look like Chicago. It looks like a prop town of cardboard under a gray haze. East St. Louis is across the river, weeds growing through cracked sidewalks, a little pocket of the 1920s . . . air lines here and there, a whiff of riverboats and hobo jungles.

I am looking at Stalin, thinking here is a man with the deaths of millions on his hands. No doubt he'd think no more of killing me than any other decadent bourgeois. But he is friendly, and it isn't the Joe Stalin I used to know in newsreels and pictures. Both are short, but this Joe has no mustache. He is unshaven, sloppy looking, middle-aged, dirty and greasy.

"The lair of the bear is in Chicago."

That's a cut-up or dream sentence from 1963 Tangier. It didn't mean anything at the time. Still doesn't. Here's another: "Captain Bairns was arrested today in the murder at sea of Chicago. Witnesses from a distance observed a brilliant flash as the operator was arrested." "Life is a flickering shadow, with violence before and after it," Ian Sommerville told me in a dream.

And what the bloody hell is Joe eating? Some sort of black meat pie, blood pudding perhaps. I can't take my eyes off it, as though I am looking at him to see the lineaments of multimillion murders. The first hundred thousand is the hardest. After that it's all downhill, they tell me. Nothing shows in his greasy dish, just nothing good or bad. He isn't even repulsive.

But he does have the look about him of someone who was somebody. . . . "Look, that's Al Capone, or John Barrymore, or Jack Buck, or Manolete." Somebody who used to be somebody . . . there, in a shirt without a collar, and even a brass stud sticking out. But yes, he was somebody . . . no doubt about that.

It isn't even a private room. Through a window I can see the cash register and the hostess leading the patrons to tables. Middle-aged men who call their wives "Mother":

"Now, Mother and I was in Mexico and we didn't like it at all. Mother's piles flared up and we couldn't get any soothing Tuck and I said right out, 'When are you folks going to get civilized?' And the druggist said, 'We don't want your syphilis, got plenty of our own,' and he shoved an opium suppository up Mother and it did ease her a bit."

The hostess looks like Olive Oyl, a long neck and a chicken head. I look at Joe. He knew the secret of power: sit long and move fast. Hitler could move, but he couldn't sit. Stalin could sit like any peasant can.

Ignore a dog and he gets desperate, whimpering and showing his teeth in little dog smiles like Gary Cooper when he is being a cute millionaire, certainly his most distasteful role. He's this eccentric millionaire, see, when he buys pajamas he only wants the tops . . . now, isn't that cute?

"Only the tops, sir? Well, I'm afraid—" Frantic signals from the manager. "Oh, yes, of course, Mr. Wentworth. I understand perfectly . . . just the tops."

Here he is at the piano, putting the make on a working girl.

"Looky looky looky, here comes Cooky."

And he keeps looking up at her with these loathsome little smirks. But she eats some spring onions and holds him off.

"Put that ring on my finger . . . and until you do, I'll fight you with every vegetable at my disposal."

Fight him with puke. It's what he deserves. You see the difference between a star and an actor. An actor can play any role. But a star always plays himself. There is that special something that only Gary Cooper can bring to a role, whether he's hanging his best friend for cattle rustling, or being Mr. Decent American.

Yes, a star sure does play himself a piece at a time. Look at John Wayne in *Red River.* Now, they'd all signed on to see the drive through . . . *moo moo moo.* But when the going gets tough, two yellow-livered skunks deserted the drive.

They is apprehended and brought before the Duke, sprawled against his saddle, shit-faced drunk as usual and nipping away as he mutters, "I'll show them all something to remember."

The varmints whine out, "All right, go ahead and shoot us!"

The Duke takes a long pull and wipes his mouth with the back of his hand and then it comes out, ugly as anything I ever sawed, "I'm gonna *haaannng* you!"

He is, of course, prevented from doing so by his PR man.

"Bad for your image, Duke. We'll have to call in the Old Man to shoot you in the leg and stop you."

The deserters slink off like the coyotes they is.

Later, in an interview, he defended his original position.

"Hell yes I'll hang the sons of bitches! I may be portrayed as a hard, cruel man, but never as a mean or petty man."

Well, now, a little pettiness might be a lot prettier. Don't rightly see how it could be any uglier.

Hollywood has filmed the species right down to the bone. There is not a dream of man that Hollywood hasn't cooked down to a hideous travesty. The human mold is broken and this you gotta hear . . . out crawls a monster centipede with the head of a Hollywood Jew and plops itself down on the front page of the *Völkischer Beobachter.*

Nazi movement compressed into three minutes of film time. The beer hall putsch . . . *Mein Kampf* . . . Olympic games . . . concentration camps . . . Blitzkrieg . . . the Russian front . . . the Bunker . . . executions at Nuremberg . . . the Executioner is trying to rig up an electric chair in Samoa . . . a blast of current reduces him to a cinder.

Old Sarge does a hula dance.

"I'd like to see some moa of Samoa."

There comes that moment in a blinding flash of bullshit when he suddenly *sees* everything, and the way it all fits together as part of the great whole. He is everything and everything is him, and there is no aloneness, no separation, just endless love. He knows all the questions and all the answers, and there is only one answer, so he wrote "Nature Boy" and got cured.

> "The greatest thing you'll ever learn
> Is just to love and be loved in return."

The Charge of the Light Brigade: We have the advantage of surprise. The virus enemy cannot comprehend elasticity. They cannot believe we can survive their seemingly foolproof broadcasts.

Scrambles. The craft are made of light and you have to keep yourself completely empty. Any solid thought will be blown to atoms by the velocity. Target is located in southern Utah . . . all squadrons zero in . . . SU coordinates 23 . . . drawing a blank . . . keep looking . . . dishes . . . a network moving up and down and sideways like a huge mechanical toy . . . magnetism in reverse . . . they can pull thoughts out of your brain and pull them in . . . wall ahead . . . very narrow pass . . . wall is black . . . the pass is like a crack . . . rowing out into Lone Star Lake . . .

The lake is empty, the marina in ruins. A few broken hulls full of water. I launch an aluminum rowboat and row out into the still black water. Frenzied attacks of screaming demons from Bosch intercut with nigger-killing, fag-bashing rednecks and snarling dogs . . . barbed wire . . . dogs . . . towers . . . *Achtung!* Machine-gun fire . . . bogged down in old war films.

I recall a game from childhood that we used to play in the school bus:

Child 1: "I'll put a copperhead snake in your house."

Child 2: "I'll put a hooded cobra in your mother's electric."

Child 1: "I'll release black widowers in your granny's out-house."

Child 2: "I'll put piranha fish in your bathtub."

Child 1: "I'll put sulphuric acid in your Listerine."

Child 2: "I'll put nitric acid in your eyedrops."

Miracles are made from the most unlikely ingredients. And miracles are the deadliest of all weapons. When all else fails, the final, the last resort is a miracle.

This is the Age of Miracles or the Age of Total Nonmagic, Nonmiracle, a completely predictable cause-and-effect universe running down to Nada.

Orgone balked at the post. Christ bled, Time ran out. Thermodynamics has won at a crawl.

The Miracle of the White Cat:

The White Cat has a million defenders who will fight to the death for their white cat.

"Death to the Board!"

"Death to the Nuclear Conspiracy!"

"Come out and say what you are doing!"

Wimpy jumps up: "You trying to kill our White Cat?"

Wimpy in my lap now, purring loudly. He has such a need for love. My little brown Wimpy beast.

Unexpected ingredient? How can any danger come from an old man cuddling his cats? Danger comes always from the most unlikely direction. Huge black cats are lapping up the Milky Way.

Come out from under the table, you Board members, and face the White Cat, and the faces behind the White Cat.

Do they fear a harmless, necessary cat? No. They stand in deadly fear of the Gods and spirits that the White Cat represents. "That male cat is Ra himself." And many other powers as well, large and small—powers they thought long dead, blocked out or blockaded.

"I tell you nothing could get through that blockade . . . nothing . . . but here it is . . . the White Cat."

A radiant cat glowing with a pitiless white light, light on secret files and ops, light on directives and memos, light everywhere. No corner of darkness left. Power shrivels and turns to dust in the light.

Light on lies and contingency plans for drastically reduced personnel, a self-chosen few who will survive the holocaust they have themselves unleashed.

Operation Clipper: Space sailcraft propelled by the blast that reduces planet Earth and its inhabitants to a smoldering cinder. It isn't good PR, not good at all.

A. J. Crump was a philanthropist. He had not always been one. Years before his conversion, he had discovered that it is more profitable to give wages than to receive them. He was too stingy to pay an accountant, and did all his accounts by hand and kept them in huge ledger books in his dingy office, from which he ran his multimillion-dollar hardware network coast to coast. Going over his accounts one Christmas Day, he decided to extend the maxim: It is more profitable to give money away than to make money.

So, he launched the Crump Fund. His first act was to endow a turkish bath with a horse trough in front of it. Why did he do this? He was clean himself, a clean old man? No, he was not clean, as he could not bring himself to bathe, for fear of sustaining a loss. But he approved of cleanliness in others. And why the horse trough? He loved animals? There is no reason to believe that he did, but he was never seen to abuse any animal in public.

And that was only one of the civic things he did. He set up a home for homeless animals. Cats he dug special. And he didn't practice euthanasia: "Can't see as you do any cat a favor by killing it." When neighbors complained that his cats escaped and killed birds, he set up a network of bird-feeding stations. And there were soup kitchens and dormitories for homeless folks. All these establishments were graced by a life-sized picture of the Founder.

So he cut his taxes to the bone. The house he lived in was the Office of International Nutrition, which specialized in food packets containing vitamins, minerals and proteins in a special Crump package, no bigger than a cigarette box and therefore easy to distribute.

It is Christmas Day. Old Crump is reviewing Christmases past. Well, he'd always enjoyed giving things away. Sure, virtue goes out, but it comes back with compound interest.

Christmas present . . . he pets the white cat on his lap. Christmases to come . . .

Some fifteen years ago I conceived a TV show to be called *On Call*. Characters are summoned to appear *On Call* and answer a battery of searching questions. The subjects may be celebrities, they may be unknown. If the subject fails to appear, we ask our questions of a dummy got up to look like the subject and supply his answers. Don't be a dummy. Come when you are called.

The idea lay fallow until this morning. It sometimes happens that a communication can put one into such a tizzy of annoyance that Satori results. This is the Crank Satori, and one of the more difficult routes, as witness Ezra Pound. One does not as a rule thank the irritating instance that has accreted a pearl. He did not intend it to do so and will, almost certainly, recoil from the Satori it has ignited.

This morning I conceived a TV program based on the White Cat. The White Cat symbolizes the silvery moon prying into corners and cleansing the sky for the day to follow. The White Cat is described by the Sanskrit word *Margaras*, which means the Hunter, the Investigator, the Skip Tracer, He Who Follows the Track. He is also the killer of forces that lurk in darkness. All hidden motives and beings stand revealed in the inexorable silver light of the White Cat.

The show could be called *Cat's Eye*. Subjects are summoned before the Cat's Eye. Like the old game of *Truth or Consequences*. It works like this: Here is a worthless shit in Warwick, Rhode Island, who killed a stray cat in his microwave oven. We find his name and address. We photograph him and his house. We interview local people.

Now we summon him to appear. TRUTH. He refuses, of course. CONSEQUENCES. We put it out on the air. We use a hideous dummy. We show his picture. We show his house. We invite the viewers to phone and write in comments. Better he should appear on TV. The consequences we can evoke are deadly. He moves. He changes his name. The White Cat will find him. We never give up.

Another program is called *Truth and Recompense*. Neglected artists, unrecognized merit, forgotten inventors and ideas and concepts, unobtrusive workers for the Djoun forces, the Little People.

Case in point are homes for animals where they are maintained in perpetuity, not killed. Oh, sorry . . . "put to sleep" is the phrase. Would *you* like to be put to sleep? Animals don't like it either. They know Death when they see it, and so-called Humane Society Shelters are death camps. I couldn't work there for any money. Oh, yes, they are doing good work. They do find homes for some of the animals, etc. Granted. But not on my show.

There are two permanent shelters outside New York City, and one in Chicago called Tree House. So we show the work they are doing, we invite contributions and make suggestions. We seek out the unknown, the unrewarded. The man who stopped and helped. Those who take in strays. The Johnsons of the world. We sanction the shits and reward the Johnsons.

Come drunks and drug takers . . . come perverts unnerved.
Receive the laurel given, though late, on merit.
To whom and wherever deserved.
Parochial punks, trimmers, nice people, joiners, true blues.
Get the hell out of the way of the laurel.
It is Deathless and it is not for you.

(Louise Bogan)

The road to the Western Lands is the most dangerous of all roads and, in consequence, the most rewarding. To know the road exists violates the human covenant: you are not allowed to confront fear, pain and death, or to find out that the sacred human covenant was signed under pressure of fear, pain and death. They can keep their covenant in case of being caught short with a million years of bullshit.

To enter the Western Lands means leaving the covenant behind in the human outhouse with the Monkey Ward catalogues.

The town of Waghdas covers a vast area around the lake, shading into suburbs and semirural districts, and there are a number of adjacent centers with a wide variety of life styles. Neph made frequent random trips, often deciding his route by the toss of a coin.

He is accompanied by Neku, a youth of blazing vitality, and by Mekem, with a body like living marble and the quiescence of stone. They come to a crossroads, and Neph catches a whiff of the centipede smell, like rotten spices on a hot wind that blisters the skin and rasps the lungs. They retrace their steps and turn at right angles.

At sundown they come to a town on a swampy lake. He feels the lake wind on his face as he rounds the corner . . . a clean, clear blue smell. In this area of Waghdas there are old red brick houses with slate and tile and copper roofs, surrounded by trees and gardens. Lawns stretch down to the lake and the jetties.

The house on Pershing Avenue is well back from the cobblestone street, worn smooth by centuries on the march. He finds his key. The lock turns. Inside he stumbles over a heap of toys . . . one Christmas after another in layers . . . a .30-.30 rifle at the top with a box of shells. A crust of broken ornaments crunches underfoot like snow.

He moves forward through the dining room, stacked with dirty dishes, into the pantry and the kitchen, pushing his way through mounds of garbage. He steps out onto the back porch overlooking the back yard and the alley. The garden is a jumble of weeds. The apartment building facing Euclid Avenue is falling in ruins, the windows broken, long deserted . . . the whole area has a smell of emptiness and absence.

Carrying the rifle he walks out through the garden and the cracked concrete of the alley into the street. For twenty or thirty years no one has walked this street. You can hardly see the sidewalk for the weeds and vines and small trees.

What happened here? Nothing happened. Cause of death: totally uninteresting. They could not create event. They died from the total lack of any reason to remain alive . . . decent Godless people.

You need your dreams, they are a biologic necessity and your lifeline to space, that is, to the state of a God. To be one of the Shining Ones. The inference is that Gods are a biologic necessity. They are an integral part of Man.

Consider the Pharaohs: their presence was Godlike. They performed superhuman feats of strength and dexterity. They could read the minds and hearts of others and foretell future events. They became Gods, and to be a God means meting out at times terrible sanctions: cutting the hand off a thief or the lips off a perjurer.

Now imagine some academic, humanistic, bad-Catholic intellectual as God. He simply can't bear to cause any suffering

at all. So what happens? Nothing. There are no horrible accidents. Not even an elderly woman killed in a rooming house fire.
No hurricanes, no tornados, no opposition, no pain, no decay.
No death. So the decent Godless people, who could neither
accept any God nor assume the prerogatives of a God, simply
crumbled away like a cookie dunked in Postum many years
ago . . . the last tremulous Ovaltine. A long pause did not
refresh.

"Professor killed, accident in U.S." This is an old cut-up
from *Minutes to Go* (1960), waiting all these years for the place
in the Big Picture jigsaw puzzle where it would precisely fit.

He levers a cartridge into the chamber and shoots out a dusty
shop window . . . *ping* . . . a hole with dust drifting out into the
stagnant air. Nobody has breathed there for many years. Not a
breath of air . . . where the dead leaf fell, there it did rest.

He walks west to Maryland Terrace and right up to King's
Highway. Phantom luggage covered with dust. The front of the
Park Plaza Hotel has caved in, looks like a bomb exploded
there, and the lobby is full of decayed leaves and dirt with grass
growing and vines. The bronze statue of a boy is green with
verdigris and streaked with bird excrement.

He crosses King's Highway and walks by the huge houses
of marble and red brick, the dusty, shattered greenhouses,
plants cascading through jagged holes in the dirty, shattered
glass. Not a skeleton in sight. A glass pane falls from a window
and shatters . . . another . . . another. Now I can see the putty
crack and break away, the wood rots before my eyes. Best to get
out of here while I still got flesh on my bones.

Across Lindell at a run, into Forest Park . . . a little pond
there where he used to come with a net and catch frogs and little
fish to put into a bucket . . . keep moving . . . head for the Zoo
and Forest Park Highlands.

Here is the St. Louis Zoo, overgrown like some ancient ruin.
You can just make out the paths, a few rusty fenceposts here

and there, a pool green with algae, but limpid. You can look down into the green half-light where the skeleton of a bear stirs slightly as a breeze ripples the water, wafting out a black stink of carrion.

He moves forward cautiously . . . a sudden reek of elephants. *Sput . . . ping . . .* silencered bullet. He drops to the ground and rolls. The cages here had housed small animals . . . wolves and foxes . . . the musky smell.

He sprints for a drinking fountain. There is a building in front of him . . . the shots are coming from the roof.

"He was caught in the zoo for position and advantage." (Old cut-up.)

This is the Berlin Zoo. Back in his Waffen SS shoes. He was foolish to agree to this meeting, where the list was to be turned over for $50,000 in U.S. currency.

He searches the roof. A flurry of movement. He edges his .30-.30 forward. The shot is loud and a jet of flame shoots out the muzzle. It takes out the agent there with the silencered rifle. Probably English.

"Halt!" A 9mm bullet whistles past him. He pivots and shoots the cop, knocking him backward as his gun flies into the air.

He can see the German cop in his black uniform with the neat black Heckler & Koch P-7 he cleans every night, the cop reeling back and the gun flying out of his hands as if it were too hot to hold. Then he is gone, fallen from sight, and the gun hits grass with a dull plump. People are shouting and pointing from further and further away, as if seen through a retreating telescope.

When you kill a cop you make a door, he reflects smugly. He did not want to reflect philosophically. Could "As Allah wills" be far behind? And it is written by a writer, reeks of nepotism at least, if not blatant fraud.

A fence . . . he hates that precarious springy barbed wire under his crotch. So he takes wire cutters from his tool chest and cuts the wire and walks through, down a steep mud slope onto the highway. How they do fall apart . . . blocks of concrete forced up by tree roots . . . they'll grow through all our bones in the end . . . and the gravel road up to the entrance . . . a blast of heat from the Midway, smell of popcorn and elephants and big cats . . . he can hear trumpeting and sullen snarls. It's hot and the cats are restless.

The Lion Tamer, the Great Armand, is hitting the sauce heavy and suddenly he's scared, and the cats can smell his fear. An elephant tramples a three-year-old child down to pink jelly. Looks like the show is cursed.

A thunderstorm on the way, the air is heavy and sullen with violence. Groups of youths, silent faces blank with a sucking hostility, looking and waiting. No laughing, very little talking.

"Any minute now they'll take the place apart . . . seen it happen before," says the old barker. He barricades himself in his boxcar and takes a fix.

"HEY RUBE!"

Next thing this pot-bellied aborigine is charging him with a tent stake and he shoots him where his shirt spills over his belt and he goes down screaming like a castrated pig.

He runs on. He has a plan. The Great Armand, the cat tamer, is in a state of abject funk, drinking Georgia lightning out of a Mason jar.

"I can't go in there. They'll tear me apart."

"You don't have to go in. Just let the cats out."

They is running this way with tent pegs and fence posts, knives, guns and axes. Then the cats come out snarling. So the rubes in front is shrinking back, screaming, and the pressure of those behind catapults them right onto the cats and there is a pile-up like a football scrimmage and the cats go full crazy and jump into the thrashing, squirming arms and legs and bodies, biting and clawing.

Now rain sluices down from darkening skies.

Joe retained fragmentary memories of the Land of the Dead: stone streets streaked with oil patches . . . a green haze of palpable menace and evil . . . tornado green. But this is a static tornado, a heavy, sucking emptiness. Faces in the street swim by in the heavy green medium, faces pressed and pulled out of all human semblance by hatred, evil and despair . . . faces torn by hideous unknown needs and hungers. Winds of searing pain sweep the dark streets in waves of screams and moans, whimpers, and the wild, maniacal laughter. Eyes glowing and sputtering blue flame . . . the streets slope downward, people slip on oil patches and plunge screaming into the green black darkness.

CHECK POINT . . . the terrible Death Police are checking, sifting. Arrest can only mean the Second and Final Death. A boy is dragged away with a thin, discarded cry of despair.

Joe's Ka, quick and light as a shadow, slips through. A Death Cop catches a fleeting glimpse and raises his death gun. It looks like a pinball death ray. Joe's Ka takes him out with a heavy air pistol, the microscopic projectile squeezed out under tons of pressure. There is only a hole where the cop was, a sucking black hole.

Run for it. Behind them the hole has sucked in the police patrol. They are running through a vast, abandoned amusement park overgrown with rank thistles and thorn-covered vines. Now he can smell the Duad, a reek of rotten citrus and burning plastic.

A shattered, burning grain elevator . . . a roller coaster bursts into flames, throwing screaming passengers like rockets across the Midway. Oil gathers into black pools . . . a reek of mineral excrements. There are eerie eddies of calm that can only be experienced in a context of total danger. For this is *it*. You are on your own. You are facing the Second and Final Death. The swampy banks of the Duad are just ahead.

The Duad winds through a vast carnival to the skies, Ferris wheels, tunnels, rides . . . whirlwind riots spring up, leaving a wake of severed limbs, blood, guts and brains ground into the oily streets . . . sinuous, weasel-like creatures with huge eyes snake through the corpses, lapping the blood and eating the brains . . . garish and deadly-real danger behind crude simulation, and seemingly-real danger that covers harmless illusion.

Hall of Mirrors, Tunnel of Horrors, merry-go-rounds, Midways, shooting galleries, animal acts, freak shows, floods, fires, explosions, cheap hotels and eating places, bars, bathhouses, tricksters, steerers, guides, pimps, bright glaring colors, pink and orange and cherry red and purple and pea green, blaring bursts of music, fireworks . . .

Joe is caught in a shower of rockets and Roman candles, a searing pain. Kim's face swims into focus.

"He could just make it."

On this scene fell a sudden chill, as the temperature dropped fifteen degrees . . . freezing sweat, and the sky turned bright green around the rim and then the big cats left their prey to slink whimpering under the boxcars and the rubes fled the stricken field, screaming down the Midway as the hail pelted down big as hens' eggs, knocking holes in the tents. The elephants trumpeted frantically, and then the sound: like a low-flying jet, as the boxcars were tossed about like matchboxes, screaming cats thrown into the air with snakes and freaks and the great tents whipping into the sky, tent pegs whistling like arrows . . . bleachers and seats and rifle ranges, Kewpie dolls and screaming railway cars, caught in a black whirlpool and pulled up into the sky.

A suburban couple, entertaining the Boss, were appalled to see a lion dropped into their rose garden, from which he leapt with a roar of rage to attack a frigid matron, Mrs. Worldly herself. She put up a hand . . . *"Ohhhhhhhh!"* . . . the lion caved her head in like a thin-shelled, rotten egg. Her brittle old bones shattered on the stone terrace as the caterers and servants fled precipitately, some taking refuge in the house, others scurrying off into the garden.

The cat has caught a fleeing fag who runs an antique shop. *"Help,"* he screams. Now his young lover, son of the host, rushes up with a double-barreled shotgun and blows his lover's head off with one barrel, kills the lion with the other.

"I didn't know what I was doing," he explained to police. "He was my best friend," and threw himself into the stony arms of an old desk sergeant, sobbing wildly.

SOCIALITE SLAYS TORNADO LION

While trying to rescue a friend attacked and thrown to the ground by the Tornado Lion, William Bradshinkle III accidentally shot and killed his friend, Greg Randolph.

Bradshinkle said he tripped as he rushed to the scene with a double-barreled shotgun. One barrel was discharged, hitting Randolph in the face. The lion ran toward him and he fired the second barrel, killing the lion.

The youth stated: "I feel terrible about this. He was one of my best friends."

Drawing room of the Bradshinkle home. It is an unfashionable district of north St. Louis, near Forest Park Highlands. However, the property is large, on a limestone hill with trees and gardens, an island of tranquility in the middle of an area of warehouses and factories and blocks of poor workers living in ramshackle frame and old brick rooming houses.

From where they are sitting they look out across a garden and a fish pool to the smoky horizon and a red sunset, a real Turner. The house seems to float over St. Louis like a magic carpet.

Billy is a strikingly handsome young man: dark hair, blue eyes, and a petulant expression of continual discontent.

("Is this supposed to be *life?* How do they dare to serve me such wretched fare? Shit, piss and stink until you get to like it. Life, my dear, is fit only for the consumption of an underprivileged vulture. What am I expected to *do* here?")

"Something jogged my arm, Mother."

"No one is blaming you, dear. Mrs. Randolph called to say she knew it was an accident and she knew you loved Greg. I told her you were under sedation."

"Good, but it was as if, just as I pulled the trigger, making absolutely sure the pellets wouldn't hit Greg . . . *something moved my arm.* . . ."

"Of course, darling. We are all controlled by the Powers. Not one, but many, and often in conflict. It is part of some Power Plan."

"And Greg was on about how he *adored* tornado green, and I looked up and saw this lion soaring through the air over the garage and I knew it was a real lion from the circus that was performing for a week at Forest Park Highlands. Greg couldn't see it because his back was turned and I was already running for the house to get my shotgun. I don't know why he didn't follow me. Just as I got to the door of the terrace I saw the lion land in some rose bushes. The thorns must have enraged him because he came up with a roar and hit Mrs. Worldly, who was about to walk down from the terrace to the garden, and she hit the terrace and I swear broke in pieces like an icicle, and a little blood seeped out, highly concentrated, like red acid. Look there . . . it can't be washed out, it's eaten into the stone. That's what she was . . . ice and acid. And I can see Greg running out toward the pool in a stupid panic. When I got back down with the gun, the lion had him down near the pool and I circled and aimed just behind the lion's left shoulder. Then, suddenly, as I pulled the trigger I see Greg's face in my sights, completely inhuman with fear. . . ."

"Let the dead bury the dead," murmured Mrs. Bradshinkle.

"But Mother, how the fuck is that possible?"

"Don't be coarse. It's just a figure of speech."

"This lion sailing in with his claws out against the green sky. Like a bit of ancient Egyptian kitsch, my dear. All he needed was luminous wings."

"I bruise easy but I heal quick," trills the parrot.

He shoots it a glance of annoyance. "Vulgar bird." As with many extremely beautiful people, his annoyance carries no weight. His presence is insubstantial, too perfect to be carnate. He seems always on the point of dissolving into a portrait.

"Mother, I want you to meet Kim Neferti Carsons, Great Pharaoh of the Two Outhouses, he who breathes in right and truth, surest gun west of the Pecos. . . ."

Kim takes her hand in both of his. . . .

"The Gods plan well."

They stroll down beyond the fish pool. A wooded hill ends abruptly in a sheer limestone cliff, five hundred feet above the lake. They are on a promontory at someplace eight hundred feet high, so that until you reach the rim there is an illusion of rolling hills.

"What happened to St. Louis?"

"I never heard of it."

"How do you get down to the lake?"

"Oh, there is a cave system . . . leads down to grottoes."

The promontory is six hundred yards across where it joins the mainland, tapering to a scant three hundred feet at the outer tip, where the garden is located in a little scoop of land. The house is the prow of a great ship anchored in the rocks and trees of the mainland.

The cave system penetrates the mainland for miles. No one knows how far back the tunnels go. Some narrow into dead ends, others open into huge caverns with underground rivers and lakes. There is a deadly stasis of impregnable grandeur, forming a dense medium, difficult to breathe. One suffocates in fairy lands forlorn, magic casements, ruined palaces.

They sit down by a marble pool where humanoid newts live.

"We had to bring them out of the more remote caverns because of cave-ins. Some died on the trip out through dry tunnels. We carried all the water we could but it was not always enough. Now only three remain. . . ."

The newts are a shimmering mother-of-pearl color, with huge limpid gray eyes reflecting the last remote, crumbling cavern where they had taken refuge millennia ago, to escape the teeming predators of water, land and air. When they first came to this cavern, there was light from a fissure in the rock. But the fissure slowly closed. Blind for thousands of years, their eyes now serve as breathing mechanisms, the irises contracting and expanding to pass water through the lungs.

They are so sad it hurts to see them, an age-old ache of hopeless blind alleys.

"Life is very dangerous and few survive it. . . . I am but a humble messenger. Ancient Egypt is the only period in history when the gates to Immortality were open, the Gates of Anubis. But the gates were occupied and monopolized by unfortunate elements . . . rather low vampires.

"It is arranged that you will meet the man who will break that monopoly: Hassan i Sabbah . . . HIS."

9

June 6, 1985. Friday. I am in Iran someplace, looking at a map to see if the secret place of Djunbara, where Hassan i Sabbah took refuge from his enemies, is on the map. It was somewhere north of the capital. It was not supposed to be on the map, but it was quite clearly marked.

Now I see a cleft in a block of limestone, and through the cleft I can see an old man of great strength, a stone man, his arms and legs of smooth marble.

The Stone Man gave HIS a base of power to shut out his enemies and regroup his shattered forces.

Danger is a biologic necessity for men, like sleep and dreams. If you face death, for that time, for the period of direct confrontation, you are immortal. For the Western middle classes, danger is a rarity and erupts only with a sudden, random shock. And yet we are all in danger at all times, since our death exists: Mektoub, it is written, waiting to present the aspect of surprised recognition.

Is there a technique for confronting death without immediate physical danger? Can one reach the Western Lands without physical death? These are the questions that Hassan i Sabbah asked.

Don Juan says that every man carries his own death with him at all times. The impeccable warrior contacts and confronts his death at all times, and is immortal. So the training at Alamout was directed toward putting the student in contact with *his death*. Once contact has been made, the physical assassination is a foregone conclusion. His assassins did not even try to escape, though capture meant torture. By the act of assassination they had transcended the body and physical death. The operative has killed *his death*.

To modern political operatives, this is romantic hogwash. You gonna throw away an agent you spent years training? Yes, because he was trained for one target, for one kill. The modern operative, then, is doing something very different from the messengers of HIS. Modern agents are protecting and expanding political aggregates. HIS was training individuals for space conditions, for existence without the physical body. This is the logical evolutionary step. The physical body is not designed for space conditions in present form. Too heavy, since it is encumbered with a skeleton to maintain upright position in a gravity field.

Political structures are increasingly incompatible with space conditions. They are inexorably cutting our lifelines to space, by imposing a uniformity of environment that precludes evolutionary mutations.

The punctuational theory of evolution is that mutations appear quite quickly when the equilibrium is punctuated. Fish transferred from one environment to a totally new and different context showed a number of biologic alterations in a few generations. But when more fish were brought in, uniformity was reestablished. Alterations occur in response to drastic alteration in equilibrium in small, isolated groups. All isolated groups are inexorably assimilated into an overall uniformity of environment.

I am the cat who walks alone, and to me all supermarkets are alike. Yes, and the people in them, from Helsinki to San Diego, from Seoul to Sydney.

What did Hassan i Sabbah find out in Egypt? He found out that the Western Lands exist, and how to find them. This was the Garden he showed his followers. And he found out how to act as Ka for his disciples.

At death the Ren, the Sekem and the Khu desert the body, soon to be a sinking ship. The Ka is stuck with his boy. He is a front-line officer taking the same chances as his men, day after day, not just once like Jesus. If his boy dies in the Land of the Dead, he dies too. Forever. So your Ka is your only guide through the Land of the Dead to the Western Lands, the most dangerous of all roads since you are facing Death itself. Don't believe the Christian God or Allah or any of that second-rate lot, in their sleazy heavens of pearls and gold with their *houris,* gods for slaves and servants, with lying promises . . . the Slave Gods.

I saw HIS many times in parks and squares and teahouses. He met a number of people, but always for a purpose. He was assembling the pieces of a jigsaw puzzle, a piece here and a piece there, like Iris reconstituting Osiris, who was cut in fourteen pieces and scattered all over Egypt. As I recall, she had a hard time finding his prick.

Cairo and Alexandria were the cultural centers of the world. Scholars came from China, India and Europe to study there. The official religion was Islam, but there were Jews and Coptic Christians and a variety of Moslem sects.

HIS had contacts among the academic elite. They did not know what he was planning. He was planning to take over the Western Lands by assassinating the demon guards, through their human representatives. Already he was drawing up lists.

Demons must possess human hosts to operate. Beneficent beings can live in woods and water and clouds. When they do manifest themselves through human operatives, they do so at the fervent and heartfelt invitation of the host. Demons, like house dicks, need no invitation. Once in, one literally plays Hell getting them out. They have the same desperate need of a host as the addict has need of opium . . . nice, warm cover . . . keeps out the cold.

Cut off a demon's host connection and you flush him out in the open. But demons keep themselves hid good. He may be a shopkeeper, a postal clerk . . . concierges he digs special, janitors and maintenance people. How do you know the ones who need killing, like the demon needs them? A competent operative can smell them out. Or one can cast a wide net.

TV program on a vaccine for hepatitis-B given to gay volunteers. Interview shots:

"How many sexual contacts have you had in the last six months?"

"Six months? [giggle] Well, I can't exactly remember, but—"

There sit the fiends. . . .

(Overheard in London while passing a Boy Scout troop: "That's where those fiends join in. They're fucking the Boy Scouts.")

And they don't look very fiendish. The more familiar something becomes, the less it will incite fear and hostility. When "gay" becomes a household word and one mama leans over the fence and confides to another: "My son is gay," the closer we are to a whole parade of parents of gays carrying banners:

MY SON IS GAY

AND THAT'S OKAY.

I'M PROUD OF MY GAY SON.

But, and it's a big But, a certain percentage of individuals, varying with environment and context, act in the opposite direction: the more gays come out into the open, the more hysterical and frenzied and often violent they become. These are the demon-occupied hosts. By their *brutes* you shall know them.

Sticker on his heap: KILL A QUEER FOR CHRIST.

Already HIS was drawing up lists. Many of the operative demons at that time were to be found among the orthodox Moslems. Demons are always found among the orthodox, those who will never round on a demon and say: "What are *you* doing here? Get your ass out of mine, chop chop."

However, we have not as yet made the first step to locate the Western Lands and to gain access. Do the Western Lands still exist? Conquerers usually attempt to destroy the old gods. Had the conquerors been Christian, this would have been unnecessary. The Egyptians take to Christianity like vultures to carrion. Both believe in the resurrection of the body. That's what mummies are all about.

But Islam is another crock of shit altogether. However, the Western Lands cannot have disappeared without leaving a blueprint behind.

We set out to find that blueprint. Myself and my two guards, HIS and his lover and bodyguard, who is, like Jesus Christ, a carpenter, and four other Ismailians, silent as shadows.

We go first to Memphis, where a house awaits us at the end of a long, crooked street in the merchant quarter. There are high walls topped with spikes around the garden. Apparently two big snarling dogs come with the house.

Hassan's face darkens at sight of them, and he says a few words to the guards in a dialect unknown to me. The guards unsheath short swords and dispatch the dogs with a few expert slashes. Barely have the dogs been buried, when a beautiful white cat appears.

We visit the temples and statues . . . ignorant caretakers looking for baksheesh. The statues are awesome, some fifty feet high, vast arms in polished granite, with fists six feet across the knuckles, larger than life and so more immortal in stone.

One thing does not change here: the river and the mud and the *fellaheen,* with mud in their souls and in their dull, blunted yellowish eyes. The *fellaheen* are the food of Osiris, the mud his excrement, the river a vast urinal where all the Gods void their urine, and from this stinking mud rose the God Kings and the

Gods who conferred the gift of Immortality on the chosen few, the priests and scribes, the viziers and princes so rewarded, to build the Western Lands as their slaves built the pyramids and tombs and temples.

To harken is good. To obey is best of all.

The Western Lands are fashioned from mud, from *fellaheen* death, from the energy released at the moment of death.

I realize now that the Mugwumps of *Naked Lunch* were Death Collectors like the Feku, the Shit Collectors. The sign for "to come into being" is the dung beetle, Khepera. From death they built the Western Lands, and from pain, fear and sickness and excrement they built the Duad as a moat around the Western Lands, lest this exclusive country club be overrun by the peasantry.

These thoughts took shape in hasheesh smoke and mint tea amid the flowers and shrubs of our garden. To maintain my cover as a traveling merchant, I made discreet purchases of rose essence and musk and the rare Pakistani berries that bring visions of exquisite, overripe corruption, of scented corpses and rotten flowers.

The Feku, the Death Collectors, are specialized beyond any human semblance. Their faces have a smooth copper sheen like a beetle's wing. The mouth is a purple beak, the huge black eyes bright and shiny with insect innocence of human feeling. A long pink proboscis can protrude from the mouth to a distance of two feet, sucking in the energy released in the moment of death. Violent death is the most nutritive, and these creatures gather like vultures at battles and riots and executions.

The first picture before the Gods . . . 1930s bankrobbers, roadmaps spread out on the kitchen table at the hideout farmhouse.

"Sure to have blocks up here . . . and here . . . we could just hole up here."

"Uh-uh . . . they don't rumble us getting out, they will close in house to house."

"Makes sense . . . let's try it here. . . . let's go."

As always he felt the cold hollow fear, his throat dry as he croaks, "Yeah, let's go. Up and at 'em." He wonders if they are as scared as he is. Sure they are, but you don't talk about it. Terrible form.

What was he leading this life for? Where any second could be his last . . . that *was* why. If you face death all the time, for what time you have you are immortal. It was always like this, the sick hollow fear, when he feels as if he is fainting . . . then the rush of courage, the clean, sweet feeling of being born. He read that somewhere, about an Old West shootist and how he felt after a shootout. But the fear can go on and on until you can't stand it, it's going to break you, and that's when the fear breaks—you hope.

What was Hassan i Sabbah like? Who was he?

For the last forty years of his life, HIS occupied the mountain fortress of Alamout in what is now northern Iran. From Alamout the Old Man dispatched his assassins when he decided they were ready and their missions necessary. It is said that he could reach as far as Paris. As for the training that the apprentice assassins received, there is no precise information. What little historical data survives tends to be misleading, such as the notorious account given by Marco Polo of a heaven of *houris* promised to the martyr, where he would be wafted when his work was done. There were no women in Alamout.

It is related that HIS had his own son beheaded for smuggling a bottle of wine into his quarters. No doubt this was not the real reason. Obviously the boy was plotting against the Old Man's life. It happens in the best Eastern families.

Beyond that, there is little. Did he ever tell a joke, or smile,

or drink? Some say that in his later years he became an alco-
holic, and that the smuggled bottle of wine was intended for
him, and poisoned. Rumors . . . but very little of the man
emerges and what we do see is not sympathetic. One can't help
thinking of these evil old mullahs with their closed, harsh faces.
I mean that his personal life, his habits, his eccentricities are
completely occluded. This may well have been deliberate on his
part.

Oh, yes, I knew him personally, but I never knew him at all.
He was a man with many faces and many characters. Literally,
he changed unrecognizably from one day to the next. At times
his face was possessed by a dazzling radiance of pure spirit. At
other times the harsh gray lineaments of fear and despair gave
notice of defeat on some battleground of the spirit. Battles are
fought to be won, and this is what happens when you lose. One
thing I know: he was a front-line officer who never asked his men
to do what he would not do himself. He was ready to fight
alongside them, inch by bloody inch.

For example, he moved in a number of Islamic circles. There
were many deviant sects, like the sentimental Sufis, too sweet
to be dangerous. And the whole labyrinthine world of Arab
learning and thought, at a time when they led the civilized
world, introducing such essential factors as distillation for
drunkenness, and the zero for business. What would Burroughs
and IBM do without it? Of all these sects, the Ismailians were
singled out for special persecution, since they commit the black-
est heresy in Islamic books, assuming the prerogatives of the
Creator—and in a very literal sense, for his aim was the creation
of new beings.

You can see the vein on the mullah's forehead stand out and
pulse like an agitated worm at the thought. Leadership is passed
along by direct contact with the Imam, in the course of which
the subject becomes the Imam. This cannot be faked. Anyone
who can see with the eye of the spirit can see it.

The human condition is hopeless once you have submitted to it by being born . . . *almost.* There is one chance in a million, and that is still good biologic odds. Start from where you are looking down the *almost* barrel. Nine tenths of your activity is purposeless fidgeting around, lighting another cigarette . . . nine tenths deadwood weighing you down . . . house odds.

Films are supposed to concentrate the few moments of meaningful action, but they still carry sixty percent of dead weight. Take a film like *The Godfather* . . . cut cut cut. Who wants to see him buy a peach, put on an overcoat, drink a glass of wine? So we have maybe ten minutes that really *move* and that is a very good film. So you can run through your life script in a week, often a lot less. Some walk-on extra blows his wad in a few seconds.

Fix yourself on the whole planet moving at that speed. Every encounter is portentous as a comet. The air crackles with danger, fear, grief and ecstasy. Faster faster round and round.

The Russian delegate tore the Atlantic Proposal into pieces, and to the amazement of the United Nations, wiped his ass with it.

"For this it is not even good," he grunted.

Red alert expected at any second . . . into the Centers . . . issued equipment . . . stand down . . . President on the hotline . . . Checking their guns and shit in and out faster faster get to the end of the checkout line and join the in-line over here . . . round and round faster shift partners round and round faster faster . . . NATO planes up and down . . . tech sergeant finger reaches for the button . . . President on the hotline . . . round and round hotter and hotter . . . finger pulls back, moves forward . . . round and round closer and closer . . . RED AL/ . . . President on the hotline . . . three Russian heads have fallen meanwhile . . . heads are rolling round and round . . . they are shooting it out in the Kremlin like old gunfighters. . . .

The Old Man, Hassan i Sabbah, stands in an ozone reek of purpose, resplendent in his Imam persona. . . .

"This future may not happen, if you all strike at the right time in the right places. So we have a human lifetime with a few moments of meaning and purpose scattered here and there . . . need not be superb pieces of deadly tradecraft, can just be the night sky over St. Louis, or anywhere. Can be a white cat on a red mud wall looking out over Marakesh . . . that male cat is Ra himself. It is fleeting: if you see something beautiful, don't cling to it; if you see something horrible, don't shrink from it, counsels the Tantric sage. However obtained, the glimpses are rare, so how do we live through the dreary years of dead-wood, lumbering our aging flesh from here to there? By knowing that you are *my agent*, not the doorman, gardener, shopkeeper, carpenter, pharmacist, doctor you seem to be."

"How many you kill today, Doc?" calls a fellow agent in Hicksville. And you feel good all over when you say something stupid and corny, you roll in the joys of deception and duplicity, the joy of being something quite different from the face you show the world, and quite dangerous.

So acting out a banal role becomes an exquisite pleasure . . . listening to a redneck's bigoted opinions. I've got *him* on my list. He *never* will be missed.

"You sure is right about them kikes. Ever read the Protocols of the Elders of Zion?"

And the Saturday night poker game . . . you always win if you want to, cool in secret contempt, and on some level they feel the contempt and it frightens them and they want to placate you by losing. . . . The whole human comedy, spread out for your amusement.

Basically, however, you are waiting for the moment of action. So when do you really move? When your Ka takes over and directs your movements and you merge with your Ka.

The Ka, the double, takes the same chances you take in the

Land of the Dead. If you die, he dies. If you are tortured, so is he. So your interests are absolutely synonymous. And that is the only basis for absolute trust. He will be there when you need him and he will know when that is.

The male Ka acts as an agent designed to further male interests in the widest sense, with particular attention to immortality. Recall dream in which women on bicycles, clad in gray shorts and jumpers, flash by a bandstand and raise clenched fists as they intone *Mortality!*

Remember that as a man your Ka must be a male, so any female Ka is sure to be a lethal impostor, happily embraced by an appalling percentage of idiotic and besotted males just aching to be turned into swine. Remember that the Egyptian glyph for poltroon is woman as man, that is, a female Ka taking over a male body.

Now, Kas is all a little different, but people who look alike, Ka alike. They may be viewed interchangeably. The basic Ka spirit, the male Ka, is in fact the Imam. The quickest manner of contact is sexual. Sex is the basis of fear, how we got caught in the first place and reduced to the almost hopeless human condition. The Ka can be freed by the act of sex when there is no fear present.

The magic rites begin: "Let the Shining Ones not have power over me."

What niggardly dealings! Are the Shining Ones your guard dogs? Do your job and get back to heaven?

So the Adept, having intimidated the Shining Ones with an amulet or two and his ivory Rod of Power, now bribes them with some Woolworth incense, jacks off or fucks his chick and they have to obey him and fill that contract.

Let the Shining Ones *enter me.* I want to shine too. That's why I evoke the Shining Ones.

Sure, I know I'm breaking every range law and flight regulation you got. So what? Time to Stop—Change—Start. The point of contact with demons, elementals and succubi, incubi, radiant boys, Shining Ones, is to mate with them and produce desirable offspring, by which I mean offspring with long-range survival potential.

In present-day Egypt, or in the areas of the Mayan and Aztec ruins, one encounters truncated history, where the present-day reality has lost all connection with the historical past, to create a solid time-block. So the last place to look for clues to ancient Egypt is in Egypt itself.

Specifically, I want to reach Egypt about a thousand years ago, when Hassan i Sabbah was there. The concept of salvation through assassination is taking shape. The first real clue is the Egyptian concept of Seven Souls. HIS sees that the Ka, the Double, is the guide to the Garden. However, the Ka must kill the False Ka in carnate form. And the False Ka, the Feku, *must* present itself when the true Ka takes full possession of the human organism. This is the function of the human organism, to serve as a receptacle for the true Ka. So the enemies of HIS are various carnate manifestations of false, parasitic Kas.

The Feku have the advantage of being infinitely prolific and virtually interchangeable, like a virus. The Feku invades the Ka and immediately starts creating falsified copies. These bear some relation to the original, as cancerous liver cells are made from liver cells. Looks like the real thing but cannot survive contact with the real thing. A cancerous cell and a healthy cell cannot occupy the same space.

Religions are weapons, and some of them act quite rapidly. Witness the explosive expansion of Islam to the gates of Vienna, up into southern Spain, east to Persia and India, west to the Pillars of Hercules and deep into black Africa. In truncated time areas like Egypt, a diving-bell approach is indicated. Time has backed up here and solidified.

"Batten the hatches, Mr. Hyslop, we are going down."

Back through layers of newspapers, cheering crowds, down through Nasser to Farouk, a fat, sad clown, down through the stuffy dining rooms in the Shepherd Hotel that was burned by rioters, flames of the burning hotel snuffed to candlelight on British Colonials, sure of themselves as actors in roles of quiet privilege and self-possession . . . down through the prayer calls, the suffocating stagnation of the Arab world, back to an explosion of energy sweeping up to the gates of Vienna, up into southern Spain, over to the Atlantic, then KLUNK. And Allah hits a thousand-year writer's block.

"Sun cold on a thin boy with freckles," Burroughs repeats for a thousand years.

Allahu Akbar . . . Allahu Akbar . . .

So Allah overwrote a thousand years, and now he can't write anything better than Khomeini. I tell you, those old mullahs got a *terrible* look in their eyes. It's a cross-eyed look, up and to the left with a completely disagreeable expression. A dead wooden texture to these faces. This is nasty writing, Allah, and speaking for the Shakespeare Squadron, we don't like it.

The most severe visitation of writer's block has fallen as my narrative comes to Hassan i Sabbah in Egypt, where he presumably learned the secret of secrets that enabled him to attract followers, establish himself at Alamout and control his assassins from a distance.

I realize that my whole approach to HIS has been faulty. I have put him on a remote pedestal; then, with a carry-over of Christian reflexes, have invoked HIS aid, like some Catholic feeling his saint medal. And when I was defeated I felt betrayed. I did not stop to think that he was also defeated, that he is taking his chances with *me*. Instead of asking about the juicy secrets, I asked another question: Did HIS have as bad a time in Egypt as I had in the Empress Hotel? Immediately I knew that the answer was Yes!

I am HIS and HIS is me. I am not an agent or a representative, to be abandoned when the going gets tough, or disowned by some Chief in a distant office. That is what HIS training achieved. The Ka of his assassins merged with HIS Ka. From that moment on, he is in as much danger, in fact exactly the same danger, as his assassins.

HIS realizes that his ill-fated attempt to become the Sultan's Vizier derived from a deep feeling of vulnerability. Some would call it cowardice. He desperately needed protection against his enemies, who hate him for what he is, but more virulently for what he could achieve. For HIS is the ultimate threat to their parasitic position. The voice of self-evident spiritual fact.

Hell is to fall into the hands of such enemies, and he had barely escaped.

Isolated in Egypt, without money and without followers, HIS's position is desperate. He can feel the hate all around him: snarling dogs and doormen, hostile officials and landlords. He walks by three old men sitting on a bench in front of a little café. They follow his passage with cold, hostile eyes. He walks on, feeling the hate like a palpable force, as a small stone thuds against his back.

He whirls around . . . a street urchin stands there with a dog's snarl on his face. The boy spits. The old men glare. No use to make an issue. He turns and walks rapidly away.

The heat is like an oven. He must find lodging with the last of his money. He has sent out some messages to followers, but he can't be sure whether they have arrived or when he can expect help, if ever.

He doesn't like the looks of the landlord, a beefy, bearded man with stale wine and onions on his breath. He agrees, however, to pay a week in advance.

"I will put the receipt under your door."

He doesn't like this either. A man's word should be enough. But he is too tired to look further.

A cubicle room with a lattice door for its only ventilation;

a pallet on the floor, a stand with a pitcher of water and a basin, some wooden pegs in the wall. He splashes the warm, fetid water on his face, takes off his djellaba and hangs it on a peg. He lies down on the pallet in a loincloth and shirt, his knife in an ornate sheath at his belt, and falls immediately into a feverish sleep.

Someone is pounding on the door. He puts on his djellaba and opens the door. The landlord is standing there.

"What do you want?"

"What do I want?" the landlord sneers. "I want my money of course."

"But I have paid you for a week."

The landlord looks at him with cold insolence.

"You paid me nothing." A foreigner, the landlord thinks. From Lebanon or further east, probably a heretic as well. Such people have no business in Cairo. "If you don't get out of here, I will call the police. I don't think you want that, do you?"

HIS sees the situation. A red tide flows up his spine, stirring the hair on the back of his neck, and comes out his eyes in a flash of light. The landlord gasps and steps back as the knife hooks up under his ribs to the heart. He turns dough-white and his mouth opens and closes.

HIS quickly puts his knife into its sheath and drags the sagging body into the room and dumps it on the pallet. He searches the body and finds a purse of coins at the belt. He goes out and closes the door.

Down the stairs and out into the street, walking rapidly. Rounding a corner he almost collides with a woman. She opens her mouth to curse him, then closes it and shrinks away.

For the first time since his arrival in Egypt he feels free and whole as he slips along through the narrow, twisting streets, letting his legs carry him. There is only one answer for people like that.

It is evening, a slight breeze comes in from the river. He realizes that he is ravenously hungry. He has not eaten in two days. He comes to a little restaurant with a bench along the side. Cauldrons of stew are bubbling over a charcoal fire and a basket of fresh bread is on a table with bowls.

"Come in."

The man has a rugged, ugly face. He is missing his front teeth, but his eyes and his smile are unmistakable as he ladles out a bowl of spicy lamb stew with chickpeas and hands HIS a loaf of flat brown bread still warm from the oven.

HIS quickly finishes the stew and asks for another bowl. When he has finished, the man brings out a kief pipe, lights it and passes it to him.

"I have come a long way from the East," HIS says, choosing his words carefully. "They call me Ismail, among other names."

The proprietor extends his hand . . . one long and one short squeeze. "It is a name I honor." He brings two cups of mint tea and refills the pipe.

HIS tells him about the landlord. The man nods.

"I know this man. He was himself a foreigner, a Hittite. He was also a police informer. It is best that you leave Cairo at once."

Memphis: a tangle of piers and stalls connected by catwalks, a reek of fish, river mud, sewage and *fellaheen* sweat. Eyes flick at him with a mudlike antagonism, cold and unfeeling as sidling scorpions. HIS is accompanied by the young boatman, Ali, a curly-haired youth with a sharp, fox face and wary street eyes. The boy gives off a faint smell of civet. He carries a heavy stick and there is a cane knife in a crocodile-skin sheath at his belt.

Moving back from the river, they come to an area of walled villas with barred gates. As always, the dogs go mad at the sight and smell of HIS, leaping and biting at the gates. HIS finds this senseless hate unnerving because he knows the dogs *see* him, not just as any stranger or intruder, but as a threat to their lives, something basically undoglike. No food, no love, no home will ever come to a dog from this man or his followers.

They turn aside into an area of modest houses, traders, artisans, merchants, scribes, embalmers, magic men and witches.

Ali knocks loudly with his club on a green door with a heavy brass lock. The door opens and an old man, quite bald, with bright brown bird eyes, motions them inside. He closes and bolts the door and leads them to a room that opens onto a small, walled garden. The old man has the same fox face as Ali and the same civet smell.

"This man wants dog amulet," says Ali.

The old man smiles, showing toothless gums. "He has need of it. I could trace your path from the river. Well, there are amulets of course . . . but an amulet is only as good as its owner. It can help, like a weapon. There is the cat goddess Bast."

He points to a picture in lurid colors on the wall, showing Bast with a scythe, up to her knees in blood . . . a sea of blood to the sky.

"For every Goddess, there is also a God. Few know of the Cat God Kunuk, and he is stronger for being unknown. A known God, you see, has so many claims that it drains his power."

Kunuk is depicted as small—five feet in height—covered with fine silver fur, with eyes like opals. He carries a scythe and he is very adept at throwing it so that it severs a head and then returns to his hand. He is a juggler and can keep three sickles in the air.

This is a wild, free spirit, capricious, swept by icy passions. In the hands of a weak or timorous man his amulet is worse than useless, attracting attacks which Kunuk refuses to deal with. Too starved an argument for his sickle, or his terrible three-inch claws that can disembowel with one quick flick. Sometimes he beheads dogs and juggles the heads in remote transient markets.

His voice is sharp as his sickle. Few can hear it and fewer still can imitate it. No dog can endure the voice of Kunuk. It is like red-hot needles jabbed into his ears until blood flows from his nose and eyes. To a cat the voice is a delicate caress. They arch and whine and purr. The quickest approach to Kunuk is through his voice.

One wall is taken up by wooden cubbyholes with animal and snake skins, skulls, potions, bottles and jars and bundles of herbs. A purple-gray cat comes in from the garden and rubs against HIS leg.

The old man comes back with a silver box, three inches by five and an inch in depth. Inside the box is an intricate arrangement of copper, silver and gold wires in crisscross grids welded to the sides and the bottom of the box. He replaces the top. At one end of the top section is a grid of glyph-shaped slots cut through the box top. He holds up the box and a thin twang vibrates through the room.

HIS can feel it down into the bones, trembling like an oud string. His skull and teeth are humming, the sharp frequency like a probe of silver light.

"I think you have the answer to your dog problem . . . and now there is the question of my fee."

"Of course. But I would like to test the device. Not that I doubt your honesty, but it may not work for me."

"Certainly. Go out the gate and turn to your right. Follow the street until you see the mosque. The dog is called Cerberus. Cerberus will come without being called."

The boy stands up, but the old man raises his hand. "He must go alone. Otherwise it is not a true test. He must also leave his knife and his stick."

HIS feels waves of sick, cold fear.

"If you do not trust this box absolutely, the box is absolutely worthless."

With numb fingers, HIS puts his knife on the table. He takes a deep breath. The fear closes around his chest tighter and tighter. His head spins.

"Remember, the box will not fail you if you do not fail the box."

HIS steps through the gate into the noon street like a man going to execution, fighting his fear and losing with every step. He feels himself near collapse. There is no strength in his arm. Even if he had the knife, he knows he could not lift it from the scabbard. He can see himself bolt and run, shit and piss streaming down his thighs. He holds the box clutched to his pounding heart. He takes a deep breath and concentrates on the One Point, two inches below the navel. He has learned this, and many other secrets of combat, from a traveler from the Far East.

Stumbling, shambling, and there ahead is the blue dome of the mosque . . . an open gate . . . a low growl . . . a huge black dog. Its eyes light up with green fire at the sight of HIS. The hairs stand up on the animal's back as it slinks forward, muscles bunched for a deadly rush. HIS brings the box out and holds it toward the dog.

Now he can feel *ki* stream down his arm into the box, and he hears the words of his teacher: "When you need me, I will be there." HIS is suddenly calm. The fear lifts from him. The dog snarls and shrinks back, then comes in again. HIS pours his *ki* into a flash of silver light. The dog leaps back, howling in pain and rage. HIS pours in more power as the dog comes rushing back. This time the dog is jerked violently back, as if he had come to the end of an invisible chain. Blood pours from his nose and ears. Yipping, howling, he turns with a despairing snarl and runs back into the garden.

HIS feels a calm, floating dispersal melting into the sunshine and shadows of the street, the white walls and doorways. An old man comes to the gate and looks at HIS with malevolent suspicion. HIS holds out the box and the janitor shrinks back.

"Keep your gate closed and your dog chained."

The gate clicks shut. The man's face and the dog's snarl are fading in his mind like dream traces.

"Well, I am convinced."

"So, now there is the matter of my fee. It is not money.

Something much more valuable. My fee is the right to serve you."

Unlike other masters, HIS *becomes* his servant. If the servant loses and fails, HIS also loses and fails. So he does not accept servants lightly. In fact, he does not accept them at all. How can an extension of himself be a servant? One maintains distance with a servant. Here is a special closeness, an identity, in fact, that is the basis of the relationship.

The function of the Guardian is to protect the child during the vulnerable period following the first death. It is a difficult, dangerous and thankless job. There are no excuses for failure, and no rewards for success. He combines a ruthless competence in carrying out his protective function with a deep tenderness for the child he guards.

The Guardian first comes into existence in the moment of conception, so he is *biologically* bound to his charge. Guardians tend to have a deep cuddle reflex. They cuddle skunks and raccoons and cats and lemurs and . . .

"A musk ox on TV in deep snow and I wanted to embrace it because it is a noble animal with huge liquid black eyes, all covered with a thick fur."

There is no question of payment. The Guardian is distinct from the Khu. The Khu is eternal and leaves the body after death. The Khu does not take his chances in the Land of the Dead. Well-intentioned, but his commitment is limited.

The commitment of the Guardian is total. His position is almost the same as the Ka's, but not quite. You can say that the Ka is the Guardian's Control Officer. The Ka must contact the Big Picture if he is to perform effectively.

There are many professional guards in Waghdas, specializing in various areas of protection. One agency sells protection against the Thuggees. These devious operatives are stock agent-types: cold-eyed, with no commitment beyond personal advancement in a game universe.

Pick up any spy book:

When Peter walked into the office, the Chief smiled. Agents have been known to get frostbite from the Chief's smile.

"Having trouble with the Jew boy?"

"He's a bit standoffish," said Peter noncommittally.

"Sure he is. We'll treat a kike like a Jew and a high-class professional Jew from Rutherford, New Jersey, like a kike. Tell him right out, 'You wanta get into a nice gentile Country Club?' We like *nice* Jews, with atom bombs and Jew jokes."

Peter could see the Chief as some cold-eyed old exterminator, deciding on the bait to poison a warehouse full of rats . . . a little molasses, a little tinned salmon and plenty of arsenic. Peter knew he was in the presence of greatness. He squirmed with the schmaltz of it and broke out fulsomely, "I'm just beginning to realize what a cold-hearted bastard you are!"

The Chief was pleased, but his voice was cool. "Well, that's one way of putting it. I call it staying on top of an op."

"Even if that means . . . ?"

"The code word is POP."

"The casualties could run into the millions."

"The billions, Peter. The billions." The Chief spread his hands and smiled. "Outsiders. None of our people will be touched. Operation Bunker."

"How long?"

"Long enough for things to cool off. Then we emerge like the Phoenix, without, of course, the inconvenience of being incinerated like the peasantry."

Peter squirmed *deliciously*. This was *true* greatness. You can't fake the real thing.

"You *are* a cold-hearted bastard!" he ejaculated.

"Just drop a few hints . . . room in the Bunker for the right kind of Jews. You know what I mean . . . *white* Jews. None of that Galician trash. Now they tell me Portuguese Jews is the best kind, like Portuguese oysters."

"He's coming around, Chief. Out of a clear blue sky he says, 'It's the kikes in our race that give us a bad name.' "

"Tomorrow is always white and blue," the Chief said enigmatically. "Any trouble with the cracker boy?"

"Not a peep. Gave him the old white schmaltz right down the old line: 'What are you doing over there with the niggers and the apes and the yids? Why don't you come over here where you belong and act like a white man?' "

"And how is our darky shaping up?"

" 'Always a place in the Bunker for the right kind of darky.' "

"Swallowed that, did he? Believes in the American Dream like all niggers . . . well, as one menstruating cunt said to another . . . 'I guess it's in the rag.' "

The Chief smiled slow and dirty.

People without any long-range commitments. They can be bought by anyone, but they have no honor in being bought. To hire such operatives as protection is to be precariously and temporarily protected from your protectors . . . the old protection racket.

"If you're smart you will protect yourself from *me*. At a price." Blackmail, and the price keeps escalating.

So other agencies protect you from the Thuggee-protectors, and so on. Hitler created the SS to protect himself from the SA, and to eliminate the SA. Had he lived long enough, he would have needed protectors from the SS, and protectors from those protectors . . . where does it end? Perhaps with only one protector, who is, of course, your deadliest enemy.

I saw a picture of a balloon suddenly and unexpectedly soaring and some people still holding onto the ropes connected to the balloon were suddenly jerked into the air and most of them didn't have the survival IQ to *let go in time.* Seconds later they are sixty, a hundred feet off the ground. Those who didn't let go fell off at five hundred or a thousand feet. A basic survival lesson is: *Learn to let go.*

Put it another way: Never hang on when your Guardian tells you to let go.

RIGHT NOW.

Suppose you were holding one of those ropes? Would you have let go in time, which is, of course, at the first upward yank? I'll tell you something interesting. You would have a much better chance to let go in time now that you have read this paragraph than if you hadn't read it. Writing, if it is anything, is a word of warning . . .

LET GO!

A word about conditions in the Land of the Dead: quarters are precarious and difficult to find one's way back to, and privacy is fleeting. Doors are flimsy, often absent, leaving your quarters open to corridors, passageways, streets, and there are always other means of access, so one is subject to find anybody or anything in one's digs, if one is lucky enough to have digs. Bathroom facilities are filthy and inadequate. One shaves in a toilet with a shard of broken mirror.

As usual I am looking for a place to have breakfast, always difficult. This time it's a cafeteria common room. Mikey Portman, deceased, falls in beside me in the line. He is broke as usual . . . be my guest. It's close to eleven. Last serving. Cold, watery Spanish omelette slopped onto a dirty plate with soggy toast and cold coffee. Why do we need to eat, being dead? I guess we are eating the concept of food.

This time our quarters are in a basement area, concrete corridors and wooden partitions with wire mesh doors. My lodgings are on a ledge fifteen feet above the concrete floor, reached by a shaky iron ladder. The ledge is six feet wide and slants downward, so that I am in continual danger of falling off the ledge. Fatima the Arab girl is waiting to come in and clean up.

Often the quarters look like hotels, with elevators that take one to the wrong floor or stick between floors. Door dogs importune one in the corridors, and some people make pets of them. The same difficulty to find a place, to eat breakfast—at one place the waiter told me the restaurant was not distinguished enough—and the same danger to one's continued tenancy.

The White Hunters offer essential protection against the extremely dangerous animals, reptiles and amphibians found in the Duad and in the pestilent lowlands, sloughs and swamps that surround it. They take a lot of killing before they know they are dead. Unlike the Thuggee Guards, the White Hunters have a code of honor. They are bound to protect the life of a client, even a client that they despise, at the risk of their own.

We break through heavy underbrush to a meadow leading down to the river. The farther bank is hidden in mist.

"Well, let's go."

The White Hunter stops his client.

"You wouldn't get five feet. Look . . ."

He tosses a rock out into the meadow. The rock breaks through a thin crust of mud, steam jets up through the hole and the grass around the rock hole writhes and twists like a Van Gogh and suddenly a steaming claw emerges.

"It's not just the mud, which is sticky as hot rubber—you can't walk in it, you can't swim. There are predators that live in the hot mud—blind, naturally, but just break the mud crust and they converge, great bloody worms with a disk-shaped mouth like a rotating saw, and crabs and snakes with incurving needle teeth. Better try the jungle approach."

We turn aside, skirting the deadly meadow with its glistening green grass. Giant trees overhead. Our path darkens. A huge centipede crawls up out of a hot sulphur spring that gushes from a limestone cleft. Wilson gives it a double-barrel shot charge that guts it from head to ass. The stinking, eviscerated body squirms around, shooting jets of poison from its fangs, the liquid dissolving the limestone.

Consider this scenario: HIS and Neph make the pilgrimage and reach the Western Lands. The knowledge they bring back could destroy the existing order founded by the Venusian Controllers, which manifests itself through all authoritarian governments and organization: the Church, the Communist Party, in fact *all* governments currently operating. It's a tight monopoly on Power.

So try seizing power in some small country and setting up a distant system, *separate* from the other systems. And that is exactly what HIS did at Alamout. For starters, no victimless crimes on the books. Someone wants to take drugs, it's his own business. Right away you have the KGB, the CIA and every other agency with orders to terminate, *stat.*

So HIS and Neph flee Egypt with every contract in the known world on their ass. Finally they reach Alamout. And HIS held it for thirty years. He did not, as some say, fail. He wasn't attempting old-style territorial politics. Alamout was never intended to be permanent. It was intended to gain time to train a few operatives for the future struggle, which is right here, right now, in front of all of you. The lines are being drawn.

"God's word says that the Occult is the enemy."

Some reborn son of a bitch is listening to his Master's Voice like a good human dog.

"Magic is the enemy. Creation is the enemy."

ALAMOUT

Sometimes it can be done in minutes. Other cases take years. Sometimes it doesn't happen. This is sad, but there is always useful work. When it does happen, they both know. You can't fake it. Neither HIS nor the initiate could fake it. Take a pure desert boy, no defensive impactions, and there is immediate access to the Ka. The Secret Name can be written, and the assassin dispatched on his mission.

He passes through a soft gate in a gush of molten gold into the Master's Garden, and he knows the Old Man will be with him and show him when and where and how to strike.

His legs take him to a lodging house. The landlord is middle-aged, rather sad-looking. They exchange hand signals. The landlord's name is Temsemani. He brings out a map of the city and shows him where the Sultan's litter will pass during the festival.

For three days Ali frequents the area, fitting into the venerable role of the mischievous street boy, yelled at and chased by shopkeepers.

Sixty years ago the Sultan had undertaken an expedition against the nomads of the western desert—a joke-expedition, since the nomads retreat ahead of his forces.

On the expedition: the Sultan, with his concubines and courtiers, is established in luxurious tents. He is a foppish, strikingly handsome youth with cold features, like chiseled marble. Scouts have found a pool of tar, liquefied and bubbling from underground heat. The Sultan gives the order to collect barrels of the tar. It is useful to pour on besieging forces.

A number of young desert boys have attached themselves to the expedition, doing menial work in return for scraps of food. The Sultan's eyes fasten on a boy and narrow with greedy anticipation. He beckons. The boy rushes up with a dazzling smile.

"Can you run?"

The boy nods eagerly, expecting a messenger job that will mean food from both sender and receiver. At an order from the Sultan, a scout pours a bucket of melted tar over the boy and applies a torch. Screaming in agony, the boy runs fifty yards and falls against a sand dune.

The Sultan strolls over, drawing the smell of roasted flesh and pungent oil deep into his lungs. The boy is lying face down, moving spasmodically. The Sultan rolls him over with a contemptuous boot. For a split second the boy glares at him, spitting hate from blackened eyes.

The music starts in the early morning. The Sultan will come by in an hour. Already the bearded Syrian guards line the streets, their staves held horizontally in both hands to keep back the crowds. Ali slips along the edge of the crowd. A great cheer goes up, and he feels a shiver run up his back to the neck and out his eyes in a flash and the Old Man is there in a mantle of light.

The Sultan is now a thin old man with a white beard, carefully trimmed. He should be magnificent, but he isn't. He looks mean and petty and ill-natured. He never looks straight in front of him, but always a little above and to the left. Whatever he is seeing there, he doesn't like it.

The Sultan has ruled long, and his kingdom has prospered. He holds audiences where any man may plead his grievances. Word of his mercy and wisdom have spread through the land. His aqueducts and grain storage bring freedom from hunger. To those without land or implements, he distributes bread and soup. His armies protect the frontiers, bringing freedom from fear.

Ali moves through the cheering crowd: just a street boy. Watch your purse. The Sultan's face is a mask of old ivory carved in lineaments of noble serenity, annulled by eyes as dead as pools of tar.

Now! Ali feels it up the back of his neck and out his eyes in a blaze of silver light. The street shifts under his feet, tilting him under the staves. He streaks toward the Sultan's litter like a shooting star.

With an incredulous wrench, the Sultan swivels his eyes to focus on the youth, four feet in front of him, and the bottom falls out of his eyes, leaving a hideous mask of crab terror. The Sultan's mask shatters in a scream of abject recognition:

"*You!*"

Ali's dagger catches him under the chin and protrudes from the top of his head. A witness said that as the dagger struck, the Sultan's eyes caught fire and burned like pitch.

The eunuch Vizier scrambles awkwardly from his litter, screaming, "Take him alive!" But the Hittite guards have already shattered Ali's skull with their staves.

"I said—"

"We did not hear, *master.*" The guard gives him an evil grin.

"I'll have you—"

"Will you, *master?*"

"Well . . . be careful . . . and remember that I give the orders."

"We will remember, *master.*"

Looking at the grinning, bearded faces, the Vizier feels the clutch of cold fear.

Wish they were all that easy. All I had to do was slip into the *hand,* like putting on a glove. It can be a tricky business, guiding a boy like that. Sometimes they freeze the controls, and there is always the problem of enemy interception. You can run into a dead blackout of enemy occupation. Usually there's a chink, a long chance, but a dead blackout always indicates the whole operation is blown. They've gotten to your agent and turned him all the way. Time to pull out fast.

The Sultan could not have lived long in any case, with the inevitable ambitious General, treacherous Vizier and two sullen sons. The Old Man knows what will happen. The Vizier will speedily poison the sons, keep the General occupied with foreign conquests and set up a moderate regime. He is a cowardly, corrupt, indolent man, but very astute. While the former Sultan was extremely rigorous in persecuting dissident sects, and made deadly enemies in consequence, the new regime will be lenient, making it easy for the Old Man to place his agents.

The old gardener blew the ash out of his kief pipe. He sat immobile on a stool in the shade of the toolshed. He seemed to be listening to something, and his head and upper body moved almost imperceptibly, like the movements of a cobra in supposed rhythm to the snake charmer's flute.

He stood up. He picked up the hand scythe and tested the edge. He walked to the pool and resumed his work of trimming the grass and weeds along the banks.

It was early evening, and the General always walked through his garden at this hour. The gardener was an excellent gardener, who made his garden something above those of his peers. The General paused to watch the gardener at work. Unhurried and old, he seemed to be moving with an inner rhythm.

"He's doing it to music," the General reflected. This cognition seemed to clear his mind of his tormenting obsession with the Old Man. He was organizing an expedition against Alamout, and had vowed to rid Persia of this heretic and stamp out his pernicious cult. His hatred ate at him so that he would wake up in the middle of the night, cursing and screaming imprecations. He saw assassins lurking behind every bush.

It soothed him now to watch the old gardener's precise movements. He was working at increased tempo, faster faster round and round, turning now in a wild dervish dance. Too late the General heard the shrill of the flutes, the menacing pulse of the drums, and reached for his sword with a snarl of rage.

The scythe glinted in the sun, cutting the General's imprecation in half as his head bounced into a rose bed and lay there impaled on thorns, grimacing. The body staggered in a clumsy bear's dance and fell, spilling a thick column of black blood.

Guards were rushing from the palace. The old gardener danced to meet them, whirling and slashing, until he fell transfixed by lances and sword points.

A. J. comes to the costume party as a Mexican bandit in filthy, torn cotton pants and shirt and a wide sombrero pocked with bullet holes.

"¡Chinga!" he screams, and pulls his machete and decapitates Lady Caroline's Russian wolfhound with a single stroke.

Now he points to the slavering head, and does a revolting imitation of the head and the body, which lies twitching in obscene spasms. A huge rubber penis snaps out of his fly and quivers, spraying the guests with a foul-smelling yellow ichor.

"If anyone does not like this thing that I have done, I can use this machete a second time."

He makes his re-entrance as a pirate with a patch over one eye, a cutlass and flintlock pistol at his belt, a vulture on his shoulder, singing lustily, "Fifteen men on a dead man's chest!"

He draws his cutlass and decapitates Colonel Greenfield, whose face, purple with rage, splashes into the lobster Newburg, spattering the guests with rich cream sauces.

"Yo ho ho and a bottle of rum!"

He slices off Mrs. Worldly's head, face frozen in a maniacal shift from icy disapproval to naked terror. The head, spilling diamonds from her necklace, bounces across the terrace.

"Scrambles!" screams an idiotic English Lord, showing his long yellow horse's teeth. Bloodstained guests scuffle and grab for the bouncing diamonds.

A.J. beheads an ambitious young politician. The mouth gapes open, dying eyes pleading to be heard as if he would catch another vote with his silver tongue, which protrudes to the root as the eyes go out.

"Drink and the devil had done for the rest."

A.J. hauls out his double-barreled flintlock loaded with iron filings and cyanide crystals and takes out two secret service guards before they can get their Uzis out of special briefcases with complex locking mechanisms.

The old gardener's dance moves out in concentric circles. Plop, a starlet's head sinks into the blue lagoon.

In Alamout the musicians and adepts take a break for mint tea. They have been concentrating to activate the distant agent with their music. The Old Man has them in stitches with his dummy. He's got this life-size dummy with a white beard and eyes of blue glass that shoot out rays of light.

"You see, my son, all present, all past and all future can be contained in a single note of music."

The dummy yacks out, "Give us more of thy wisdom!"

"Since music is registered with the whole body it can serve as a means of communication between one organism and another."

A CIA man leans forward, sweeping the room with laser eyes. "A viable means of conveying instructions to and receiving information from agents in the field."

Musical intelligence. Agent attends a concert and receives his instructions. Information and directives in and out through street singers, musical broadcasts, jukeboxes, records, high school bands, whistling boys, cabaret performers, singing waiters, transistor radios.

"Red sails in the sunset
'Way out on the sea . . ."

Red alert coming up.

> "Oh! carry my loved one
> Home safely to me."

All agents return to Center.

A team of dedicated Russian agents disguised as rednecks roar out "The Star-Spangled Banner" at a political rally.

> "And the rockets' red glare"

Russian rockets are on the way.

> "At the twilight's last gleaming"

RUSSIAN MISSILES HIT WASHINGTON D.C.
"Head for the hills!"
What hills? Geiger counters click to countdown. Decaying lead spells out the last syllables of recorded time. Orgone balked at the post. Christ bled. Time ran out. Radiation has won at a half-life.

"When metal goes rotten, everything goes," said a wise old Texas sheriff. The young deputy wondered how you could keep lead straight. Maybe it just needed the love of a good woman, and apple pie. It's just as simple as that, he thought, as the jail disintegrated. This was more than the sheriff could take.

"What can a man depend on when his jail falls apart? Get back in there, you sidewinders!" he screams, reaching for his melted shotgun with no hands.

" 'Only fools do those villains pity who are punished before they have done their mischief,' " Kim quotes, as he shoves a horrid rednecked oaf out of the lifeboat. The sharks cut his screams to a bearable pitch and period.

"I wonder how long it would have taken him to reach the same conclusion about me? Just so long and long enough."

He takes a long pull from his brandy flask and opens a tin of beef, thanking Allah for eyes to see and hands to push. The sun lays a crimson path across the darkening sea that stretches to the sky in all directions. Another pull at the brandy flask, to celebrate and savor a blessed absence.

Occasionally the boat undulates slightly, as if the ocean bed has shifted without disturbing the surface, like moving an aquarium slowly, being careful not to break the film that holds a sprinkling of fish food on the surface. And that is what he is. A sprinkling of fish food.

He recalls the Shark Spirit, a little wooden figure carved somewhere in the South Pacific. He'd seen it in the Burlington Museum in London . . . sly, enigmatic, very old and patient, driven by a cold, deadly, implacable hunger for anything its big mouth can tear off and swallow. Any individual shark is expendable, but the hunger remains to find another receptacle. Three hundred million years the shark has survived, with a big mouth to tear off chunks and a gut to digest almost anything.

It is inconceivable that Homo sapiens could last another thousand years in present form. People of such great stupidity and such barbarous manners. And what do years mean, apart from human measurement and perception? Does time pass if there is no one there to register its passing? Of course not, since Time is a figment of human perception.

Ahead and to the right Kim sees a black shape rising from the sea, clearly an island, though he can't see any lights. He stands up and rows toward the distant land, facing his objective in the Mediterranean rowing style, leaning forward with a long stroke that sends the boat gliding forward, then relax, feather oars, lean forward. Less than an hour till dark.

A book with glowing roses twined around the words and growing through the words. He can see the roses growing through his body, the aching red translucent thorns growing from his fingers and toes, his penis a single glowing rose.

Across the street he can see men in white robes standing by a doorway. The men step aside, and he enters an empty white space illuminated by the radiance that flows from his body. His eyes are shaded purple roses with glistening black rose pupils, his mouth is full of thorn teeth. He grows from place to place on swift silent vegetable currents. He comes to a white-walled room, one side open. Hawks glide against a fragile eggshell-blue sky. The room opens on a cliff with a sheer drop of three thousand feet to the valley below.

An old man stands in front of him with an instrument like a paintbrush open in his hand. He is writing instructions back through the door, way past the two doormen and take the left fork. The road leads steeply upward to the familiar land of giants and dwarfs and castles, doors that pop open on steps leading down and slam shut, spider magic, mirror magic, card magic, coffee grinder magic, fork and spoon magic.

He turns into a medieval inn, and cold hostile faces turn toward him. He sits down and drapes his arms on the table.

"Barkeep!!"

A slovenly brute looks up from the bar he is mopping with a filthy rag.

"You talking me?"

"I am. Bring me a beer, cheese and bread, quickly."

"Maybe you wrong people, wrong place."

"Wrong people *learn* place."

Rose speaks in a blur of movement. Hands, fingers, palms, sprouting needle-sharp thorns close lightly on the barkeep's neck. Rose grows back to his table. The barkeep touches his throat and looks at the blood on his hands.

"Right away, sir," says barkeep, looking behind Rose's table as a man in palace guard uniform steps forward and unsheaths his sword.

"You must come with me, stranger. Your papers?"

Rose points the outstretched fingers of his left hand, squeezing out thorns that thud into the guard's chest. The guard's face turns bright red, then dead pale. He slumps gently to the floor.

Outside it is getting dark, and the wind is rising from a cat's whine to a shriek. Rose spreads his cloak like a gliding lemur, sailing on gusts of wind out across the valley faster and faster on a jet of sulphurous, blazing farts, streaking across the sky like a comet, propelled by millennia of animal farts tearing and burning through him.

I come to light in a muted bar, dining-room set, discreet conversation, well-dressed patrons who are obviously walk-on extras. The maître d' is exceedingly respectful, as he should be, showing me to the best table.

"The Doctor phoned to say he will be a few minutes late, sir. Would you like a drink?"

I order the martini with a dash of absinthe for which the establishment is renowned. These martinis are kept chilled in the freezer. Anyone asking for rocks would be immediately thrown out into the cobblestone alley.

Now the Doctor slides into the seat opposite. Fine-looking old whitey, phony as Yellow Kid Weil. Two martinis materialize on the table.

"Sorry to keep you waiting, Bill."

He lifts his glass. We drink. He smiles knowingly over his drink. "Well, things have gotten out of hand."

"Out of whose hands?"

"Out of my hands of course." He looks down into his empty glass, twirling it. "I don't know what I'm going to do about you, Bill. I really don't."

"When in doubt, do nothing."

"On the contrary . . . when in doubt, always do *something*. It may be your last act before doubt paralysis sets in. In the terminal stages you have to be force-fed, because you can't decide to eat—so many reasons not to." The old fraud ducks and laughs and punches me on the shoulder.

A perfect venison steak with wild rice appears on my plate, and the old man gets this half smile on his face, shaking his head and looking down at the table. And I don't like it at all. It's creepy and corny and deceptive . . . very deceptive.

"Now Bill, you know you've gotten out of line and caused a lot of important people a lot of concern. Gave old Countess ———— a sick headache, and brought on Monsieur ————'s ulcers. Now if you'd just listen to reason."

"I'm listening. Talk some reason."

"That's what I mean. You want us to tell you what we want. And that's not reasonable."

"Depends on who decides."

"We decide, Bill. We decide."

"Prove it. Right here. Right now."

He ducks around, holding up his hand in mock defense. "Don't blast me, Bill. Always played fair with you . . . just an old showman."

"Good sir, to the purpose."

"Well, put it this way, Bill." He is pacing around the patio of a run-down 1920s Spanish villa. Could be Florida or southern California. A balmy night, with the scent of night-blooming cereus, stars like wilted gardenias in the sky. "I can make you an offer."

"In return for what?"

"Well, look at the *offer* first: nice secure place, shooting range, swimming pool, and full of *anything* you want, Bill. We are men of the world. Sure, you're a bit worn out. We got serums will fix that."

What is life worth when the purpose is gone? Skulking in an ill-fitting body from a shabby bargain long void, he is, if anything, the carrier of the child formed from his mind and body.

Every assassin he trained became his child. He *became* his agents, his messengers.

The Old Man's voice is a thin, dry rustle, like a snake shedding its skin.

"The real struggle is yet to come. What we are doing here is simply an exercise. You have known the pure killing purpose that comes from the total awareness of what you are killing."

The desperate days of pursuit and flight, the ambush sensed just in time, the quick knife in an alley, the after-kill feeling, sweet and clean like rebirth, the constant alertness, the crushing fatigue, a different lodging every night, the shifts of identity: a merchant, a holy man, a scholar, a beggar, a doctor, a man of no trade, a traveler on precarious roads of shifting alliances, partial commitments, treacherous loyalties. (He knows this man will betray him. There must be no outcry.) Safe houses that are not safe. (He knows he can't go back there tonight. An ambush will be waiting.)

He is safe here in Alamout. No one can touch him. But safety is the most dangerous of all conditions.

10

THE VALLEY

There is no way in or out of the Valley, which is ringed with sheer cliffs with an overhanging ledge. How did the people of the Valley get in there in the first place? No one remembers. They have been there for many years. Children have been born, grown old and died in the Valley, but not many children. Food is scarce. A stream runs through the Valley, and they have dammed up a large pond to raise fish. There is an area along the stream where they grow corn. Sometimes they kill birds, a few lizards and snakes. So most children must be killed at birth. Just an allotted number to continue the line.

Maybe, some say, they will be seen, and people will lower ropes. There is a legend that one man built a flying machine from lizard, snake and fish skins sewn to a frame of light wood. It took him all his life to build it, and he was seventy when the machine was finally finished. It looked like a gigantic dragonfly with sixty-foot wings.

The currents rising from the Valley on certain hot afternoons, he calculated, could bear the ship aloft. It could carry only one person, and that person must be very light. A boy of thirteen was chosen. The Builder was by then comparatively corpulent, since he was granted extra rations for his work, which they hoped would be their means of deliverance: *Esperanza*.

The Builder had a device like a dowser's wand, carefully constructed of the lightest fish bones. He would hold the wand out, testing the air, and the wand would seem to be an extension of his hands, gnarled and twisted by their years of painstaking work. He would shake his head.

But finally the rod seemed to leap and vibrate and point straight up to the sky beyond the cliffs. He nodded.

"The time has come, but you must act quickly."

The boy took his place. No time for goodbyes. The men and women of the Valley gently lifted the huge craft above their heads as high as their arms would reach.

"*¡Ahora!*"

They launched the craft into the air. It sailed forward and seemed about to crash, then the current caught it, wafted it upward, further and further, almost up to the vast overhangs now, as the scales of the fish and snakes and lizards caught the late sun and sparkled with iridescent lights, for the Valley was already in shadow.

A powerful updraft from the darkening Valley, up, up, riding the wind like a vulture . . . then one wing tore loose and the craft dipped and veered. The other wing broke against the top of the cliff and the boy plummeted down, trailing gossamer rags of the torn fuselage, down, down into darkness.

That was many years ago. How many, no one knows. There is no point in keeping any sort of time here. Only the old men remember, and no one knows how old the old men are. No one has tried to build such a craft since.

The Valley is narrow, only six hundred yards across at the widest point, so that there is sun in the Valley for only a few hours each day. They have developed a strain of corn that grows by the light of the moon and the stars, a pale blue corn with a metallic taste, that emits a faint luminescence. The corn is nutritious, but it rots the gums, the teeth fall out, and the corn attacks the palate . . . finally the tongue and gums and lips are eaten away to the bone so that the Corn-Eaters resemble grinning skulls, their contaminated flesh glowing in the dark. Most of us avoid the deadly corn, knowing where it leads as the corn attacks the bones, until the spinal column is eaten through . . . even so, the head still lives for some hours.

The only thing that keeps us alive is music, and in this the Corners excel. They sing through their rotting gums, a strange, viscous sound, exquisitely sad, a lament of living protoplasm, and they strum delicate instruments of feathers and fish skin and leaves and insect wings . . . the instruments disintegrate under their hands, the delicate flutes split and flutter to the ground. . . .

At one time we were able to grow chilies, but a blight killed the plants. I think we would all kill ourselves except for the *grifa*. We have planted it where it will reach all of the sun each day, in the middle of the Valley by the stream. The plants are of a very dark green, almost black, and oily. One whiff on the pipe is enough for hours. Like everything, the *grifa* is carefully rationed. How is this enforced? There is no need to enforce anything here, where we all know the precise limitation of needs. The fish, the *grifa*, the nettles, the ants, the lizards and snakes, the moss from the edge of the cliff, the birds, everything is precisely doled out. Those who are working on instruments take precedence and are allotted extra rations. Sometimes a Corner will spend years on an instrument, preparing a single song.

How else do we occupy our time? Every day we must plan for the food of the day. This involves elaborate calculations: counting the fish, the number of moon-corn plants, the nettles, the moss. A miscalculation could mean starvation and the extinction of our line. We must believe that our line is precious, and that it must be maintained.

Often the word comes: "No food today." Or there may be just a meager allotment of boiled nettles. Fire is a problem, but we have the Burning Crystals. Occasionally there is a feast, perhaps two large snakes have been killed and one fish can be spared. On these rare occasions the Corners perform, and some of them die the following day. Their bodies must be hacked up and used to fertilize the moon-corn patches for future Corners.

Corners have the calling, like a priest. It is both an honor and a disgrace to have a Corner in the family. But at the age of puberty, the mark of the Corner can be perceived: a look of dreamy despair, the look of a hungry ghost in time of famine, but a noble resignation that transcends the hunger. At first the Corners are supple and strong. At this stage many attempt to climb out of the Valley. A few have been known to reach the overhangs.

Soon the rot sets in. They wake up spitting teeth and blood and pus. It is time for them to learn the ancient songs and music, time to start making their instruments. They also make a mooncorn beer to be used at the festivals. The Death Brew is lethal. One cup will kill in three days . . . three days of agonizing bone aches and hemorrhaging through the skin, literally sweating blood. To avoid this horrible death the Corner chooses someone to kill him at dawn. This is done by thrusting an obsidian knife under the rib cage and into the heart.

Escape from the Valley occupies our life. We could tunnel out, perhaps. Such a tunnel was undertaken, but after five years of work there was no way to supply air and the tunnel workers suffocated. The tunnel has long since fallen in, but you can still see the entrance. It's a good place to catch snakes and lizards.

Some devote themselves to exercises to escape from the body and soar out of the Valley. The Soarers receive extra rations of *grifa*, but many feel that they are simply lazy parasites.

"Well, man, I gotta get it together, you understand?" And they go on getting it together, as the light comes and goes, babies are born, old men die.

There is no possibility of sending messages out of the Valley. Tied to the leg of a bird? We don't even know what that is. And we have tried smoke signals, but we must ration our meager supply of fuel.

The Soarers are into mind-to-mind sending. One of them rigged up a contraption with a piece of quartz crystal and some wire he had made by putting certain rocks in a fire and some bright nodules melted and ran out. These he pounded into thin

---

strands, and he formed fish gills into caps for his ears and ran the wires from the crystal and wire unit to the ear caps. With the ear caps you could hear crackling sounds and snatches of music and human voices. We could hear them . . . they could not hear us. But we knew they were there.

It was occasion for a festival. Everybody was drunk. The rations of moon-corn beer were brought out, and extra *grifa*. We didn't go overboard, but this was something to celebrate. *We are not alone!* Others live *outside* the Valley. They will find us. They will lower ropes. They will take us out of the Valley, to where the sun shines all day. We will have enough to eat. We will be in *Heaven*.

One day it happened. We heard a roaring noise overhead and looked up to see what looked like the legendary Dragonfly, hovering there in the sky. We waved and shouted. The craft hung there and then turned and headed away. Next day it was back over the Valley, with several more just like it.

Now one came down past the overhangs and landed by the stream. Immediately the Soarers rushed forward as two men got out of the craft.

"Mucho gusto . . . buenos días . . . muchos años aquí."

The men explained that we would all be evacuated, but that they could only take five at the moment. And five Soarers got into the craft, which lifted off.

Now another settled, but the pilots started back at sight of the advanced Corners.

"These gooks will have to be quarantined."

"They don't go in *my* chopper."

"We'll contact Atlanta."

Gingerly they tossed out some food packages.

A strict quarantine was imposed . . . soldiers were stationed around the Valley. Armed helicopters stood by to turn away any attempt to approach the Valley by air. A helicopter chartered by the Press was turned back, having been warned that there were orders to shoot down any aircraft that violated the quarantine.

The entire population of the Valley, forty men and thirty-five women, was transported to Atlanta by technicians in protective clothing, and placed in isolation. The Valley itself was in Colombia, but the local authorities were glad to turn matters over to the *gringos* rather than risk responsibility for some horrendous epidemic.

The Corners were found to be suffering from some form of radiation sickness. However, neither the corn itself nor the lesions responded to the most sensitive and advanced radiation detectors. The investigators concluded, "If radiation is the etiological factor we must conclude that it is some form of radiation unknown at the present time."

The Press, of course, wallowed in speculation and clamored to be allowed to interview the Valley people and take pictures. They were firmly admonished that the possibility of a virgin soil epidemic imposed emergency conditions. No one but scientists and doctors from the CDC would be allowed access to the Valley people, unless or until there was no danger of an unknown disease agent getting loose in the world's population.

The Press grumbled and prowled around the Center, thrusting their microphones at anyone who came in or out. Exhaustive tests determined that the Corn Disease was not directly contagious, but resulted from some substance in the corn or in the soil upon which it was grown. But this substance defied isolation.

Finally the Valley people were released, and a press conference was held. The Soarers took over the conference, recounting the legend of the Dragonfly, *Esperanza.* The question as to how they got into the Valley was a subject for endless conjecture and speculation: the Valley had been sealed off by an earthquake and a landslide—the Valley people were survivors of a wrecked spacecraft—they or their ancestors had entered the Valley by rope ladders, which pulled loose from their moorings.

The Corners formed a rock group called "Glowing Corn" and became fabulously wealthy. When they stopped eating the contaminated corn, the disease was arrested. They resorted to plastic surgery. The other Valley people scattered, gravitating to the Hispanic *barrios* of Los Angeles and New Mexico. A few went to New York.

In a few years the Valley was forgotten.

Relative Einstein, known as Uncle in the family, wrote matter into energy and some of us think he should have been murdered in the bulrushes. He also wrote the speed of light as 186,000 miles per second. The earth is losing light at that speed. Any factor that can be measured is quantitative, and any quantitative factor runs out in a time universe. The process has been greatly accelerated by photography. A photo has no light of its own, but it takes light to be seen. Every time anyone takes a picture, there is that much less light in circulation. Slowly at first, the gathering darkness on the margin of vision . . . the mutters of voices at the edge of hearing.

Daring light holdup . . . escaped with a million kilowatts, easily worth a hundred million on the black light market. The Light Units, or LUs, are small rectangular sections, rather like a thick credit card which you can insert in your Converter to produce so many units of light.

You want to keep your house and garden lighted during the day? (You have to, according to the zoning regulations.) And you got a little hunka sky over your trap like an umbrella? Solid middle class, just a jump ahead of the Big Blackout . . . precarious trades . . . one day lit up like a Christmas tree, next day fading into total eclipse.

Black market light dealers . . . Joe's Lunch Room, the sign went out years ago. A ten-watt bulb lights the bar, the booths are in shadow. A boy slides into a booth.

"Got some light here. Want to trade it for shit."

The boy's eyes are going from the continual darkness. You don't know what darkness is until there isn't any light. No light from anywhere. He blinks in the dim light with heavy shades. All he cares about is light enough to shoot by. He'll be blind soon and need a Light Boy to lead him around.

You can make a certain amount of light from your own substance, if you have any left, and light transfusions can be had for a price. Politicians is trying to convince the public they got a system for eating votes and shitting out light. But the light is running out and everybody knows it. It's leaving this planet at 186,000 miles a second and nothing can bring it back. The time is coming when no amount of light units will buy any light.

> Day is done
> Gone the sun
> From the lake
> From the hills
> From the sky.

Joe's first encounter with the Land of the Dead: the first thing he notices is oil patches in the dim streets, or perhaps just patches of greasy darkness, but the feel of oil is there, and the smell of coal gas. The sky is black and dark green.

He comes to the house at Pershing Avenue. His mother is there and a long reptilian neck rises up out of him, curls over his mother's head and starts eating from her back with great, ravenous bites, some evil predatory reptile from an ancient tar pit. His mother rushes in from her bedroom screaming, "I had a terrible dream! I dreamed you were *eating* my *back!*"

Smoker, the gray cat, is an ally in this dim, oily area. The night Ruski got lost and I was thinking I shouldn't have brought him out here, Smoker found him and brought him out, just as Fletch brought the Russian Blue kitten down from the tree.

There are many other places . . . a restaurant/hotel/station area, where one is always in doubt about his room reservation and rarely able to find his way back to his room if he leaves it in search of breakfast, which is always difficult to locate.

Le Grand Hôtel des Morts: escalators, stairways, a multilevel complex of rooms and restaurants and shops. I glimpse Ian Sommerville several times on an escalator, or passing in the corridors and waiting rooms. There is a long line of people at a reception desk waiting to get rooms. I have a reservation for room 317, but can't be sure of it with all these souls pouring in. Many of them look American, with crew cuts and rucksacks, undoubtedly servicemen from Vietnam. I hear there was a terrible pile-up.

This area is a vast airport, seaport, train station, hotels, restaurants, films, shops. I find Ian on a mezzanine in front of a boutique. He is vague and wispy and cool . . . excuses himself and goes inside. He is a curious combination of a mathematician (he really understands things like quantum theory) and a cold, bitchy woman. Being older and wiser, he is willing to leave it there. But I follow after a moment and ask the girl for Ian Sommerville.

"Oh, yes," she says and he comes out. We exchange a few dead sentences. It doesn't matter who says what.

"Is Brion here?"

"No. He's not coming."

"I wonder if my room is still reserved?" I moan plaintively. Ian does not have an opinion.

"Last night I slept on a couch in a room with four or five other people."

"Well, that's pretty frank," he says flatly, and turns away.

The boutique is an arrangement of booths according to some cryptic design. Several black girls enter, and Ian is talking shop with them but it is a shop I don't know . . . wrong turnings, tracks lost, bring us to this boutique on an alien planet where he is at home and I am not and nothing can ever bridge the gap. He has business here of which I can have no conception.

The name of the hotel is La Farmacía, but I can't find a

farmacía to buy codeine. Seems to be a European city. . . .
Looking for a place to eat breakfast. This always poses a problem. Wander around out to the end of a subway line, then back
to the hotel. It must have a restaurant. Go into one, fairly full,
and the waiter tells us, "This is not really a suitable place. Not
very distinguished." I am somehow reminded of the Madame
Rubenstein anecdote:

"Ah, Richard, so sorry you weren't at my party last night."
He walks right into it. "But, Princess, I wasn't invited."
"It was a very *distinguished* party."

A neat little fillip of insolence from the waiter, who is an
ugly, angular Italian with bony knees and sunken chest and
rank chest hair sprouting out between the shirt buttons, long
scruffy hair, a filthy black suit.

Find my way back to the hotel room. Two little dogs in the
corridor follow me into my room. One is brown and one is gray.
Obviously these are Door Dogs, but since I am in the Land of
the Dead I don't have to worry.

The Land of the Dead: a long street with trees on both sides
that almost meet overhead. He walks to the end of the street,
where there is an iron stairway going down. On the stairs he
finds money, which he dutifully deposits in a trash receptacle
as he intones, "Littering is selfish and dirty. Don't do it."

In the Land of the Dead quantitative coinage is worthless,
and anyone proffering such tender would reveal himself as totally unchic. But at the bottom of the stairway, which leads to
a stone promenade by a river, I spot a coin about the size of a
silver dollar. The coin is of silver or some bright metal. Two
shoulder blades in bas-relief almost meet in the middle of the
coin, just as the shoulder blades of a Russian Blue cat almost
meet if the cat is a star. This is a Cat Coin, more specifically a
Russian Blue Coin, for in the Land of the Dead coinage is
qualitative, reflecting the qualities the pilgrim has displayed
during his lifetime. A Cat Coin will only be found by a cat lover.

There are Kindness Coins: the bearer has helped someone without consideration of payment, like the hotel clerk who warned me the fuzz is on the way, or the cop who laid a joint on me to smoke in the wagon. There are Child Coins. I remember a dream child with eyes on stalks like a snail, who said, "Don't you want me?"—*"Yes!"*

There are Tear Coins, Courage Coins, Johnson Coins, Integrity Coins.

Are there things you would not do for any amount of money? For any consideration? For a young body? The Integrity Coin attests to the bearer's inaccessibility to any quantitative bribe. The coin certifies that the bearer has definitely refused the Devil's Bargain.

A coin cannot be stolen or transferred to anyone who has not earned the right to use it. They cannot be counterfeited. A stolen coin will often tarnish and blacken. It will always ring false on the fork. Every shop and innkeeper has a tuning fork to test the coins proffered in payment. A true Cat Coin will ring out harmonious purrs. A false or stolen coin will hiss and spit. So each coin rings with its special quality.

The Coin of Truth, on which is inscribed the Chinese character of a man standing by his word, rings with truth. You don't need a receipt. If false, it rings hollow and false as Jerry Falwell. The lies slither out.

"Receipt please."

"I'll put it under your door."

"Excellent. I will give you the money at that time."

Certain coins are prerequisite for obtaining certain other coins. Only the coinage of cowardice, humiliation and shame can buy the Coin of True Courage. Child and Cat and Kindness Coins can only be bought with Tear Coins, and Cat and Child Coins can, in turn, buy the very rare Contact Coin. This coin attests that the bearer has *contacted* other beings. There are coins attesting to Cat Contact, prerequisite for the Animal Contact Coin.

Coins of the Long Chance, the horse that comes from last

to win in the stretch, the punch-drunk fighter who comes up at the count of nine to win by a knockout, Samson pulling the pillars of the temple down. The expendables, the last desperate gamble, the Coin of Last Resort. It's a one-time coin.

So many coins, and none that can be bought with money or any quantitative factor. The Devil deals only in quantitative merchandise.

"Anything you wouldn't do for money? For a young body? For *Immortality?*"

"Yes—dig out a cat's eye . . . and a lot of other things."

Immediately the deal is off. "Well, if you are going to be like *that.*"

I am. I'd rather slug it out in my seventy-year-old body than agree to some shabby fool's bargain.

Another store is there. Kiki, what house? Half-club interruptions. Renew an alliance which does not amuse?

Aquaintance circumstances a police informer.

(Pause for word from me.)

The dream *pensions* whisper out from Mexico to Paris . . . dust of nights without sleep.

(The Indian is out.)

Lymphatic gray winter walk in the season of pause.

I go in for rat thick boy.

"Hisss." Animal slob planet.

Hummingbird spirit, you have made no fruit.

(A little cold snigger.)

They are gone away, leaving a shutter clattering in the wind. Tire tracks in freezing mud.

A bandana stiff with jissom in a dry drawer of the empty hotel with the desiccated corpse of a cockroach.

Rain in cobwebs, empty lavatories of summer schools.

Eggshells, wet bread crusts, hair combings.

A large empty loft: a dust of plaster falls on my shoulder like the first stirring of a sail in a storm gathering out of dead sick calm. Plaster is falling all over the room now. Get out quick!

With a boy from the magazine making it in a ditch. Summer

night breathes through salt-encrusted gills, the porous taste on his tongue in the rubble of wing sheaths and shells, rose-patterned stone under the archways, blue shadow cool on the silken bed, the scent of hyacinths. Mother and Dad will drive me to Liberty, Ohio, a student town. Kiki doesn't like it.

A warm wind winter stubble
Late afternoon in the 1920s
Room over the florist shop by the vacant lot where I could find
    snakes under rusty iron
A little green snake nuzzles lovingly at my face.
A whiff of speakeasies, white silk scarves, tuxedos, 1920
    wraiths that fade from the paper.
Christmas was warm soot on melting snow
walking by granite walls on Euclid
and I said to my cousin
"I can't believe it's Christmas."

The night before Christmas
And all through the house
Not a creature is stirring
Not even a louse.
A room with high ceilings
Lobsters in a room with
high ceilings
There's a party down the road
had to be restrained
Mick Jagger and I think
pulled the curtains closed
There was more
I am off to a hunt
Remember it
Last night dogs howling
A dog to feed
Lightning in the south of Spain

Let me tell you some crystal
and pineapples . . . lobster last
have a lobster?
Make luff with you
in a room with high ceilings
Sweet rosebuds dear old prince
Fat and twinkly in his shades
Dead on the toilet seat
Selective historians, come on
Don't be touchy
Umbrageous in the apartment
I glimpsed obligingly a modicum of central heating
A modicum whippet and the central heat
Honky foolery yet if I could
The telephone's ringing through the sky
Littered with silver and BOOM BOOM
Giff any champagne?? When did I?
My God it's all so—
Lobster. . . .

White bears graze in lush green meadows. A shrieking black
boy dances around in civilian bones . . . emerald whirlwinds.
  "It's always her toes to be left alone."

These magical visions are totally devoid of ordinary human
emotion and experience. There is no friendship, love, hostility,
fear or hate. There are no rules, no series of steps by which one
can be in a position to see. Consequently such visions are the
enemy of any dogmatic system. Any dogma must postulate the
way, certain steps that will lead to the salvation which the dogma
promises. The Christian Heaven of pearly gates and singing
angels, the Moslem paradise of eternal whores and plenty of
water, the Communists' heaven of the worker state. Otherwise

there is no place for a hierarchical structure that mediates between dogma and man, that dictates *the* way.

To endure in time, any structure must present predictable recurrences. The visions, the glimpses of the Western Lands, exist in space, not time, a different medium and a different light, with no temporal coordinates or recurrences. The medium bears some relation to holograms.

I remember seeing an exhibit of early holograms, mostly chess pieces in little glass cases. There is something strangely oppressive about these objects, a feeling of something that doesn't belong there. The vision medium can be faked. A hologram can fake it. But when faked, it becomes quite disorienting and unpleasant. A hologram is the illusion of magic without magic.

One of the rarest of all spirits, and the most difficult to see, is the Deercat, half deer and half cat. The grass-eater and the flesh-eater are united in this spirit. It is a bright green color with the head and horns of a deer and the claws of a cat. It can climb trees and run with great speed. It can eat flesh or grass at will. When it eats flesh, it has the teeth of a cat. When it eats grass, it has the teeth of a deer. It can be seen only in forest glens in a black-green light, tornado green.

For the Deercat is a spirit of tornados and whirlwinds, with the agility and strength of a cat and the speed of a deer. Its eyes are green-black and crackle with lightning. It has the power to move any weight of despair and hopelessness, of fear and apathy and death. Once evoked, all the weight of black magic and negative forces are whirled back to the source and sucked up into a black funnel. There are no words to evoke this spirit, only total emptiness.

You must find a small, round glade surrounded by bushes and trees, but open at the top. In the center of the glade place a barometer of crystal on a pyramid of black stones. The stones are smooth and polished with dream semen. Stand now at the northern edge of the glade. Empty all thought and all feeling, voiding thought and feeling out through the tail of the spine. This will leave you a skeleton of crystal bone. As the flesh melts into moss the temperature will drop 20 degrees in 23 seconds and the barometer will drop and drop and finally implode in black light. Then you will see the Deercat, in the green-black tornado light.

He stands there for a second of arrested time. Then you will hear the wind whistling through the trees with a cat's whine rising to a shriek as the black stones break free and whirl around the Deercat. Sky and trees, lake and river, are pulled into the whirling funnel. Not one stone will be left standing on another. The Deercat is the spirit of total revolution and total change. The Deercat is the spirit of the Black Hole.

I WORK FOR THE BLACK HOLE, WHERE ALL NATURAL LAWS ARE INVALID.

Working for the hole
I'll get a mule to foal
I'm the uninvited mole
The errant lawless soul
I pop out here
and I pop out there
I have no human goal
I'm a singularity
I have no human MEEE
No man can pay my fee
No man can set me free
I'm a lock without a key
A singularity.

The trees are two and three hundred feet in height. Looking up, he can see what at first glance look like brightly colored leaves, but the colors shift and change as the color winds mix and swirl, red, orange, yellow, russet, leaving the green leaves and blue sky sharp and painful. There is a path under the trees, very old, a trough three to four feet deep. Here and there tree roots jut from the sides and cross at the bottom . . . have to watch your feet.

But he finds that his body is avoiding obstacles. He is very light on his feet, moving in long strides. His clothes outline muscles, the toes separated, genitals cupped. It is a second skin, made of some light, strong, smooth material, dappled green and yellow, it changes color as he moves through light and shadow.

Silence soaks through him, he cannot formulate "Where am I?" Going and arriving are both present at the same moment, not separated in linear word sequence.

He is walking now by a long, low building. The gutter stretches away into the distance. What look like railroad tracks run along the side of the building and fan out to the side in complex patterns. There are keeps in this labyrinth which only those who live there know, for the labyrinth patterns are built into the soul. Anyone with different maze patterns could never find his way.

He sees canals and paths and bridges, a network to the sky with an intricate series of locks and sluices, gardens and houseboats pulled by huge turtles with eyes for ropes in their shells. The turtles have webbed feet and move with surprising speed and power, pulling barges of produce and passengers.

In the distance he can see a vast lake in milky light. There is no sun or satellite visible. It must be reflected light that gives such a soft, even distribution. Occasionally he meets people on the path. He can feel their bodies as a precise displacement.

He did remember now. Every other time he had been unable to get the dream straight in his waking mind. He had been walking among a great crowd of people, something Eastern about them. There was a terrible bright sun, and the people were half naked. They were silent and slow and their faces had a look in them of starvation. There was no sound, only the sun and the silent crowd of people.

He walked among them and he carried a huge covered basket. He was taking the basket somewhere, but he could not find the place to leave it. And in the dream there was a peculiar horror in wandering on and on through the crowd, and not knowing where to lay down the burden he had carried in his arms so long.

He walked until he reached the railroad tracks. On either side there were rows of dilapidated houses. In the cramped back yards were rotted privies and lines of torn, smoky rags hung out to dry. The earth itself seemed filthy and abandoned. The endless fluid passage of humanity through endless time. A warning . . . a shaft of terror, a future of blackness, error and ruin between radiance and darkness. A terrible dream, groaning and shuffling his feet on the floor, and maybe even more than that.

December 25: Yesterday I copied out the dream section from Carson McCullers's *The Heart Is a Lonely Hunter.* I was running through the dream in my mind, when I experienced the familiar chill that presages surprised and terrible recognition. . . .

"What is in the basket?"

Recurrent dream of coming into a darkened room. Someone is there on a bed. I wake up screaming, *"No! No! No!"*

A basket case. Terrible bright sun stuck in the sky. No place to put down the basket, as he moves on and on through the silent crowd of people with starvation in their faces. Not hungry for food, hungry for something else. Something that isn't there. Not knowing where to put down the burden he has carried in his arms for so long.

A child is dying in the basket. And there is no help here under this stuck sun in an old film from which life is draining away slowly and silently like the moving crowd.

Sayings of the old White Hunter:

You never have real courage until you have lost courage. Lost it abjectly, completely . . . bolted, crawled. And there is no exhilaration equal to courage regained. That is why it is almost always fatal. How can you top it? And if you haven't got anything left to top, what are you waiting around for?

Never fight fear head-on. That rot about pulling yourself together, and the harder you pull the worse it gets. Let it in and look at it. What shape is it? What color? Let it wash through you. Move back and hang on. Pretend it isn't there. Get *trivial*. And what will they serve at this faculty party? Some lethal acidic punch no doubt, just the thing to bring on my hiatus hernia. A dreary parade of faculty parties and office parties to remind you that acute fear and boredom are incompatible.

There are many ways to distance yourself from fear. Keep silence and let fear talk. You will see it by what it does. Death doesn't like to be seen that close. Death must always elicit surprised recognition: *"You!"*

The last person you expected to see, and at the same time, who else?

When de Gaulle, after an unsuccessful machine-gun attack on his car, brushed splintered glass off his shoulder and said, *"Encore!,"* Death couldn't touch him. You don't say, "Oh, you again!" to Death. Death can't take that.

Francis Macomber and Lord Jim: courage lost. They both bolted. Courage regained: Death.

THE WISHING MACHINE

The old writer lived in a converted boxcar in a junk heap on the river. The junk heap was owned by a wrecking company, and he was the caretaker. Commander of a junk heap. Sometimes he sported a yachting cap. The writer didn't write anymore. Blocked. It happens.

It was Christmas night, getting dark. The writer had just walked a quarter mile to a truck stop that was serving hot turkey sandwiches with dressing and gravy to go. He was carrying his sandwich back when he heard a cat mewling. A little black cat stepped into his path. As he put down his shopping bag and leaned toward the cat, it leaped into his arms and snuggled against him, purring loudly.

Snow was coming down in great soft flakes, falling like the descent of their last end on all the living and the dead, the writer remembered. So he brought the little black foundling back to his boxcar, and they shared the turkey sandwich.

Next day he walked to the nearest convenience store and bought a supply of cat food. He called the foundling "Smoker" after the Black Smokers. These are clefts in the Earth's crust, two miles under the sea—no oxygen, no light, and enormous pressure. It would seem axiomatic that no life could exist there. However, abundant life teems along the cleft of a Black Smoker: huge crabs and tuber worms four feet long, and clams as big as dinner plates. One brought to the surface is said to have given off an incredible stink like nobody ever smelled before. These creatures eat minerals and suck nutrients from rotten-egg gas.

And Smoker was a strange cat. His fur was a glistening soot-black, his eyes a shiny white that glittered in the dark. He grew rapidly. Smoker, a creature of the lightless depths, where life as we on the surface know it cannot exist, brought light and color with him as colors pour from tar. From the total lack of air, from pressures that would crush a submarine like a flattened beer can, he brings a compressed variety of life. Nourished on phosphorescent minerals, his eyes glitter like diamonds. His body is molded from the absence of light. And Smoker loves the writer with a special affection from his special place, with a message urgent as a volcano, or an earthquake, that only the writer can read.

And the writer begins to write again. Animal stories, of course. He leafs through *The Audubon Society Book of Animal Life* for his characters . . . the Flying Fox, with long thin black fingers and its sharp sad black face, just like Smoker. A Fishing Bat peeks out of a turtle shell. A Pallid Bat creeps forward, the only ground feeder. The writer caresses the pictures as he turns the pages and pulls them toward him, as he's seen a mother cat reach out and pull her five kittens to her.

At sight of the Black Lemur, with round red eyes and a little red tongue protruding, the writer experiences a delight that is almost painful . . . the silky hair, the shiny black nose, the blazing innocence. Bush Babies with huge round yellow eyes, fingers and toes equipped with little sucker pads . . . a Wolverine with thick, black fur, body flat on the ground, head tilted up to show its teeth in a smirk of vicious depravity. (He marks his food with a musk that no other animal can tolerate.) The beautiful Ring-Tailed Lemur, that hops along through the forest as if riding a pogo stick, the Gliding Lemur with two curious folds in his brain. The Aye-aye, one of the rarest of animals, cat-size, with a long bushy tail, round orange eyes and thin bony fingers, each tipped with a long needle claw. So many creatures, and he loves them all.

Then Smoker disappeared. The old writer canvassed the neighborhood with Smoker's picture. He offered a fifty-dollar reward. Finally he bought a Wishing Machine. Directions for use are simple. You put a picture, nail clipping, hair or anything connected with the subject of your wish between two copper plates activated by a patented magnetic device that runs on standard current. Then you make your wish.

"Well, mister. I don't say it *works,* but I knowed a man cleared the acne off his daughter's ugly face. Nobody seen just how ugly it was till he cleared the acne off, and maybe he shouldn't have done it like that. Then he wished the hemorrhoids of his grandmother to recede perceptibly. Before, they was nightcrawlers, now they is like little red worms you play hell threading on your hook. Another bloke kilted a tapeworm in his maiden aunt and her gained ten pounds in one week."

"Will it do anything *positive,* like bringing back a lost cat?"

"Well, I don't rightly know, but I figure with this artyfact the sky might not be the limit."

" 'All is in the not done, the diffidence that faltered.' "

"How's that?"

"Ezra Pound."

"Tell Ezra to pull down his vanity. And bear in mind that this *is* a murder machine. This you gotta hear: man wished his neighbor dead. Neighbor went full crazy and come after the wisher with a chain saw, cut him in two sections like the lady-sawed-in-half act, difference being the wisher was in no condition to take a bow. And then the neighbor dropped dead from the glory of it. So think, before you wish out some rotten-weed wish."

The old Wish Machine peddler drops to his knees and clasps his hands. "Giva me womans, maka me rich!" he mocks.

The Gods of Chance don't like whiners, welchers and pikers. Feed a whiny wish through the Machine, and you will soon have ample cause to whine. And from half-assed wishers shall be taken even that which they have.

"I only want one thing."

"In that case you'll likely get it, one way or another."

"Well, here's your machine, all gift-wrapped for Christmas. Just a few more calls to make."

Back in his boxcar, the old writer unpacked the machine and plugged it in. He sat down in front of the Wishing Machine and formulated a silent, unconditional wish for Smoker's return, dead or alive, regardless of any consequences. He knew that the fulfillment of his wish might occasion an earthquake (unknown in this area) or a winter tornado. Might even rip the known universe apart.

"Let it come down."

From the boxcar window he could see the snow swirling down like flakes in a paperweight. His wish is a giant arm. He can reach out and turn the paperweight upside down. He can break it in two. He can see Smoker racing through the winter stubble, crystals of snow in his fur, closer and closer. Then, incredibly, a scratch at the door and Smoker's chittering cry. He slides the door open and blackness pours in.

"Looks like he opened the door to get some air and suffered a coronary and died from the exposure," a police spokesman said.

An alert, ambitious reporter did some research and came up with a feature story that proved to be his passport to New York and fame as an investigative reporter specializing in the borderline supernatural.

Bizarre Story of Writer's Ghost Cat

"It was like something out of 'Twilight Zone,' " a neighbor recounts. "I couldn't believe what I was seeing."

When William Seward Hall took up residence in Lost Fork a year ago, only one man here knew who he was and where he came from. That man is Eugene Williams, a retired professor of English literature. The following account is derived from an interview with Professor Williams:

Thirty years ago, Hall wrote a book called *The Boy Who Whittled Animals Out of Wood*. The story concerned a crippled boy who fashioned animals in wood and finally animated his creations by means of masturbatory rites. When his creatures reverted to wood, he achieved one final animation through his death, and the animals scampered away. This book made him famous. It was bitterly attacked and extravagantly praised. Hall never wrote again.

During his time here, Professor Williams was his only visitor:

"He was a good conversationalist, but I learned not to refer to his writing another book. He looked very sad and asked me please never to mention the subject again, the way someone might feel about a bereavement, and I guess that is the way he did feel. He had killed himself in the story.

"I'd been out of town over the Christmas holidays. When I got back in early January, I went to see Bill. He told me he had found a cat on Christmas Day and had named the cat 'Smoker.' I heard a strange, chittering, mewling noise, but I couldn't see anything. Then I realized Bill was making the sound without opening his lips. It gave me a funny feeling but that was nothing compared with what happened then.

"He opened a can of cat food, all the time making that sound, and I could almost *see* a cat there. And then he gets down on all fours and rubs himself against invisible legs, purring. Straightens up and puts the plate of cat food on the floor. Next thing he gets down on all fours and eats it.

"I couldn't take any more, and it was a week before I could bring myself to visit him. I found him in despair. Smoker, he told me, had disappeared. He was going to offer a reward and show Smoker's picture to the neighbors. The picture was just a black blur of underexposed film, but people humored him and pretended to see a cat. 'Sure is a *black* cat.' I thought of getting a black kitten and claiming I'd found it nearby. But before I could do this, he told me about the Wishing Machine that could bring Smoker back.

" 'Well,' I said, 'it's worth a try.'

"And there's nothing more to tell. I guess he got his wish, one way or another."

"What happened to the Wishing Machine?"

"I have it. Police found a handwritten will, leaving all his personal effects to me. Wasn't much: cooking utensils, cat food, a few tools, a machete, a Ruger Speed-Six Magnum, a Rossi double-barreled 12-gauge shotgun, and the Wishing Machine."

"Do you intend to use it?"

"No . . . but then who can refuse the monkey's paw?"

It was a hectic, portentous time in Paris, in 1959, at the Beat Hotel, No. 9, rue Git-le-Coeur. We all thought we were interplanetary agents involved in a deadly struggle . . . battles . . . codes . . . ambushes. It seemed real at the time. From here, who knows? We were promised transport out of the area, out of Time and into Space. We were getting messages, making contacts. Everything had meaning. The danger and the fear were real enough. When somebody is trying to kill you, you know it. Better get up off your tail and fight.

Remember when I threw a blast of energy and all the light in the Earl's Court area of London went out, all the way down to North End Road? There in my five-quid-a-week room in the Empress Hotel, torn down long ago. And the wind I called up, like Conrad Veidt in one of those sword-and-sorcery movies, up on top of a tower raising his arms: *"Wind! Wind! Wind!"* Ripped the shutters off the stalls along World's End and set up tidal waves killed several hundred people in Holland or Belgium or someplace.

It all reads like sci-fi from here. Not very good sci-fi, but real enough at the time. There were casualties . . . quite a number.

Well, there isn't any transport out. There isn't any important assignment. It's every man for himself. Like the old bum in the dream said: Maybe we lost. And this is what happens when you lose.

But in those days there were still purple patches, time eddies by the side of the river. I remember a Gypsy with a baboon that jumped through a hoop to an old, foul tune, and a muzzled dancing bear, and a trained goat that walked up a ladder, a German piper boy with a wolf's face and sharp little teeth. Gone, all gone now . . . and soon, anyone who might regret their going will be gone too.

So here I am in Kansas with my cats, like the honorary agent for a planet that went out light-years ago. Maybe I am. Who will ever know?

The Director reels around on an empty deck giving meaningless orders. The radio is out. The guns stopped working light-years ago. The Shadow, Memory, horribly maimed, clings to the Remains, Sekhu. The spirit that must remain in the body after all the others are gone: the Remains, that enabled the others to leave, by giving them a receptacle to occupy in the first place.

Palm Beach, Florida. 202 Sanford Avenue. Mother and I take Old Fashioneds, which I mix every day at 4 P.M. We are trying to keep my son Billy from getting into more trouble before his trial, on a charge of passing forged speed scripts.

Mother comes into my room with a bag full of empty paregoric bottles from Billy's room, just lying around for the narcs to find. I take the bag down to Lake Worth and throw it out with a stone for ballast.

Every day I walk out to the end of a sandy road by the sea, to wait for 4 P.M. Once a police car stopped and drove part way out on the road, looked at me, backed up and turned around.

"Just an old fuck with a cane and his trousers rolled."

At least I dare to eat a peach.

The dream is set right there in the sand and driftwood. An L-shaped building with an open door. Standing by the door is an old bum who says, *"We lost!"*

There were moments of catastrophic defeat, and moments of triumph. The pure killing purpose. You find out what it means to lose. Abject fear and ignominy. Still fighting, without the means to fight. Deserted. Cut off. Still we wore the dandy uniform, like the dress uniform of a distant planet long gone out. Messages from headquarters? *What* headquarters? Every man for himself—if he's got a self left. Not many do.

I am looking at a big book, the paper made of some heavy, translucent material. The pages are blue, with indistinct figures. The book is attached to the floor of a balcony. I am looking at the book when two Chinese girls intervene and say to someone else I can't see clearly, "This is ridiculous. After all, he is just an *old bum.*"

Battles are fought to be won, and this is what happens when you lose. However, to be alive at all is a victory.

Soul Death takes many forms: an eighty-year-old man drinking out of an overflowing toilet clogged with shit.

"We lost!"

Cancer wards where death is as banal as a bedpan. Just an empty bed to prepare for the next Remains. The walking Remains, who fill up the vast medical complexes, haunted by nothingness.

The door closes behind you, and you begin to know where you are. This planet is a Death Camp . . . the Second and Final Death. Chances of getting out are maybe one in a billion. It's the last game.

The ally Smoker is not lightly invoked, a creature of lightless depths and pressure that could flatten a gun barrel. Smoker emerges in a burst of darkness.

Remember, Smoker will take you at your word. . . .

Newlyweds Killed in Flash Fire . . .

"Not *that* way!" the foolish wisher exclaims in horror. "He left me paralyzed from a botched operation, and then took my bloody bird. All I wanted was to ruin him with a malpractice suit, to see him barred from practice, eking out a meager living as a male midwife, and her peddling 'er dish in Piccadilly. Didn't mean to *burn* them. Hmm, well, I did say 'damn his soul to hell and she should fry with him.' But I didn't mean . . ."

Be careful, and remember there is such a thing as too much of the goodest thing, like a wise guy who wishes all his wishes would be immediately granted. Wakes up, has to shave and dress—no sooner said than done, breakfast already eaten, at the office another million dollars, faster and faster, a lifetime burnt out in a few seconds. He clutches at Joy, Youth, Innocence, enchanted moments that burst at his touch, like soap bubbles.

Mr. Hart wanted the ultimate weapon so he would always be safe. His is a face diseased and covered with pustules, bursting to communicate a secret so loathsome that few can learn it and live. They flee before him in blind panic or drop in their twisted tracks, tongues protruding to the root, eyes exploded from their sockets. Perhaps those eyes saw Smoker.

As Joe moves about the house making tea, smoking cigarettes, reading trash, he finds that he is, from time to time, holding his breath. At such times a sound exhales from his lips, a sound of almost unbearable pain. It is not a pain he can locate in bodily terms. It isn't exactly *his* pain. It's as if some creature inside him is suffering horribly, and he doesn't know exactly why, or what to do to alleviate the pain, which communicates itself to him as a paralyzing fatigue, an inability to do the simplest thing—like fill out the driver's license renewal form. Each night he tells himself firmly that he will do it tomorrow, and tomorrow finds that he simply cannot do it. The thought of sitting down and doing it causes him the indirect pain that drains his strength, so that he can barely move.

What is wrong? To begin with, the lack of any position from which anything can be seen as right. He cannot conceive of a way out, since he has no place to leave from. His self is crumbling away to shreds and tatters, bits of old songs, stray quotations, fleeting spurts of purpose and direction sputtering out to nothing and nowhere, like the body at death deserted by one soul after the other.

First goes Ren, the Secret Name. Destiny. Significance. The Director reels out onto a buckling deck. In shabby theatrical hotels the Actors are frantically packing:

"Oh don't bother with all that junk, John. The *Director* is onstage and you know what that means in show biz!"

"*Every man for himself!*"

Then Sekem, Energy. The Technician who knows what buttons to push. No buttons left. He disappears in a belch.

Then Khu, the Guardian, intuitive guide through a perilous maze. You're on your own now.

Then Ba, the Heart. "Feeling's dull decay." Nothing remains to him but his feeling for cats. Human feelings are withering away to lifeless fragments abandoned in a distant drawer. "Held a little boy photo in his withered hand . . . dim jerky far away someone has shut a bureau drawer."—(cut up, circa 1962–63).

Is it the Ka, the Double, who is in such pain? Trapped here, unable to escape, unable even to formulate any place to escape to?

And the Shadow, Memory, scenes arbitrarily selected and presented . . . the badger shot by the Southern counsellor at Los Alamos, sad shrinking face rolling down a slope, bleeding, dying.

Joe is galvanized for a few incandescent seconds of rage. He jerks the gun from the man's hand and slaps him across the face with it.

"But it might have bitten one of the *boys!*"

The boys? Even lust is dead. The boys wink out one by one, like dead stars. The badger turns to bones and dust. The counsellor died years ago, heart attack in his sleep. A shadowy figure stands over him with an old .45 automatic pointed at his chest.

"But, but—I, I—"

The bullets crash into his chest, knocking the breath out. Standing on an empty hillside, a rusting gun in his arthritic hand, like an old root growing around the cracked handle.

"Gibbons," the Director A. J. Connell called his boys. Tailless apes. Ugh! Your gibbon is a very dangerous animal. A friend of mine pushed his pet gibbon gently aside, and the gibbon whirled with a scream of rage and severed his femoral artery with its canines. He knew what to do. He lived. He gave the gibbon to the zoo. Wouldn't you? Bits and pieces.

The Big House at Los Alamos. God it was cold on those sleeping porches. "Get down and waddle like a duck!" says the counsellor, who directs fifteen minutes of exercise before breakfast. Wind and dust . . . where the balsam breezes blow . . . Los Alamos. A vast mushroom cloud darkens the earth.

Ashley Pond is still there. Joe is catching a trout, a big trout, twelve inches. You eat the meat off the back . . . trout bones.

A whiff of incense. He used to burn incense in his room at Los Alamos and read Little Blue Books.

Back in the 1920s, looking for an apartment in the Village. I am wearing a cape and hold a sword in my hand, a straight sword three feet long in a carved wooden sheath with a brass clip. Will it go on the right side, so I don't have to take my belt all the way off?

A sword: *"Je suis Américain, Catholique et gentilhomme. I live by my sword."*—"The Golden Arrow," by Joseph Conrad.

To wail the fault you visualize. What form would surface with an explosive separate being, desperate last chance? The 12-gauge number 4 or never explosive honesty. You see that comes from sincerity the punch-drunk fighter commitment at the count kid. *Bang* and your hybrid is there, speed of light *splat*. Ace in the hole the cats scrap way buried your own laws of nature we create our layout trigger by will. Some of HIS blew up in the sky what of the hybrid? Yes nodded primitive unthinkable not time. Guardian is the saddest shot has a tear in it. Big Bang shotgun art an orgasm of any solid only one of its kind. Chance the hopeless message flashes with the sky final desperate gamble Ruski blow the house layout challenge the immutable results as simple as squeezing energy directed accented brush work.

I want to reach the Western Lands—right in front of you, across the bubbling brook. It's a frozen sewer. It's known as the Duad, remember? All the filth and horror, fear, hate, disease and death of human history flows between you and the Western Lands. Let it flow! My cat Fletch stretches behind me on the bed. A tree like black lace against a gray sky. A flash of joy.

How long does it take a man to learn that he does not, cannot want what he "wants"?

You have to be in Hell to see Heaven. Glimpses from the

Land of the Dead, flashes of serene timeless joy, a joy as old as suffering and despair.

The old writer couldn't write anymore because he had reached the end of words, the end of what can be done with words. And then? "British we are, British we stay." How long can one hang on in Gibraltar, with the tapestries where mustached riders with scimitars hunt tigers, the ivory balls one inside the other, bare seams showing, the long tearoom with mirrors on both sides and the tired fuchsia and rubber plants, the shops selling English marmalade and Fortnum & Mason's tea . . . clinging to their Rock like the rock apes, clinging always to less and less.

In Tangier the Parade Bar is closed. Shadows are falling on the Mountain.

"Hurry up, please. It's time."

THE END